Déjà Voodoo

A Cajun Magic Mystery
Book 3

ELLE JAMES

Twisted Page Inc

This book is a work of fiction. Names, characters, places, and incidents are the product of the author's imagination or are used fictitiously. Any resemblance to actual events, locales, or persons, living or dead, is coincidental.

Twisted Page Inc

Manufactured in the United States of America

First Edition June 2013 – Entangled Publishing

Second Edition Mar 2016 — Twisted Page Inc

Ebook ISBN: 978-1-62695-049-8

Print ISBN: 978-1-62695-050-4

This book is dedicated to my daughter Megan, who keeps me young by allowing me to live vicariously through her. Follow your dreams, Megan!

Author's Note

Enjoy the following books by Elle James:

Cajun Magic Mystery Series
Voodoo on the Bayou (#1)
Voodoo for Two (#2)
Deja Voodoo (#3)

Bayou Brotherhood Protectors
Remy (#1)
Gerard (#2)
Lucas (#3)
Beau (#4)
Rafael (#5)
Valentin (#6)
Landry (#7)
Simon (#8)
Maurice (#9)
Jacques (#10)

Visit www.ellejames.com for more titles and release dates

DEJA VOODOO

A Cajun Magic Mystery Book Three

New York Times & *USA Today*
Bestselling Author

ELLE JAMES

Chapter One

B*AYOU MISTE, LOUISIANA*

"Boyette, I hope this idea works." Edouard François Marceau scrunched his smartphone between his ear and shoulder as he sat on the bench by the back door of the rental cottage. With his hands free, he pulled off a muddy boot and dropped it to the porch planks. "If it doesn't, we may have us one dead witness on our hands, and that bastard Primeaux will get away with murder."

"Don't worry, it'll work," Ben Boyette, his partner in the Special Criminal Investigations Unit in Baton

Rouge, reassured him. "Did you have any trouble finding the old trapper shack?"

"Did anyone ever tell you GPS devices work best on roadways, not waterways? Still, we managed with a few dead ends and switch-backs. If I lose this thing, I'll have to hire a tracking dog with gills to find them. Holy Jesus, that swamp is a freakin' maze! Marcus and I counted no less than nine alligators while we were out there. And those were the ones we could *see*."

"Did you point them out to our witness?"

"You bet." Ed shifted the phone to the other ear and attacked the laces on his left boot. "That ought to make even *her* stay put."

"You think? After the drug-running, backstabbing, mafia thugs she's been shacking up with, the alligators probably looked tame."

"Good point." One-handed, he tugged at the remaining muddy boot. The phone slipped, and he grabbed for it. "Tell me again why we're playing babysitter to a witness and why you didn't take this assignment?"

"Number one, I don't trust anyone else to get our witness to the courthouse alive. I suspect we have a mole in the force. And I'd have done it, but I'm up to my neck in trials over the serial rapist case." Ben sighed. "Since I did all the legwork, I'm the one in court. God, I hate courtrooms. But, we have to nail this guy so it sticks. Otherwise, I'd be there in a heartbeat. Oh, and I have a pregnant wife at home."

"Oh, yeah. That. Guess you're right. Although, I'd switch with you in a second. You're the one with all the experience wrestling alligators."

"You'll survive. Hopefully, the only alligator you have to wrestle is my moth—" Ben stopped in mid-sentence as if he changed his mind about what he was going to say next. "By the way, how are your digs? Mom buy your story?"

"Yeah." Ed padded through the small cottage, appreciating the homey feel of it. This was the kind of house he'd always pictured belonging to his grandmother. If he'd ever known her. "I hate lying to your mom, though."

"She'll get over it. Did my share of fibbing to get out of doing the lawn a couple times growing up." He chuckled. "Come to think of it, I can still taste the soap. That woman could see right through every lie. She always caught me. But she loved me anyway."

"Yeah. She had to love you, you're her son." And Boyette was damned lucky to have her.

"I'm sure your mom did the same."

"Don't bet on it. Never knew her." His voice was a little harsher than he'd intended. A twinge of longing flickered across his subconscious, which he quickly squelched. No use pining after something he never had.

After all these years, he hadn't realized how much he missed having a mother until he'd met Ben's. Barbara Boyette was the consummate maternal figure. Care and concern written in every smile, wrinkle, and gray hair.

Ben cleared his throat. "Oh, by the way, do you like kids?"

Ed pushed his boots to the side and stood. Did he like kids? "Never thought about it. Why?"

"No reason. Did mom invite you to dinner already?" Ben asked.

"Nope."

Ben laughed. "Don't worry, she will."

"Is that bad?"

"Uh, no, not at all." Ben's answer was a little too swift for his comfort. "She moves quickly with single men."

"I'm not single, I'm divorced. There's a difference. Is there something you're not telling me?" He tamped down a sudden urge to get out of town. Fast.

"No, no. Nothing at all." Now Ben's voice sounded entirely too cheerful.

He should definitely run from this small town stuff as fast as his Nikes could take him.

"Mom's a great cook. She just sometimes cooks up more than her guests are ready to swallow."

Now he knew for sure Ben was keeping something from him. "What the hell do you mean by that?"

"Okay, so you're all set, then." Ben ignored his question. "Lay low and go fishing enough to keep Marcus and our girl fed and happy."

"Gotcha." He looked around the tiny cottage, the walls closing in on him already. "One question."

"What's that?"

"What the hell am I supposed to do with my time for the next few days?"

"Keep an eye open for suspicious characters. Otherwise, make like a vacation, and relax."

"I don't think I've ever taken a vacation." He scratched his head and thought back. No, he'd hung out at the office even on annual leave. All that use-or-lose vacation time got lost each year. "What do you do on a vacation?"

"Sleep until noon, girl-watch, you know, the usual thing."

"Maybe on Cocoa Beach, but in Bayou Miste? I'd go so far as to say the alligators outnumber the people. I don't think I've seen one live human besides your mother and the marina owner. Tell me, Ben, do they count the alligators in the census?"

Ben's outright laughter blasted Ed's ear. "Bayou Miste isn't that bad. Think about it, you arrived in the middle of the day, right?"

"Yeah. So?"

"School and work should be getting out by now." Ben chuckled again. "Just wait."

He didn't like the sound of his partner's laugh, it had a devilish quality. "Wait for what?"

"To meet the family. You're gonna love them."

"I thought it was just you and your mother."

Ben snorted. "Oh, no. I have eighteen brothers and sisters."

He fumbled the phone and almost dropped it. "Holy hell!"

"Yeah, that's what it's like around my house after school."

The introverted halls of Monti-Ed-zuma crashed around his ears.

Nineteen children in one family? What were his parents thinking? Obviously, they hadn't been thinking, they'd been—

"What have you gotten me into, Boyette?"

"You're a tough guy, you can handle it."

As the tune to "When the Saints Go Marching In" played on Alexandra Belle Boyette's phone for the sixth time in thirty minutes, she lay down on the couch and crammed a pillow over her ears. "Please leave me alone."

"Why don't you answer it and get it over with?" Calliope sat across from her, scraping the silver coating from a scratch-off lottery ticket, her long, wild, light red hair fanning across her shoulders like a cape. She wore a halter top and an ankle-length, tie-died peasant skirt, her legs tucked under her. No matter the circumstances, she always looked relaxed and carefree.

"No way." Alex sat up and leaned her face in her hands. "She'll ask me again if I've been seeing anyone, or she'll invite me to dinner at the house and drag some poor slob to the table with the family."

"So? What's wrong with that?"

"Even if I liked the guy, one look at my family and he'll run screaming into the bayou."

"Damn." Calliope frowned at the lottery ticket and tossed it onto the table. Then she looked across at Alex with a smile. "Your family's wonderful."

"Yeah, all nineteen of them." She rolled her eyes. "In this day and age, who in their right minds would have nineteen children?"

Calliope grinned "Your parents."

"Yeah, and what did it buy them?" She sat up. "An early grave for my father and insanity for my mother." Despite her flippant words, she still felt the pain of loss. Her father had been the rock in their lives and she missed him terribly, even two years after his passing.

"Alex, your mother loves every one of you and only wants to see you happy."

"I wish she could love me a little less."

"You don't mean that."

"Yes, I do. She won't leave me alone about love and relationships. I'm happy with the way things are. I have my own business, I'm in the best shape of my life. I have this great house. What more does she want?"

"Grandchildren?"

She snorted. "Big Brother Ben has that market nailed. She'll have her first grandbaby in three months. Lucie's getting as big as the bayou."

"Speaking of Lucie, I saw her yesterday when I was in Baton Rouge. And you're right. She *is* getting big." Calliope smiled. "She looks great. Pregnancy must agree with her."

"Yeah, and Ben's over the moon. His chest is swelling so much, I doubt they can find shirts to fit him." Alex was happy for her brother. At the same time, a stab of intense longing hit her right in the gut. She had to suck in air to relieve the pressure.

"Oh, I almost forgot." Calliope jumped from her seat on the couch. "Lucie asked me to give you something."

She cringed. "Oh God, what now?"

Calliope fished in her pocket and dug out a small red velvet drawstring bag.

When Alex peered inside, she almost gagged. It smelled like something the cat dragged in from the swamp. "What is this stuff?"

"She didn't say. I bet five bucks it's some Voodoo remedy."

"Egad!" She dropped the bag on the end table. "You remember the last time she dabbled in Voodoo she almost had the entire town of Bayou Miste under her wacky love spell."

"But it all worked out in the end. Lucie married Ben, Maurice and DeeDee scheduled a Christmas wedding and Elaine and Craig eloped. The whole magic thing couldn't have turned out better. And, she's been taking lessons from her grandmother."

"Maybe that spell worked out all right, after a considerable amount of bad luck and a few murder attempts. But the one she put on Mo's pet alligator gave the poor beast a bad case of puppy love for

Granny Saulnier's poodle. T-Rex still hasn't gotten over it."

"I don't know what it is. She asked me to give it to you the next time I saw you. I did and now my duty is done." Calliope blinked, all innocence. "Maybe it's a sachet you're supposed to put in your drawer to make your clothes smell good."

She wrinkled her nose "Not this stuff. It could make a grown man weep. I swear it has that rank odor of stump water." She shoved the bag toward her friend. "Take it back to her. I don't want to risk getting caught up in one of her crazy spells."

"Oh, no." Calliope held up her hands. "I'm not carrying that thing around. It might give me hair in places I have no business growing hair. Or worse, maybe it'll make me lose hair that I shouldn't. No, if you want her to have it back, you'll have to give it back yourself."

"Fine, I will. Next time I'm in Baton Rouge." She frowned at the sachet bag. "In the meantime, I have to put up with it. I hope it isn't anything dangerous."

The phone sang again and she flopped down on the couch pulling the pillow back over her head. "Why couldn't I have had Lisa and Lucie's mother, who stays gone for twenty years at a time?"

Calliope stood at the sound of the third ring.

"Because your mother loves you, and you should be nicer to her." She reached for the phone.

"Don't do it, Calliope," She warned. "If you value our friendship, you won't touch that phone."

Calliope cocked an eyebrow and punched the talk button. "Hello?" She listened. "Yes, Mrs. Boyette, Alex is right next to me. Sure. I'd be happy to relay the message. Seven o'clock? I'm sure that would be fine. Me, too? That would be nice. Good to talk to you, too, Mrs. Boyette. Bye, now."

"What did she want?"

"You and I are invited to dinner at her house at seven tomorrow night. Oh, and put on that slinky red dress you wore to Lucie's bachelorette party."

"My mother said that?"

"Well, most of it." Calliope grinned. "I added the part about the dress."

"Thanks, Calliope. Don't know what I'd do without you." She dripped sarcasm. "But I'm willing to try it."

Her friend dropped into the chair and tucked her legs underneath her. "I heard Lucie's Grand-mère LeBieu has been coaching her on Voodoo, again."

She punched her pillow and set it against the arm of the couch. "Should we consider moving to another state?"

The redhead tipped her head to the side as if considering her jest. "Possibly."

"Geesh. I just got the gym operating in the black, I hate to sell and start somewhere else."

Calliope's eyes lit up. "We could move to Biloxi."

With a very unladylike "Ha!" Alex stood and paced around the room. "That's the last place you need to move."

"Why?"

"Don't play dumb with me." She stopped in front of Calliope, planting her hands on her hips. "Biloxi would be entirely too much temptation for you. What, with a casino on every corner, it would be like navigating a minefield."

"I'm not that hooked on gambling. Besides, I could get a job in one of the casinos." Calliope's eyes twinkled and an excited grin spread across her face. "The pay and tips would beat what I get at the Raccoon Saloon."

"You should be happy you landed Lucie's old job. She got great tips."

"I guess moving is out of the question." Calliope's smile turned downward and she heaved a sigh. "I miss Lucie."

"Me, too," Alex said. "Why do things have to change?"

"Yeah," Calliope sighed again. "Why do people have to get married and move away?"

"Although, Lucie seems very happy." She could still picture Lucie's glowing face at the wedding. How had she lucked into finding the love of her life here in Bayou Miste?

Calliope's eyes got all dreamy. "Do you think we'll ever find someone to love as much as Lucie loves Ben?"

"Not me. I only date the guys from hell."

"Like Theo?"

Alex rolled her eyes. "Why can't that bonehead take the hint?"

"Still botherin' you?"

As if to prove her point, her phone sang the theme for Jaws, the da dum, da dum sound grating on every last one of her nerves. She launched herself across the coffee table, snatched the phone, and cocked her arm to throw.

Calliope grabbed the device from her hand before she could let go. "Hey, don't ruin a perfectly good cell phone because of a guy."

She drew in a long breath and let out the tension with her exhale. "You're right. You're right. I'd miss my phone more than Theo."

"Not all guys are like Theo, you know," Calliope pointed out.

She snorted. "You haven't seen the ones my mom keeps throwing at me." She settled back on the couch and hugged a pillow to her chest. "I don't know where she gets them, but they've all had major 'me' hang-ups."

"What do you mean?"

"It's all about the guy." She wandered around her tastefully decorated living room where everything had a place and everything was in it. "Why can't I find a guy who thinks *I* hung the moon? A partner who will love me even when I'm majorly PMSing. Someone who will love me unconditionally, no matter how bad a day he's had."

As if he sensed how upset she was, Sport, Alex's golden retriever, trotted across the room and sat at her feet, his tail sweeping the floor in a steady rhythm. He stared up at her, mouth hanging open like he was smiling at her, his eyes pleading, "pet me".

She reached down and scratched behind his ears. "I don't think I'll ever find someone to love me like that."

"Sport loves you like that." Calliope giggled.

She laughed. "You know, Calliope, you're right. I need a guy like Sport. One who will greet me at the door, always happy to see me. Someone who can forgive me for forgetting his birthday. Someone who's happy no matter what I feed him or how fat I get." She squatted next to Sport and hugged him around his neck.

"Wouldn't it be neat if Sport were a man?"

"Yeah." She loved the silky feel of Sport's coat against her cheek. He loved her no matter what. "I wish he were a man. Then maybe my mother would quit trying to set me up."

"Hey, Sport." Calliope snapped her fingers. "Come here."

The dog laid a long wet tongue across Alex's cheek and wiggled loose to go to Calliope.

"How would you like to be a man?" The redhead rubbed her hand in his thick fur. "I bet you'd be really sexy, huh, boy?"

Alex stood and brushed the dog hair off her workout pants. "I have to get ready for work. Would you mind taking Sport out for a walk?"

"I'd love to." Calliope leaped from her chair. "Wanna go outside, boy?" She reached for the leash hanging on a hook inside the coat closet.

"Just don't let him whiz on Miz Mozelle's rose bushes. She never says anything, but I'm sure she doesn't appreciate it. I don't know what it is about her rose bushes that inspires him to grace them."

"We'll steer clear." Calliope snapped the lead on Sport's collar.

"And watch out for Granny Saulnier's poodle."

"FeFe?"

"Yeah. Sport has a thing for her. If you're not careful, he'll yank your arm out of its socket going after her."

"I'll be careful." Calliope paused with her hand on the front doorknob and looked back with her eyebrows raised. "Anything else before we go for a nice walk?"

"Get out of here." Alex lobbed a pillow at Calliope as she and Sport exited.

Later that night, Alex lay in her bed, Lucie's Voodoo pouch lying on the pillow beside her. She'd had a particularly tough aerobics session at the gym and her muscles ached.

She lifted her cell phone and dialed.

"Hello?" Lucie's sleepy voice answered.

"Did I catch you doing something I only dream about?" she asked.

"Sleeping?"

"Never mind." She stroked the red velvet bag. "Is Ben home?"

"No, he's putting in a late day with the prosecuting attorney. You know, his criminal investigation stuff."

"What, and leaving his pregnant wife to fend for herself? Who's going to make the run to the convenience store for your latest cravings of sardines and pickles?"

"He's got orders to pick some up on the way home. How are you, Alex?"

"Great. I'm in the best shape I've been in a long time, I'm healthy, my business is booming and I've never been happier." Geez, she sounded like a broken record. A pathetic broken record, at that.

"Lonely, huh?"

That empty feeling gripped her belly and she automatically reached over the side of her bed to pat Sport's head. His wet nose nuzzled her hand. Was she lonely? Was that why she'd called Lucie in the first place? "Yeah, a little."

"Consider yourself hugged."

"Thanks." But a real hug would have been much warmer. From a real man—even better.

"Did Calliope give you the present?"

"Yeah. Actually, that's why I called." Alex lifted the pouch in her hand. "What is it?"

"A little Voodoo good luck for one of my best friends."

She grimaced. "Uh, gee thanks, Lucie. I can't tell you how happy it makes me."

"Relax, Alex." Lucie laughed into her ear. "You won't wake up as a frog or anything. My grandmother helped me with it, so don't worry."

"I can't tell you how relieved I am." Only slightly. Madame LeBieu knew her stuff. As the well-renowned Voodoo queen of the bayou, her spells always worked the way she intended. Unlike Lucie's.

"I can tell you're not thrilled." Lucie laughed. "Gran watched me every step of the way. She loves you like another granddaughter. Why would she propose something that would hurt you?"

"Let me remind you, she turned Craig Thibodeaux into a frog," she said, her voice flat.

"Yeah, but it all worked out in the end, didn't it?" Lucie sighed. "I love you, Alex. I just want you to be happy."

"I'm happy." Her hand tightened on the phone. "Why can't everyone figure that out?"

"Maybe you protest too much?"

"I'm not protesting." Alex realized, as she said it, she was doing just that. Her lips clamped shut.

"Is it a crime to want all my friends to be as happy as I am?" Lucie's voice drifted off.

She could imagine Lucie patting her swelling

belly, and a sudden surge of maternal longing struck her right between the breasts. Why was she mooning over having a baby? Hell, she'd helped raise all her younger brothers and sisters. "I'm happy. Really." Even to her own ears, her voice wasn't very convincing.

"Give the Voodoo charm a chance, Alex. That's all I ask."

Lucie's voice cut through her ill temper and she relented. "Assuming I give it a chance, what is it supposed to do?"

A long pause met her question. Not a good sign. "I'm not exactly sure. Gran LeBieu said it would bring you good luck."

"In terms of what?" A chill swept down Alex's spine.

A whimpering sound rose from the floor beside her. Sport must have sensed her unease.

"It's okay, really. Gran LeBieu wouldn't give you anything that would hurt you."

"I'm shaking in my sheets here."

"Look, if you don't want it, bring it back with you the next time you're in Baton Rouge."

"I will."

"And when will that be?" Lucie demanded.

"As soon as I can break free from the gym." She knew that was an excuse. The thought of visiting

Lucie in all her happy, pregnant glory made her own life look boring, lackluster, and downright sad.

"You're working too hard, Alex. Let Harry take over for a weekend. You need some down time."

She straightened her shoulders, refusing to give into downheartedness. "No, I like being busy."

"And you like going home alone?"

"Yes."

"Alex, it'll happen for you," Lucie said. "When you least expect it, love will knock you over."

"Like it happened with you?" She snorted. "I don't want to fall in love because of a Voodoo love potion. I want a man who loves me for me."

"Much as I'd like to take credit, my love spell never worked. Gran LeBieu confirmed, it had to be cast by a love bug, not a lady bug. If you remember, we couldn't find any love bugs, so we used a ladybug. She let me think it worked to teach me a lesson."

"What?" She shook her head. "You mean my dumb brother didn't need a kick in the pants to tell you he loved you?"

"Maybe he needed that kick in the pants, but he didn't need the love spell."

"I knew that," Alex said. She didn't know whether Lucie's news was good or bad. If the love spell didn't work, what were her chances at love? She fingered the velvet bag. "So, Lucie, what is this bag, really?"

"Gran LeBieu said it would help make your wishes come true."

Alex shuddered. "Kinda like my genie in a bottle?"

"I'm not entirely sure. I just thought you needed a little push, a boost to get you started."

"Look, Lucie, just because you're in love and that makes you happy, doesn't mean I have to be in love to be happy." But she had been pretty lonely since Lucie left. And she hadn't had a decent date in...When her visual memories started dating back to high school and she couldn't name a single unforget-table—happily they'd been forgettable—date, she grimaced. "Okay, I'll keep your gift for now, but I'm still not convinced I need it."

"Which makes me all the more convinced you do."

"I have my own business, my own home and a wonderful, if a little meddling, family. I don't need a love interest."

"Oh, Alex. You're my best friend in the world and I only wish you could feel how I feel."

"That's you, honey. And I'm happy for you." She didn't add, *and I miss you like crazy. Why mar Lucie's happiness?*

"Oh, Ben just walked in," Lucie said. "Hey, *mon cher*, anything you want to say to your baby sister?"

The distinct sound of smacking noises carried across the line and Lucie giggled. "Beeennn, I'm on the phone with your sister." Another giggle.

A pang of longing twisted in her gut. Again. What the hell was going on?

"Alex? That you?" Ben's voice blasted into Alex's ear.

"Yeah, bro."

"Lucie's gotta go now."

More giggling erupted in the background and an indignant, "Ben! What about the baby?"

"Look, I have some ironing to do," she said. Suddenly, she couldn't stand listening to their playful antics on the phone.

"Yeah, okay," Ben said, obviously distracted.

"Tell Lucie I'll call tomorrow."

"Gotcha—damn..." A loud clunk was followed by dead air of being disconnected.

Alex plugged the phone into the charger on the nightstand and turned off the light.

She fought the strange pressure in her chest. What was wrong with her? She was happy. She sniffed. Was she coming down with a cold? Were her glands swelling in her throat, choking off her air?

A tear slid down her cheek. *Oh hell.* She didn't need this. Self-pity was for weenies, not for black belts in karate or really kick-ass business owners.

She flung her hand out, bouncing it off the empty pillow beside her. The velvet pouch bumped against her fingers.

"Sport?"

After a brief pause, a cold, wet nose poked up over the side of the bed.

"I'm so lucky to have you." She ran her hand over his velvety snout. A long tongue snaked out and licked her fingers.

Sport was always there for her without being annoying or obsessive. Alex shivered. She'd had her share of boyfriends and stalkers. She'd rather remain celibate than go through that again.

But deep down, she ached for that closeness. And hell, she hadn't had sex in so long she wondered if she remembered how. Was she going to die one of those frigid old maids destined to read erotic romance novels to get her jollies?

I'm Pathetic.

And her mother would drive her stark-raving mad if she didn't quit shoving fresh meat at her every chance she got.

"Oh Sport, I wish you were a man. That would solve all my problems." She settled against her pillow and closed her eyes. "It would take a lot of magic to get my mother to back off. I'm not even sure having my own choice of a boyfriend will satisfy the woman." She yawned and snuggled in, pulling the comforter up to her chin to ward off the chill of the air conditioner.

As she drifted into a half-awake, half-asleep state, the bed sank down on the far side. Sport had leapt up beside her.

Too tired to tell him to get down, she gave up and let go.

A thrumming sound filled her dreams, building into a full bass echo of drums. Somewhere in the back of her sleep-numbed mind, she recognized the drums as those played at the Voodoo ceremonies Madame LeBieu conducted on those rare occasions when a little extra umph was needed to initiate one of her spells.

Just as she succumbed to oblivion, an eerie chant echoed through her head, "Wishes come true. Wishes come true. Wishes come true."

Alex sighed and gave in to the magic.

If only wishes really came true.

Chapter Two

The dark-haired stranger lay warm against Alex's back, the fur on his chest tickling her arms. A sexy tongue teased at her ear, sending tingles across her skin. Ummmmm. That felt good. She knew it was a dream, and she didn't want to wake to an empty bed, so she forced her eyes to stay closed so that she could enjoy the fantasy until her alarm blasted her awake.

She snuggled deeper in her sheets, imagining the heated skin of her dream man pressing against the back of her thighs. How long had it been since she'd slept with someone—well besides one of her siblings in her crowded family home?

Her man whimpered softly and the errant tongue traced the side of her neck.

She scooted back to snuggle against the man in

her dreams only for him to drape a heavy arm across her waist and lick her cheek

Ew! Some dream man. Who ever heard of a full throttle tongue-swipe across the cheek as being even remotely sexy? Maybe it was time to wake from this dream and kick Mr. No-more-manners-than-a-dog out of her dream and bed. Through the thick haze of slumber, she had an oh-duh moment.

Sport.

Sport had sneaked into her bed right as she'd fallen to sleep. He usually did whenever they had a thunderstorm or if he sensed her loneliness.

Eyes still closed, she raised her hand to her cheek. Yup. It was wet, all right. Double ew. Dog slobber. That's when she opened her eyes to the gray light of dawn sneaking around the blinds shuttering her window.

She rolled to her side and faced the culprit. Where her ninety-pound fraidy-cat of a dog should have been, lay a full-sized man with a startling resemblance to a young Brendan Frazier. And he was naked from the top of his broad shoulders down past the limp—well she tried not to look—to his toenails.

A shocked moment passed before her sleep-fogged brain engaged and then registered with a blinding flash of *intruder alert, intruder alert!*

Screaming at the top of her lungs, Alex leaped

out of the bed with her feet still tangled in the sheets. Instead of hitting the ground running for the door, she hit the hardwood floors face-first, cursing her brother for talking her into removing the carpets.

Before she could disentangle her legs, a thump sounded on the other side of the four-poster bed.

Oh crap, oh crap. He was coming after her.

Frantic now, visions of being raped raced through her head as she was being trapped by her Laura Ashley sheets. She peered beneath the bed wishing she could see through the clutter of boxes to the other side.

Then a whimper sounded from the floor between the bed and the outside wall. "Sport?" Where was her dog? "You better leave my dog alone, you son of a bitch!"

With the determination of a mother wolf guarding her cub, Alex finally shed the constricting sheet, leaped to her feet and grabbed for something to clobber the man threatening her dog. The only item she could find was her color-coordinated pillow that resembled a light blue giant tootsie roll. Like she could beat a man to death with a pillow. Oh well, she only had to hold him off long enough to free Sport and make a run for the door.

Another whimper sounded from the other side of the bed, spurring Alex into action. "I said, leave my dog alone." She inched around the post and braced herself for attack.

Pushing up to his hands and knees was a man with light cinnamon hair and soft brown eyes. And yes, she hadn't been seeing things—he was completely naked.

When she screamed, the man yelped and pressed his face to the floor, cowering like a whipped dog, with his hands covering his head.

While the man crouched, staring up at her with wide, nervous eyes, she committed his features to memory. A girl never knew when she'd have to identify a man in a police line-up. His hair was the same soft reddish-brown color of Sport's and his eyes threatened to melt her when they rounded all scared-like. Sport had that same look when he was hiding in a closet because of a booming thunder storm.

Get a grip, woman. This is a naked man. In your house. And he had his arm around you, in your bed! "Holy Jesus! Get out, or I'll call the police."

The man trembled all over but backed into the corner instead of fighting his way out.

Great. Out of all the houses—okay so there weren't that many in Bayou Miste—why did this crazy man have to crawl naked into hers?

Because you live alone—vulnerable to any bare-skinned man's sex-fetish whim.

Her heart beat so fast, she couldn't hear past her pulse pounding in her ears. No wait, that was pounding on the door.

"Out! Get out!" she yelled, pointing her fiber-filled weapon toward the bedroom door.

The man glanced past her, his gaze nervous as if he was afraid of her. Alex, all five feet, six inches of damned tough, angry girl. Good, he was afraid, as well he should be.

"Out!"

The banging carried through from her living room to her bedroom. Oh, thank God. For once, Calliope was on time for their morning jog.

Alex backed toward the door holding her pillow in front of her like a weapon. "I'm going into the living room and I *will* call the police. Unless you want to go to jail, you'd better leave."

"Alex, what's going on?" Calliope called through the thick wood paneling. "Was that you screaming?"

The man's head shot up and he rose onto his knees, peering over the top of the bed, his eyes wide, his face intent on the doorway.

Then before she could do anything but stand there like a lunk, the man leaped over the bed and loped for the living room.

Oh, no! Calliope had a key to the front door. She

prayed this once she wouldn't use it, or psycho-man might hurt her.

Alex raced after the intruder, chasing him down the hallway. She nearly wiped out on the loose throw rug at the corner.

A few steps ahead of her, the man sped through the kitchen and dove for the doggie-door. He yelped when he hit the floor, and struggled to squeeze through anyway. But the door was built for a medium-sized golden retriever, not for a broad-shouldered man. He backed out and stood, his gaze darting right and left.

The crashing sound of the front door banging against the wall indicated that Calliope had used her spare key.

At the sound, the man's head perked to the side and he sniffed. Then he charged through the other entrance to the kitchen heading for the front door.

"Look out, Calliope!" she cried.

A scream ripped through the air, followed by complete silence.

"Calliope? Oh, God. Calliope!" She ran through the kitchen, her heart in her throat. "That bastard better not have touched—" She screeched to a halt.

Her redheaded friend stared at the open doorway, her mouth hanging wide open.

"Calliope?" Alex frowned when she didn't

respond. "Did you see him?" She began to wonder if the naked man was all part of her pathetic spinster imaginings.

"Did I see him?" Calliope held a hand to her chest. "I saw every glorious inch of him."

Too late, she realized it wasn't shock registering on Calliope's face, it was full-fledged gaw-gaw. "Holy shit, Calliope, you're drooling over a naked intruder."

"Yes, ma'am, until I run out of spit." Her mouth still hung slack. "He was gooorrrrgeous."

"That man is guilty of breaking and entering and you're ready to jump his bones?" She slammed the door and turned to face her friend. "Are you that desperate?"

"Yes, oh yes. Did you see those muscles, sinews, and organs? Ah yes, organs..." Calliope walked toward the door as if in a trance.

"Hellloooo!" She waved a hand in front of Calliope's face. "Are you missing the part about breaking and entering? The man might have hurt—" Alex's eyes widened and she squealed. "Sport. Ohmigod! Sport!" She spun on the same small throw rug almost shooting it out from under her and charged down the hall back to the original scene of the crime. "What has that son-of-a-bitch done with my dog?" she wailed.

As soon as she entered the room, her eyes

scanned the space end to end, while her heart pounded against her eardrums. Neither hide nor hair of the dog could be seen. She leaped up on the bed and peered over the other side where she'd heard whimpering earlier. Nothing.

"Where's Sport?" Calliope appeared in the doorway, a worried frown marring her freckled forehead. "Sport? Here boy?" Her voice trailed off as she stared into Alex's eyes. "Where is he?"

She climbed off the bed and checked the window. Locked. "He couldn't have gotten out this way. And the man couldn't have gotten in."

"If Sport is outside, he wouldn't have gone far. He always comes home," Calliope said, her hopeful tone choking the air out of Alex's lungs.

"That bastard." Tears welled in her eyes and she sank onto the side of the bed and then jumped up. "My bedroom has been violated by a strange man. And where is Sport? If that jerk—"

"Why would he take Sport's collar off?" Calliope's words cut through her fog of pain. She fingered the bright read nylon band lying among the sheets. "And why would he take the time to reconnect the clasp?"

The man's eyes flashed in her memory. They were the same deep brown as Sport's.

Why the thought of her Voodoo dream sprang

into her thoughts, she didn't know. The lingering reverberation of thrumming drums and magical chants sent a lone chill slithering across her skin, raising gooseflesh.

She hopped up from the bed and ran through the house. "Sport! Sport!"

"He's not in here, Alex." Calliope hurried to the front door and threw it wide. "Sport? Sport! Come here, Sport!"

Alex joined her and they stepped out on the porch calling out in unison, "Sport!"

A bush on the corner of the house shook and whimpered.

She looked at Calliope. "Did that bush just whimper?"

Calliope's eyebrows rose. "Sport hides in that bush when he's scared." She nudged Alex with her elbow. "Why don't you go check it out?"

"Me? Why me?" She shrank back. A naked stranger accosting her once in her lifetime was enough. She didn't feel like risking a second flashing. "Sport." Her voice dropped an octave and she did her best I'm-the-big-sister-threatening-your-life voice she could muster. "Come here. Right now."

The bush shook again. But a hairy head pushed out and half of the body emerged.

The naked man.

Alex grabbed Calliope and shoved her behind her. "Go away!"

The man's gaze darted from side to side and he whimpered like an abused animal.

"Don't be so hasty." Calliope tried to push her away. "Let me handle this."

"No, Calliope. The guy is obviously a pervert."

Although the bush covered the man from the waist down, Alex could still see enough to know the guy was still without clothes.

"How do you know? He could be someone who got lost from a nudist colony." With a determined shove, Calliope manhandled Alex out of the way and held out her hand. "Hi, I'm Calliope. And you are?"

"Woof!"

She stepped back. "Did that man just bark? Tell me he didn't just bark."

Calliope laughed. "I believe he did."

A scary thought wiggled its way into her subconscious, growing into a crazy, outlandish, completely idiotic idea. "You don't suppose...I mean..." She shook her head. "No, that's ridiculous...Lucie wouldn't... Hell, she's not trained in that kind of thing."

Without taking her gaze from the man standing so hesitantly in the bush, Calliope said, "What are you talking about? You think this man is Lucie's Voodoo gift?"

"Could it be?" She peered closer.

"If so, I say don't look a gift horse in the mouth. There are much better places to stare at a horse." Calliope vamp-walked across the porch and down the stairs. "Come on, *bebe!*"

The man frowned and crouched lower in the bush, darting glances at Alex as if pleading with her to save him from the fiery redhead stalking him.

"If this is Lucie's so-called gift, what happened to Sport?" she asked.

As soon as she said the name Sport, the man's head jerked toward her and he stood taller.

Huh?

She stared hard at the soft brown eyes and reddish brown hair. "Sport?"

The man's eyes widened and he opened his mouth, "Woof!"

She screamed, and Calliope jumped back and screamed, too.

The naked man shot out of the bush and barefooted it as fast as he could across the gravel drive and out into the street.

Her friend turned toward her with a hand on her hip. "Don't scare me like that!"

Alex's shocked brain reengaged and she yelled, "Ohmigod. Calliope, we have to catch that man."

Calliope grinned and rubbed her hands together. "Now, you're talking."

Chapter Three

Ed peeked out a window at the house next door. Still early on a Saturday morning, he might escape before his neighbors spied him. He liked a solitary morning jog to clear the sleep from his brain. And he wasn't so sure he was up to Barbara Boyette's unrelenting cheerfulness this early in the day. Ben's mom was terrific...in small doses.

As far as he could tell, the coast was clear. He could make a hasty escape if he left now.

He had to hurry, before the masses of Boyettes caught him and reeled him in for the inquisition.

He ducked out the back door, turned to stick the key in the lock. By the time he swung back around, two identically beautiful young women stood facing him. Each wore their thick, black hair pinned at the back of their heads with long loose ringlets trailing down over their exposed shoulders. But it was their dresses that made him think he'd taken a step back in time. They wore beautiful peach-colored ball gowns that looked as if they walked straight out of the late eighteen hundreds.

"Hi," they said in unison.

He slapped a hand over one eye and refocused. No he wasn't seeing double. There were two of them. Damn, Ben had mentioned the bayou was said to be magical. But time travel and seeing double?

"Let me guess," he said, "your last name is Boyette."

"Yes!" Again, both girls answered in unison, their smiles practically blinding him.

One of them stepped forward. "I'm Dolley, and this," she pointed at her replica, "is Madison."

He frowned, glancing from one to the other. "You're kidding right?"

Both dark heads tipped to the right. And Thing One—was she Dolley—said "About what?"

"Your names." He smiled when they continued to look confused, and added, "You mean you're really Dolley and Madison?"

"Oh yes!" both said, the stereo frighteningly in tune.

"Okay, I'll buy that. Now, if you'll excuse me..." he moved past them.

"Wait, Mr. Marceau," Dolley said.

Madison finished with, "Mom wanted us to invite you to dinner tonight."

Dinner with eighteen kids? Did she think he was insane? "Please tell her thank you, but I have plans."

"Mom told us not to take no for an answer." Thing Two—Madison—or was she Dolley—smiled and stepped in front of him.

The other twin grinned. "And we'd like you to come, too."

"Yes, we would," Madison chime in.

Pre-jog, pre-coffee, Ed wasn't up to handling the combined enthusiasm and he was feeling just a little outnumbered by sunny faces. He was not a morning person and he couldn't stomach those who were irritatingly cheerful before nine o'clock.

"So? Can we expect you?" Dolley-Madison asked in unison.

He inhaled and prepared to say a firm "No."

But they turned some incredibly bright smiles on him. "Please?"

His opened his mouth, and knew he couldn't disappoint this early in the morning. "Okay."

Two bouncing cheerleaders in ball gowns hopped up and down, clapping their hands, their dresses ballooning out with each movement.

His temples throbbed. If he didn't get away soon,

his head would spontaneously combust. "If you'll excuse me, I'm going for a jog."

"See you at seven?" they asked.

He forced a smile. "Seven it is." Then he made his escape, taking off at an all-out run designed to put as much distance between him and the southern belle twins as possible. Holy hell! What had he agreed to?

He rounded the end of the block, glancing back to make sure the girls weren't following him. Thank God! He'd left them behind.

When he turned to face front, he ran into a brick wall, head first. Wham!

He staggered backward, his head reeling. When his vision cleared, he realized the wall hadn't been a wall at all, but a man.

A naked man.

"What the fu—"

The other guy was still flat on his naked ass, shaking his head like a dog shakes the water off his fur.

"Hey, buddy, you all right?" He reached out a hand to help the man up, and cringed. What kind of pervert ran around in the nude in a small town? Did he have some funky disease that would rub off on contact? Or had he escaped an awkward tryst with a married woman?

Ed needn't have worried. The man completely ignored his outstretched hand.

Out of the corner of his eyes, a flash of powdery pink flashed past his ankles. He ripped his gaze from the naked pervert to follow a ball of pink fluff skittering down the sidewalk.

He looked closer to determine the cotton candy was in actual fact a toy poodle dyed an outlandish shade of pink.

The man in front of him leaped to his bare feet and chased after the animated powder puff, shouting, "Woof!"

Ed shook his head. He must be hearing things. Had that man woofed?

"Sport!" a female voice called out.

"Sport!" yet another feminine entreaty split his eardrums.

The yelling voices preceded the appearance of two women from the end of the street. One was wearing skin-tight biker shorts and a sports bra, and had her fiery red hair caught up in a ponytail. The other...

Holy hell.

His jaw dropped. The collision must have hit him harder than he'd thought. Suddenly he couldn't breathe and was seeing things.

Her hair was as black as his brand new Mustang

convertible parked in the garage at his apartment building. Her eyes were bright blue and she had smooth, creamy skin that reminded him of a cup of pale, milky mocha. And boy was there a lot of skin showing. She wore a frothy blue baby-doll nightie. The gown did nothing to cover the black, lacy string bikini panties peeking out with every step as she raced down the street barefooted. And oh, those luscious breasts bobbed unfettered beneath the filmy fabric.

The jogging beauties slid to a stop in front of him. Apparently, they were real, not just a figment of his imagination.

The redhead spoke first. "Did you see a do—" she didn't get the chance to finish her sentence when the black-haired beauty jammed her elbow into her gut.

"Man. Did you see a man run by?" demanded the woman in the blue baby-doll nightie.

Interesting. Even without his usual five-mile jog and gallon of coffee, his senses were now on full alert.

Standing this close to that short, sheer, blue gown was doing crazy things to his gray matter and other parts of his body.

The women looked flustered. But then one of them had a reason. Hell, she was running around in an outfit that couldn't be licensed for public consumption in the free world.

He loved seeing her worry her full, ruby mouth and made it a point to worry it more. "Can you describe this man?" he stalled.

The dark one squirmed. Wow, she even squirmed beautifully. If he weren't careful, he'd be making a tent of his jogging shorts.

The redhead jumped into the silence. "He has reddish-brown hair, brown eyes, and a body to die for." She paused and added, "Oh, and did I say he was naked?"

He let an eyebrow inch upward. "Naked?" He asked the dark-haired one. "Any particular reason a man is running around the town naked?"

The black-haired beauty's eyes flashed, but she didn't answer.

"We scared him," the redhead supplied.

Since she'd stopped in front of him, the dark one hadn't uttered a word.

He considered it a challenge. "Do you always run around Bayou Miste in your...black string bikini underwear?" He trailed his gaze down her front to the dark shadow of her underwear barely visible beneath the filmy skirt of her nightgown.

A blush started in the vicinity of her cleavage and traveled up her neck into her cheeks. Score! "Come on, Calliope, this man doesn't know anything." The dark-haired one grabbed the redhead's arm and tried to drag her away.

"But Alex, I'm enjoying the show." She smiled a wicked smile and eyed the front of his shorts.

Too late, he'd been too intent on making Miss Naughty Nightie squirm, he'd forgotten about his own arousing reaction to her delights.

She glanced down, color brightening in her cheeks. But her mouth curved on the ends. "I take it by show, you mean comedy?" A thin, dark brow winged upward. "I've had my laugh. Ha, ha. Now, come on, Calliope. We have to catch Sport."

His ego flagging, Ed couldn't help tossing a parting shot. "What, is this some kind of kinky game you're playing?"

"And if we are, did you want to be invited?" the one called Calliope asked, her grin widening.

"Maybe." He answered the redhead, his gaze fixed on Alex.

"Too bad." Blue nightie actually tsked her tongue. "We're a little more selective of our playthings." With a dismissive sweep of her gaze from his head to his feet, she put him firmly in his place.

Then she was racing down the street, her firm buttocks even more interesting in the black lace bikini.

Ed turned to jog after her. He had to know who

she was. More important, he wanted to get to know those lace panties more intimately. After two steps, he had to pause and adjust. Nope, he wasn't jogging in the next five minutes. Not in his...uh...condition. Later. In a town as small as Bayou Miste, he'd easily find her.

Then he thought of his busybody neighbor. Perhaps Mrs. Boyette would know who the dark-haired babe was.

Wow. Who was the hunk of macho male? Alex fought to keep from looking back at the man who'd been eyeing her favorite sexy underwear. If she was going to be caught running around half-clothed in Bayou Miste, at least she had on her best. Somehow, she didn't think the present situation was what her mother had in mind when she told her to "always wear good underwear...you never know."

In her jogging shoes, Calliope was making better time at catching up with the naked man. Alex hobbled along as fast as she could, her bare feet taking a beating on the gravel.

If by some freaky quirk of fate and Voodoo hexes, Naked-Man wasn't a man at all but her dog transformed into a man, she had a huge problem on her hands.

How the hell was she going to keep him under wraps until she could get Lucie back to Bayou Miste to undo the spell? She couldn't even catch the man...er...dog.

Poor Sport. He must be terrified.

Calliope disappeared around the next corner. Alex hoped she'd catch Sport before he did something to hurt himself.

Before she neared the street they'd turned on, she could hear shouting and high-pitched barking.

With little regard to her bruised feet, she picked up the pace and rounded the corner in a gut-splitting sprint. Then she had to dig her sore heels into the pavement to keep from tripping over an eight-foot alligator stretched across the middle of the road.

Pandemonium would have been less crazy than what was going on.

At the business end of the alligator, the one with the jagged teeth and lethal jaws, stood Granny Saulnier's toy poodle, FeFe, yapping her little head off with as much ferocity as a five-pound, pink powder-puff could muster. At the other end of the alligator was Naked-Man, woofing at the top of his human voice.

She recognized the alligator as Maurice Saulnier's pet, T-Rex. He was probably coming to woo FeFe when Naked-Man interrupted.

Calliope stood near where Alex had come to a halt, shouting, "Shoo, T-Rex! Shoo!" She flapped her hands trying to scare the alligator away from the dog and the man. *As if!*

"Calliope," she called out over the commotion.

"Stop that alligator." Calliope grabbed Alex's hand and pulled her up beside her. "You have to stop him before he hurts our gorgeous man."

"He's not our gorgeous man, and T-Rex isn't a bad dog to be shooed away."

"Well, I want that man, and T-Rex thinks he's a dog. Please get him to leave, before something important gets hurt."

The poodle continued yapping non-stop, her high-pitched staccato voice grinding on every last one of her nerves. "Oh, T-Rex, eat the damned poodle, already."

"Alex Boyette, I heard that. How dare you tell that darned-fool alligator to eat my poor little FeFe." Granny Saulnier tottered out onto her porch shaking a broom. When she spied Naked-Man, her squinty little eyes went as round as shiny new dimes. "Prevert!" For a four-foot eleven package of spindly bones and bright pink hair, she moved fast. Down off the porch she came like a whirling pink dervish whacking at the air with her straw broom. "Get some clothes on, you pre-vert."

T-Rex got one look at the broom and scrambled backward, away from the crazy woman wielding it. Naked-man's eyes rounded and he whimpered.

When T-Rex backed right into him, Naked-man yelped and jumped straight in the air, his feet churning before they hit the ground. He leaped across the alligator's tail and raced straight for her and Calliope.

Before they could move, he ploughed through the middle of them, knocking Calliope flat on her butt and spinning Alex around.

"Alex Boyette, I don't know what you're up to, but I'm telling your mother about this." With one hand, Granny Saulnier scooped up the yapping pink poodle from in front of the gaping jaws of T-Rex. With the other hand, she applied the stick end of the broom to the alligator's head. "And you! Go back to the swamp where you belong." With that, she turned and marched back to her sunny yellow house.

Alex shook her head for a moment, too over-whelmed by the events to react. Then she grabbed Calliope's hand, hauling her to her feet. "Come on, we gotta catch him before he gets into any more trouble."

Which meant going back the same way they'd come and possibly passing the he-man-macho guy in the tented shorts. Warmth surged throughout Alex's body, her nipples tightening into pointy headlights, poking out of the diaphanous fabric like twin pencil erasers. Wow. All that for a stranger whose name she didn't even know. She wondered if he'd be in town long and, if so, if they would run into each other again.

She and Calliope resumed their hunt of Naked-Man. Hopefully, he was headed back to Alex's little cottage.

Disappointment hit her like a wet blanket in the face when she didn't see her handsome stranger again. Oh, well. She didn't have time to stop, and he probably thought she was wacky anyway, chasing after a naked man while wearing nothing more than her skimpiest nightgown.

The people of Bayou Miste were used to crazy things happening, what with their very own Voodoo queen a mere hop-skip-and-jump away on the bayou.

She slowed to a walk, her tender feet having had enough of the gravel and already warming pavement. If Naked-Man, whom she suspected might be her dog, wasn't back at the house, she would definitely get dressed before she ventured any farther afield in her search.

"Sport!" Calliope called out ahead.

Alex trailed behind, convinced she lived in the

twilight zone of jokes and wondered when the punch line would hit her in the face.

When her house came in view, she heaved a sigh of relief. Calliope was talking to the bush in low, soothing tones.

Naked-Man shook the bush with every quiver of his large body crouched beneath.

"*Mon Dieu*, Alex." Calliope turned, her face beaming. "I think you're right. I think that's Sport."

She shoved a hand through her hair. "What did I do to deserve this?"

"I don't know, but when you figure it out, I want to do it, too." Calliope stared back at the shaking bush. "Then whenever I needed a date, all I'd have to do is visit the local humane society."

"Don't go making plans yet. We don't even know if this is Sport."

"It is. I just know it."

Alex stepped closer to the bush and held out her hand like she did when she was trying to coax Sport out of the closet on a stormy night. "Sport? Come here, boy."

The man with sad-puppy eyes rose just enough so his head was clear of the azalea blossoms, then he whimpered.

"Come on, boy." She couldn't believe she was standing in her front yard in her baby-doll nightgown coaxing a naked man out of her bush. "I'm soooo going to have words with Lucie."

The man crouched back down.

"It's okay, boy," she said in the soft singsong voice she used when she wanted Sport to drop the sparrow he'd been chewing on. "I'm not mad at you. I'm just mad at that sorry excuse for an amateur Voodoo priestess."

Her soft words and gentle tones were doing the trick, because the man inched out from behind the bush and walked toward her.

Her heart rate jumped to what it was after a particularly tough session at the gym. What was she thinking? This guy was a man, not a dog.

He was tall and muscular, not short and furry. And all that naked skin was... well...intimidating in full sunlight.

She took a step backward with her hand held out, inching up the steps to the front door. "Want a biscuit, boy? Want a treat?"

The man's eyes widened.

When she opened the door, he shoved past her and ran for the kitchen, the same way Sport did when he knew he was getting a special dog yummy.

Alex groaned and stared at her friend. "I'm going to kill Lucie."

Calliope's eyes glowed. "Did you see those gorgeous glutes?"

Chapter Four

Ed jogged to the end of town on one side of the canal, crossed over a bridge and jogged back on the other side. He took his time studying the clapboard houses, some on stilts, others hugging the ground, daring to take on another storm surge like they'd experienced in Katrina and even more recently during torrential rains that had afflicted the bayous. Everywhere there was old metal, there was rust, and paint seemed to be in a constant state of mildewing or peeling.

He might have found it rather depressing if not for the optimism of the azalea bushes and flowers planted in front of every other house. With the constant humidity and abundant rain, flowers bloomed in wild abandon.

Though he studied the town for potential dark,

shadowy areas and henchmen hideouts, his mind couldn't help but drift back to his strange encounter of the naked and near-naked kind earlier. After bumping into the sexy lingerie kitten that morning, he'd had to wait a good ten minutes for his hard-on to subside before he could resume his morning workout. That didn't keep him from looking around every corner in hope of catching another glimpse of the naughty nightie. Alas, no luck. At least the town was quiet and so far there was not a threat to be found.

A cool shower helped wash away the sweat and residual attraction to the sex kitten in blue. Once he'd slipped into a white polo shirt and jeans, he decided he'd better get what he needed to establish his cover. Having grown up in Baton Rouge, he should know everything there was about fishing. Yet none of his foster parents had ever taken him.

Lucky for Ben, his father had been a shrimper. His father no doubt had taught him all there was to know about shrimping and fishing in the bayou and along the coast. Apparently, his dad had passed away a couple years ago.

The single good thing about losing his parents at a young age was that Ed didn't still mourn their loss. He'd barely known them.

He could see the sorrow in Ben's eyes whenever he spoke of his father. They'd been close. Well, as close as a man with nineteen children could get. Holy hell, had they really had nineteen children?

As he stepped out the front door of the cottage he'd rented from Mrs. Boyette, he felt the vibration of his phone in his pocket. He dug it out and hit the talk key. "Marceau."

"Ed, how was your night?" Ben said in his usual too-cheerful-in-the-morning tone. Must be a Boyette trait.

"Great."

"Mom get around to inviting you to dinner?"

"Hey, I'm supposed to be keeping a low profile here. How am I supposed to do that having dinner with the biggest family in town?"

"You'll be one of the family by the end of the meal. The better to blend in with the locals."

"Yeah, yeah."

"So, who'd she send?"

"Huh?"

"Which one of my brothers or sisters came to deliver the invitation?"

"A couple of southern belles in old-fashioned dresses, talking in stereo."

Ben chuckled. "That would Dolley and Madison, home early for summer vacation from Tulane University. Probably on their way to work at the Beauregard Plantation. They lead tours through the old plantation house during the summer. Make an impression on you, did they?"

"They don't take no for an answer," Ed groused. "And way too cheerful before nine in the morning."

"They get that from Mom. Have you had a chance to look around town?"

"Yeah. Took me fifteen minutes." He slid into the nondescript, gray Jeep they'd rented for the mission and closed the door before continuing. "Not much to the town."

"It's usually pretty quiet, but we do get tourists coming in to do a little fishing and the occasional bayou tour."

"I'll be on the lookout for the strange-looking tourists then." Ed twisted his key in the ignition. "Speaking of strange, is streaking a part of the norm in Bayou Miste?"

"Streaking?" Ben paused. "What do you mean?"

"As in men running naked down the street followed by women in their night clothes."

Ben laughed. "I have no idea what you're talking about."

"Never mind. I'm on my way to Morgan City for a fishing pole and whatever it is I need to look like I'm going fishing."

"You could get that stuff at Thibodeaux's Marina right there in Bayou Miste."

"I want to at least appear to look like I know what I'm doing." He backed out of the driveway and headed north. "And that I own my own gear."

"Wait a minute," Ben said. "You mean you've never been fishing? Ever?"

"I tried to tell you, this bayou vacation isn't my thing."

"You're in for a treat. Make sure you hook up with Joe Thibodeaux. He'll take you out and show you what fun real fishin' in the bayou can be."

"I'm here on a mission, not to have fun."

"Man, you have really got to lighten up. You're an old man at what...thirty?"

"Thirty-two. Same as you, man." He drove out of town and headed up the highway toward Morgan City. "Anything new on Leon Primeaux?"

"Still sittin' pretty behind bars."

"Anyone been in to visit?" Ed asked. "Are they monitoring his calls?"

"So far he's been quiet."

"I don't like it. That man has so many minions scattered over the state of Louisiana and beyond, I'll bet he's already contacted one of them to put a hit on our witness."

"Exactly the reason why we have her in such a remote location. Keep your eyes open. Could be just about anyone after her. Or more than one. It's easy to hide a body in the bayou and there are plenty of people willing to do just about anything for a buck."

"That's why I'm here running interference for a witness, instead of investigating murders and corporate espionage."

"Got you out of the office, didn't it?"

"I'd rather be investigating a double homicide in the seedier side of Baton Rouge. At least then I'd know what I was looking for."

"Look, Ed, I gotta go. I'm appearing in court in a few minutes," Ben said. "Let me know how dinner at the Boyette house goes."

"Yeah, if I survive. Somehow, I get the feeling I'm the main course to be served up."

"You don't know how true that might be."

"Wait, what do you mean?"

"Out, here." The line went dead.

Ed dropped his smartphone on the seat beside him as a speed limit sign flashed by. Hell, he'd been speeding. All he needed was to get hauled into jail for reckless driving and his cover would be blown. He eased his foot off the accelerator and reminded himself he was supposedly on vacation. A mile out of Bayou Miste, he noted a dingy, run-down shack of a barn with a sign perched precariously over the entrance. *Raccoon Saloon.* Since when did raccoons drink beer?

It had a well-worn gravel parking lot with fresh trash scattered around the building. Probably the local watering hole. At least he'd find some entertainment there. If it was a popular gathering place, he might have a chance to study the people, maybe look for those that looked as if they didn't belong.

Hell, by the time he finished dinner with the Boyettes that evening, he'd be ready to toss back a beer or two.

In Morgan City, he purchased hooks, a bag of plastic worms, and a cheap tackle box. Although he went for the least expensive of the accessories, he sprang for the nicer rod and reel. Hell, he'd never owned a fishing pole.

He juggled his purchases as he clicked the button to release the locks on the Jeep.

"Dat dere's a nice pole ya got, mista." A tall, burly man with dark curly hair and brown-black eyes climbed out of an old pickup. He wore a coverall with Littington Refineries embroidered on the front and a matching baseball cap rimmed with greasy fingerprints.

"Thanks," he said, lifting the hatch.

The young man stuck out his massive paw. "Name's Theo Ledet."

He shifted his fishing pole to his other hand with

the tackle box and clasped the man's hand. "Ed Marceau."

Theo crushed his fingers in a bone-crunching grip. "Goin' fishin'?"

No, I'm going snipe hunting. "That's right." He pulled his fingers free and shook blood back into them. *What did they feed these bayou bumpkins?*

"Hear dose largemouth bass be bitin' in Bayou Black." Theo leaned against his truck, as if settling in to chat for a while. "Where ya be takin' out at?"

Not exactly sure what the guy was asking, Ed answered with his canned response, "I'm vacationing in Bayou Miste."

"Dat so? Where you from?"

"New Orleans," he responded, also part of the lie, since he lived in Baton Rouge.

"Bayou Black's just a hop, skip, and a jump from Thibodeaux's Marina." Theo shoved his cap to the back of his head. "Tell, ol' Joe, Theo said hey, will ya?"

"Will do." He shoved the tackle box into the rear of the Jeep. "Thanks for the tip."

"Who ya rentin' from in Bayou Miste?"

"Renting a cottage from Ms. Boyette." Not that it was any business of Theo's.

"Mighty fine woman." Theo pushed his hat to the back of his head. "Dat be my gal's mamma."

"Really?" Ed glanced up. Best to know who to

stay away from. Theo looked like he would be the winner of any barroom fight. Ed had no intention of poaching on the big lug's territory. Again, not that he was interested in dating any of the bayou princesses. An image of a dark-haired beauty in a baby-blue nightie popped into his head. Well, it wouldn't hurt to talk to one. Might help establish his cover better. "Which one is your gal—girl?"

"Alex. She and I been goin' out fo' a couple months, now."

"That's nice." He slid his pole into the back of his vehicle, leaning the end over the back seat, then he shut the hatch, hoping the man would get the hint and leave.

"It's dolla beer night at de Raccoon Saloon tomorra night, if ya got a hankrin'."

"Just might." He edged toward the driver's door. "If you'll excuse me, there's a largemouth bass with my name on it out there."

The man scratched his head. "You shore 'bout dat?"

Ed shook his head. The man was a few fries short of a Happy Meal. "Just a saying. Nice talking with you." He dropped into his seat and shut the door before Theo could say another word. With a wave, he backed out of the parking space and headed back to Bayou Miste, praying Mr. Ledet wasn't going to show up for dinner at the Boyettes that night. Dinner with eighteen kids and their boyfriends would be like eating at a school cafeteria with all the noise and food fights he'd found annoying when he was a kid himself. He wondered if he could bow out of the invitation without incurring another visit from Dolley and Madison of the perpetually synchronized variety of twins.

"How'd it go, today?" Alex called out as she strode into her house. Exhausted from leading two aerobics sessions, one kick-boxing, and one black belt karate class, she'd done nothing but worry about what was going on back at her house with Sport and Calliope. Thank God, Calliope was off that day from her job at the Raccoon Saloon. Alex wouldn't have known what to do with Sport while she ran her business in Morgan City. Her sister Harry helped out at the gym, but she had her own classes to lead and the bookkeeping to attend.

"We're in the kitchen," Calliope called out.

Before she could set her purse on the hall table, the man she'd chased through town that morning burst through the doorway to the kitchen and ran full-out at her.

Alex backed away, her hands held up. "Down, Sport."

Unfortunately, Sport had never learned any manners, and he hit her square on, planting his hands on her shoulders.

She bumped against the door and squinched her eyes shut as Sport licked her cheeks, his entire body shaking.

"Ew! Stop." She braced her hands on his shoulders and pushed him away. "Damn it, stop!"

Calliope laughed. "We'll have to work on that." She leaned against the wall, smiling. "He catches on quickly, if you work with him."

"I'm sure." When Alex had Sport at arm's length, she scrubbed a hand across her wet face and looked at her dog...er man.

He wore baggy jeans, cinched at the waist with a thick black belt, an equally baggy shirt half-tucked into the jeans and nothing on his feet.

"Where'd you find the clothes?"

"In a bag marked 'dirt bag' in the hall closet." Calliope grinned. "I assumed they were some of Theo's."

She nodded. "Yeah, I meant to give them back weeks ago, but I didn't want to get into another argument with him. I can't believe I went out with him in the first place. What was I thinking?"

"You were drunk and thinking you hadn't been laid in a year."

Alex's lips twisted. "Thanks for the reminder." She shrugged. "He wasn't even that good."

"So why'd you dump him?"

"What do you mean?" Alex glared. "We weren't exactly going together."

"He thinks you were."

"One night in the sack and he thought we were practically married. I'm mean really. He left extra clothes at my house like he was moving in. After one night." She pulled the ponytail out of her hair and ran her fingers through the curls. "Shit, I'll never, ever get that drunk again." She reached up and pushed a hank of hair out of Sport's eyes and got her hand licked for the effort. "No."

Sport frowned, his shoulders sagging.

"Your mom called to remind you about dinner tonight," Calliope said.

Alex rolled her eyes. "You told her we couldn't make, right?"

"She wouldn't hear of it. Said she had a surprise for you."

With a groan, Alex flopped onto the recliner in the living room, extending the leg-rest to raise her aching feet. "I'm too tired to deal with family tonight. Besides, what are we going to do with Sport? We can't leave him alone until we find a way to undo the spell."

"Any luck getting hold of Lucie?" Calliope circled the recliner and stood in front of her.

Alex sighed. "I called no less than twenty times. She wasn't answering her phone."

"We could make a trip out to Madame LeBieu's place."

"Since you didn't cancel on Mom, we can't until after dinner." She pinched the bridge of her nose to ward off the headache threatening to explode there.

"Then I guess we're stuck." Calliope sat on the other end of the couch.

Sport dropped to the floor beside her and laid his head on her knee.

She patted his hair, smoothing her fingers through the reddish gold strands.

"So how did it go today?" Alex asked again.

Calliope grinned broadly. "We made progress."

"What do you mean, progress?"

Still petting Sport's head, she continued, "Since Sport is physically a man, I've been teaching him how to act like one." She sat forward and patted the seat beside her. "Sport, sit."

Sport glanced up, his dark eyes gleaming. He pushed up to his hands and knees and stood, then plopped on the couch, like a sloppy teen.

"Good, boy." Calliope pulled something out of her pocket, unwrapped it and popped it into his mouth.

As Sport chewed, his eyelids drooped and he leaned into Calliope with a sigh.

"What did you give him?" she asked.

"Chocolate." Calliope dug another out of her pocket and tossed it to her.

She caught it with one hand. "You're not supposed to feed dogs chocolate."

"But he's not a dog." Calliope jumped up, grabbed Sport's hand and pulled him to his feet. "And come see what else we've been working on."

Convinced she was living in some really bizarre nightmare, Alex dragged herself out of the lounge chair and followed her friend to the kitchen table.

"Look what Sport can do." Calliope handed the man a fork and stuck a plate of spaghetti in front of him.

"Are those my leftovers from Salianos? I was going to take them for lunch today and completely forgot."

"Shh. Let him show you his new trick." Calliope stood beside Sport. "Eat."

He glanced up at Calliope and down at the plate. His hand shook and the fork tilted sideways as he dug into the spaghetti and then lifted it to his face. Some of the spaghetti made it into his mouth, some landed on his lap. But he smiled as he chewed.

"Good, boy." Calliope patted his head and brushed a napkin across his cheek. "And he can talk."

"You're kidding me."

"No, listen." Calliope took the fork from him and laid it on the table. "What's your name?"

"Woof!"

Alex shook her head. "I don't know why you're bothering."

"No really, he can do it." Calliope faced Sport and bent to get at eye-level with him. "What's your name?"

Sport stared from Calliope to Alex.

"It's okay," Alex said.

He turned to Calliope and puckered his lips. "Sport!" The sound was more like a bark, but he'd done it. He'd said his name.

Alex's brows shot up. "Wow. For a dog that just became a man last night, I'd say he's making progress. Can he say anything else?"

"He knows six words." Calliope waved a hand at her. "You try. Say Hi to him."

Feeling a little silly, as if she was talking to a child when the figure before her was clearly a man, she said, "Hi."

"Hi!" Sport said in immediate response and so forcefully, Alex jerked back and laughed.

"Very good, boy." She reached out and caught herself before she patted his head.

"He can say bye, please, thank you, and good."

"I am impressed. All in one day?"

"Just think what he could do in a week."

She shook her head. "He's not going to be human for a week. Not if I can get hold of Madame LeBieu or Lucie."

Calliope's smile faded. "Ah, but I like Sport like this."

"You liked him as a dog."

"But this way I have a man to hang around with." She smiled again. "And he's pretty darned good-looking for a man, don't you think?"

Sport smiled, baring shiny white teeth.

"Still, it's not fair to Sport to be stuck in a man's body. He's not cut out to live as a human and we don't know how long the spell will last. If you teach him how to be human, how will he feel when he goes back to being a dog?"

Calliope pouted. "Ah, Alex, you take all the fun out of things."

She pulled Calliope into a hug. "I'm sorry. It's the practical side of me. The one that took care of a dozen siblings for years."

"And here you are trying to take care of me." Calliope sighed and stared down at Sport sitting so naturally at the table. "And Sport."

"I'll give my mother a call and see if I can talk our way out of dinner with the family."

"Good idea. Maybe you'll have better luck than I did. I can't say no to your mother."

"I think she's got a little Voodoo magic in her." Alex headed back to her purse in the hallway, calling over her shoulder, "No one can say no to her." She dug her phone out of the bottom and hit the speed dial for 'Mom,' noting all the missed calls she'd had from her and Theo.

Why couldn't he get it through his thick head she wasn't interested?

"Hello," a bright female voice answered.

"Let me speak to Mom," she demanded.

"Nice. I'm home for one day and my big sis doesn't even say hello. I see how it is."

Alex prided herself on recognizing each of her sibling's voices over the phone. As the oldest daughter, she was always the one calling to remind them of someone's birthday. "Sorry, Amelia. When did you get in?"

"I drove up from New Orleans this morning. I'll be here a few days."

"Good. Why don't you come by the gym while you're in town?"

"I will. I could use a good work out."

"Is Mom around?"

"No."

"No? Where is she?" Her hope of getting out of dinner dwindling, she stared across the room at Calliope and Sport.

"She should be back any minute. Had to run a pot of soup to Mrs. Badeaux. Apparently she's laid up with the gout."

"Tell her to call me when she gets back, please."

"Why don't you talk to her when you come to dinner?"

Because I don't want to come to dinner. Alex bit down on her tongue. She hadn't seen Amelia for several months.

"Oh, wait." Her sister laughed. "You don't *want* to come to dinner, do you?"

She sighed. "How'd you guess?"

"Dolley and Madison told me about the man Mom's got lined up for you."

"So it *is* another match-making attempt. I knew it."

Amelia chuckled softly. "Dolley and Madison were all excited. They said he's really cute. Even I'm looking forward to meeting him."

"Good. You can have him. I'm perfectly happy single."

"Honey, you're preaching to the choir. But Mom means well."

"I know. I've just had something come up and well..." How did she explain over the phone about her dog becoming a man? No one would believe it.

"The only way you're going to get Mom off your back is to bring a guy home."

As if a light bulb went off in her head, she stood with the phone in her hand, staring straight ahead, ideas exploding within.

"Alex? Did I say something wrong?"

"No. No, you didn't. In fact, you said something so right, I can't believe I didn't see it for myself."

"What did I say?"

"Nothing. Just tell Mom I'll be there for dinner."

"I'm taking it that it's not on my account, although I'll be happy enough to see you."

"Of course I'm coming for you, sweetie." *And to parade a man in front of Mom to show her I'm capable of getting one on my own.* Perhaps Lucie's Voodoo was exactly what she'd sold it as, the answer to her prayers, her dreams come true. "And tell her to set an extra plate at the table."

Finally, she'd get her mother off her back.

She clicked the cell phone off and called out,

"Calliope, we've got work to do if we're going to dinner at Mom's house."

Chapter Five

Ed stepped into the marina before five o'clock in the evening, hoping to catch Joe Thibodeaux before he called it a day.

A white-haired man stood behind the counter, digging through a box of what looked like junk to him.

"Mr. Thibodeaux?" he called out.

"Ain't no mister here," the older man grumbled and jerked his hand out of the box, a hook buried in his thumb. "Name's Joe."

"Joe." Ed closed the distance. "Need help getting that out?"

"Got it." Joe jerked the hook out and stuck the bleeding thumb into his mouth. "What can I do for ya?"

"I need a fishing guide."

"*Mais*, now maybe I can help you out." Joe studied him. "What kind of fish are you hopin' to catch?"

Thinking back to his encounter with Theo Ledet, he answered, "Largemouth bass."

"Been bitin' pretty good back in Bayou Black." Joe rubbed his thumb on his jeans. "Wanna go with a group or solo?"

Being in a group would advertise his inexperience. "Solo."

Joe set the box on the floor and straightened. "When you figurin' on going out?"

Ben had said something about the locals knowing the optimal times to fish, and Joe was supposed to be one of the best guides around. "I understand you're the expert in these parts. What time is good for you?"

"Anytime's good time for me. But if you wanna catch largemouth bass, the water levels will be right in the early morning or late at night. Gotcha some spinners or buzz bait?"

He had no idea what the man was talking about, but didn't want to let on. "Not yet. I have my pole but hoped to get bait here." He glanced around the dingy interior of the marina. Racks of every kind of lure, hook, line, and bait stretched before him in a daunting array. "You've been fishing these bayous, Joe, I trust your knowledge. What works for you?"

With a quick glance at the older man, he let go of the breath he'd been holding throughout the whole bait question.

Joe led him down the aisle and picked out several spinners and buzz bait combinations. "These oughta work. And if you plan on catching flathead catfish while we're out, you'll want some of these." He pulled a plastic container from the glass-front refrigerator on the side wall, opened it, and grabbed a couple of balls of something nasty looking.

The stench nearly knocked him to his knees. Eyes watering, he pulled his shirt up over his nose. "What the hell is that?"

"Best stink bait in south Louisiana." Joe's leaned his nose over the container and sniffed. "My own recipe. Stinks like hell. Just the way catfish like it."

A recipe Ed had no intention of ever using. "I'll stick to bass for now, thank you."

Joe shrugged. "Missing out on some good catfishing. Mozelle Reneau has a mighty fine recipe for fried catfish and okra. Might even get her to fix up a mess, if you get a hankerin' while you're here."

"Thanks, but I'm just here to fish." He didn't think he could ever eat catfish again, knowing what these people used for bait. "Bass fishing, if it's all the same to you."

Joe sealed the lid on the stink bait container and

placed it back in the refrigerator. "So when do you want to head out?"

"How early is early morning?"

"We'd leave at five. Gotta be here by four-forty-five to stow your gear."

He was really wishing he'd been volunteered for any other job but this one about now. "Then I guess I'll see you at four-forty-five tomorrow morning."

When he walked out of the marina with his purchases, Joe walked out with him, locking the door behind him. "Speaking of fried catfish..." The marina owner tipped his nose into the air.

He did the same and the scent of fried fish made his stomach turn over.

"That would be my dinner callin' me," Joe said.

A four-door Ford Fusion pulled up to a house two doors down from the marina. A gray-haired man got out, reached into the back seat and pulled out a small suitcase.

"Another tourist?" Ed asked, trying for casual curiosity.

"Yup. Called this mornin' looking for a cottage to rent. Just lucky I had a cancellation or he'd be out of luck."

"Is he from around here?"

"Said he's from New Orleans. We get a lot of folks out from New Orleans. They like to get away from the hustle and bustle." Joe's lips twisted. "I certainly understand that. Usta live there myself."

"You did?" He faced the older man, sure he was pulling his leg. He acted as if he was part of the bayou, born and bred.

"You'd never know it by looking at me, but I was a high-fallutin' lawyer back in the day."

"And you gave it up for this?"

"Damn right I did." Joe scratched his scraggly beard. "Ain't never looked back."

"Why?"

"You know what lawyers are like." Joe hitched his jeans. "It just wasn't me."

Having gone up against some of the slimiest attorneys Louisiana had to offer, Ed nodded. But then he wasn't sure he got the lure of the bayou. Not yet. So far it was hot, steamy, and full of insects and other less savory creatures. The sooner Leon Primeaux went to trial, the sooner the Ragsdale woman could leave the swamp, and him with her.

"The man say why he's here?" Ed asked.

Joe rocked back on his heels, digging his hands into the back pockets of his faded, ragged jeans. "Same as you."

He did a double-take before he realized what Joe was talking about. "Avid fisherman, huh?"

"*Mais*, he said he was looking for some good fishing." Joe's mouth twisted. "Not sure about avid. Have ta wait and see."

"Has he hired a guide yet?"

"I asked him, but he said he just needed a boat, no guide." Joe's brows dipped. "Don't like renting my boats until I know whoever's taking it knows his way around the swamp. Mr. Mills said he can get around on his own. Hope I don't have to go lookin' for him."

Interesting. A tourist wanting to get out on the bayou by himself. He made a note to keep an eye on the man. "Mills, huh? A common enough name."

"First name's not so common."

"Oh, yeah?"

"Oscar." Ed shook his head. "Reminds me of one of those kids' puppet shows on TV." Joe hitched up his pants. "I better get going. Don't want to be late to Miz Mozelle's dinner table. See you in the morning."

Ed glanced at his watch. He had just enough time before dinner to get back to his cottage and make a call to Ben.

He made it back to the rental without being accosted by alligators or Boyettes. As soon as he entered, he placed a call to Ben, leaving a message for him to run a search on Oscar Mills, assuming that was his real name.

With thirty minutes left to kill, he thought he might use it to figure out what the hell all this stuff was he was expected to use at the butt-frickin' crack of dawn.

He sat on the front porch and spread out the equipment he'd purchased. "This can't be all that difficult." Hell, if those folks on the reality shows could fish in the bayous, an educated man from Baton Rouge ought to be able to do it. He pulled his computer tablet out and cursed at the lack of WiFi. Okay, so he was on his own. With a half hour to go before the dinner gauntlet at the Boyette cafeteria, he was determined to make it work.

He started by trying to let out a little line from the rod and reel combo. After several attempts, he leaned back with no more line out than he'd started with. Short of tearing the reel apart, he didn't have a clue.

"You have to press the lever on the side to loosen the line," a small voice said from beside him.

He jumped and nearly decked a boy with black curly hair and bright blue eyes.

Beside him stood a girl with softer features but of the same height and with the same blue eyes.

"Let me guess," Ed said. "Boyettes?"

They nodded in unison.

"Do you all come in pairs?"

Again, in unison, they shook their heads.

"Do you have names?" he asked.

"I'm Teddy," said the girl and she pointed at the boy. "He's Roosevelt, but everyone calls him Rosie."

The boy's eyes narrowed and his fists clenched. "Only if they want a fat lip."

Ed raised his hands in surrender. "Okay. I'm not looking for a fight. Roosevelt it is."

The two sat on the porch at his feet and stripped the lures from their packaging.

"I take it you've done this before," he stated.

"Our oldest sister's been taking us fishing since we were little," Teddy offered. She released the line from the reel with practiced ease and threaded it through the rings along the length of the pole.

Since the twins couldn't be more than six or seven themselves, that meant their sister had been taking them fishing since they were toddlers, barely out of diapers. "She must be pretty good at it."

"She is," Rosie said. "Knows all the good places to go." He tied a lure to the end of the line and hooked it to one of the rings.

"Does she guide fishing tours?"

Teddy reeled the line in until it grew taut, the hook on the ring anchoring the line so that it didn't fly around. "No, she owns a gym in Morgan City."

Ed made mental notes about the kids' handling of the rod and reel so that he could do that later without looking completely inept. "She owns her own gym?"

"Yes, sir." Rosie arranged the other hooks, lures and spinners in the tackle box. "We go there for Karate lessons."

"Sounds like she's looking out for you," Ed observed. He hadn't had any older siblings to look out for him. Since his own parents had died when he was four, he'd been pretty much on his own to figure out important things like tying his shoes, let alone lures on fishing lines. Some things he'd mastered on his own, others he apparently had to learn from seven-year-old strangers.

"You're coming to dinner aren't you?" Teddy stood and brushed the dust from her cutoffs.

"Yes, ma'am," he said.

She nodded, all serious. "Good, 'cause we came to get you."

He put the pole and tackle box inside the door and locked the cottage before setting off across the yard to the Boyette house, Teddy's little hand in his and Rosie marching alongside, too much of a man to hold his hand. He marveled at how small and yet trusting Teddy was and how good it felt to have a child's hand in his. Made him feel big and somehow more responsible. He shook off the unwelcome idea and concentrated on what lay ahead. Kids...who thought they'd be...well...not so annoying? Or was it only in small doses?

Having an escort reminded him of the nightmare of what he was in for that night. Dinner with an army of children who all looked and sounded alike. So much for escapes. The Boyettes had him surrounded. He'd have to wring Ben's neck next time he saw him. This place...this family...should have come with a warning label.

"With the new clothes, shoes, and haircut, it'll work," Calliope said. "Trust me."

Her stomach churning, Alex slowed the closer they got to her mother's house. "I don't know. It seemed like a good idea two hours ago, but now I'm getting cold feet."

Sport walked upright between them, his gaze darting around at every movement, his feet still clumsy in the over-sized shoes they'd borrowed from Maurice Saulnier. Once, Calliope had to jerk him back from going after a cat. Alex had to hold him steady when a squirrel raced up a tree in front of Miz Mozelle's house.

This is a really bad idea. She almost turned and ran back to her house at least half a dozen times in the few blocks they'd gone. "He has the attention span of a..."

"Golden retriever. Give him time, he's been human for less than a day." Calliope hugged Sport's arm. "You're a good boy, Sport."

"He *is* a good boy. Poor, baby." She could imagine the dog's confusion after waking up a man and then having her wave a decorative pillow at him when he'd done nothing wrong. She hugged his other arm, partly out of love for her dog, and partly to keep him from seeing Granny Saulnier's pink poodle out of the corner of his eye.

They'd come all the way across town without any major incidents. They could make it through one meal at the Boyette house. It wasn't new territory for Sport, just a new perspective. Armed with the training they'd given him throughout the early evening, he should be able to handle one evening with the family. With so many people at the table, Sport wouldn't be required to say much.

Unless...

"God, I hope Mom doesn't go all Inquisition on Sport." Her cold feet got colder. "If she starts giving him the third degree and he answers with woof, I'm sunk."

"Why don't you just tell your mother what really happened?" Calliope leaned around the man in the middle. "She might be of help getting Sport back to where he belongs."

Torn between lying and dealing with yet another dud her mother dragged off the streets, Alex was ready to try anything. "I really hope by bringing Sport over as my manfriend that I can put the kibosh on Mom's matchmaking."

"You could have done that with Theo," Calliope said.

She shuddered. "I didn't want Theo at the dinner table with my family. I care more about by family than to subject them to that creep."

"Point taken, but you and I both know that if your mom doesn't like Sport as your *manfriend*, she'll keep pushing men at you."

"I have to do something. She's making me crazy." Alex held tight to Sport as a bird flew down in front of them, snatched a bug off the road, and flew away. Maybe it wasn't the best idea to use Sport for this lie. She had never been good at lying to her mother. The woman was psychic or something. She could see right through her and every one of her children. The taste of soap in her mouth lingered in her memories of the times she'd been caught telling lies.

As they approached her childhood home, Calliope whispered, "Last chance to back out."

On the verge of performing an about-face, she ground to a stop.

From the opposite direction, Teddy and Rosie

led the tall, dark and handsome man she and Calliope had run into early that morning when they'd been chasing Sport through the streets.

"Oh, my God," Alex muttered. "Of all the people she could be trying to set me up with..."

"The man from this morning." Calliope giggled. "I can't wait to hear the conversation at the dinner table."

"Mom will be mortified if she finds out I was out chasing a naked man through the streets in my night-gown." She tried to turn, dragging Sport with her. "Turn around before he sees us. Quick!"

Sport tensed and refused to go the other way. Apparently he recognized the twins and wanted to greet them as always.

"Uh-oh. We accounted for Sport being comfortable at your mother's house, we didn't take into account that he'd want to jump all over your siblings, like he usually does." Calliope strained to hold the man back as Alex dug her feet into the ground.

"Holy hell. Heel, Sport," she said as quietly and firmly as she could.

Sport's body trembled from head to foot, but he heeled.

"Think that man will recognize us from earlier today?" Calliope asked.

"Pray he doesn't."

With the strength of his one-hundred-seventy-pound body in his favor, Sport dragged the women to the door of the Boyette home, arriving at the same time as Teddy, Rosie, and the stranger.

"Alex!" Teddy dropped the man's hand and rushed forward, hugging her around the middle.

Rosie, with a little more restraint, hurried to hug her as well, leaving the man standing alone by the steps.

Teddy remembered her manners first. "Come meet Mr. Marceau."

So the man had a name.

She glanced across at him, guarding her expression. "Mr. Marceau."

"Call me Ed." His gaze locked on hers, a smile tugging at the corners of his lips. "So we meet again...Alex, is it?"

"Alex Boyette," she said in a rush, her nerves compromised by his devastating half smile. She wondered how much more disturbing a full smile would be. The widening grin let her know he remembered her from that morning. So much for going unnoticed in a small town. She held out her hand. "Nice to meet you."

"Nice to put a name to a...face." His warm tone and the strength of his fingers curling around hers sent a rush of electric current washing over her. She yanked her hand free and turned to Calliope. "These are my good friends, Calliope and Sport."

Ed shook Calliope's hand and reached out to shake Sport's.

Sport stared at the hand.

She nudged him in the side and whispered, "Shake!"

Sport's brows furrowed and he lifted a limp hand.

Ed shook it and let go.

One more hurdle passed. She let out a breath and turned toward the house. "Let's go in," she said, her voice high, strained. "This was a really bad idea," she muttered beneath her breath.

Ed climbed the stairs beside her, "Did you say something, Ms. Boyette?"

"No, no." Her cheeks burned. She was a terrible liar. "I just can't wait to see what Mom has fixed for dinner."

Inside offered no relief from outside. Hugging Sport close to her, she led the way through the hallway and into the large dining room where it looked, to the untrained eye, like the Boyettes were having a family reunion. The only one missing was Ben. And her father. A pang of sorrow pulled at her heart. Frank Boyette had loved every one of his nineteen children and made it a point to talk to and hug each of them at least once each day.

A tiny hand slipped into hers. "Alex, sit by me, please."

She smiled down at the littlest of the Boyette brood. "Hey, Molly." She lifted her five-year-old sister in her arms and hugged her close. "How's my sweet baby girl?" Her mother constantly reminded her that she could have had children Molly's age by now. Even Teddy and Rosie's age, if she'd started having kids right after finishing college.

"You look so natural holding a child, Alex. You need some of your own." Barbara Boyette sailed into the room, carrying a large platter of fried catfish, setting it down in the middle of the oversized table her husband had made out of an antique door he'd found in a building they'd been tearing down in Morgan City. He had prided himself in making something out of nothing and never lost an opportunity to instill in his children a sense of thrift and ingenuity.

God, she missed him. She could have moved to a larger city where she would have made more money and put her marketing degree to better use. But she had a lot of reasons to hang around and help her mother. Eighteen reasons to be exact.

Her mother swooped in to nab Ed. "Oh, you did make it. Good." She hooked her arm through his and led him to the seat next to her usual spot and pushed him into it. "You'll sit, here." She glanced at Alex. "Alex, honey, put your sister down and come introduce yourself to Mr. Marceau. I believe you two are closest in age."

Holding Molly like a shield, she shook her head. "Mom—"

"Doesn't she look like she'd make a great mother? She's single, you know." Her mother rested a hand on Ed's shoulder and smiled across at her. "Hurry and sit, dear, the fish is getting cold."

Barbara rounded the table and hugged Calliope. "Oh, dear, it is so good to see you." Every time she saw Calliope, her mother embraced her like a long lost relative. Even though she'd seen her two days earlier. "And who do we have here?"

Calliope smiled, her lips tight. "What's your name?" she said to Sport.

Sport's eyes grew wide and he barked, "Sport!"

Her mother laughed, "Well, then Sport, nice to meet you. I'm so glad you could come to dinner with Calliope." She squeezed Calliope's arm. "Nice to see you dating again."

Calliope shook her head. "I'm not—"

"You two can sit across from Mr. Marceau and Alex."

Alex swallowed a moan as her mother sat her

friend and Sport across the wide table from where she was expected to eat.

"Ed, Sport, meet the family." Her mother pointed as she went. "Ben's the oldest, and he's not here right now, but you know him already. Alexandra Belle is next, then Harry and Truman, Amelia, Abraham, George Washington, Dolley, Madison, John Kennedy, Thomas, Edison, Paul Revere, Susan B, Woodrow, Eleanor, Teddy, Roosevelt and Molly B." She breathed in and sighed. "Did I leave anyone out?"

"No, Mom," Alex said. "That about covers it." This was always the point at which any halfway interesting man her mother coerced to the dinner table got that glazed look and found a convenient excuse to escape as quickly as possible.

Her mother shooed some of her siblings into the kitchen to fetch the rest of the meal.

She studied Ed. His eyes weren't glazed and he didn't have that deer-in-the-headlights look. In fact, his lips were twitching with what looked like the beginning of a smile. He wasn't bad-looking. Some women would find him very attractive. Ah, hell, who was she kidding? He was sexy, handsome, and had a great smile.

Alex's biggest problem with him was that her mother had set her up, once again, and she wasn't interested in a relationship. Not now when she barely had time to run her business. Between the deal she was working to provide hospital employees access to her gym and now Lucie's hex, she was booked. No time for love or dating. Still...he was nice-looking and his grip had been firm, not limp like that of some of the men Alex had met. Never mind the electric current that had zipped up her arm at his touch.

"Is there something I can do to help?" she asked, rather than take her designated seat beside the man who'd seen her practically naked in the street that morning.

"No, no, Truman and Amelia are—well, bless my soul, there they are now with the fixin's."

Truman and Amelia entered through the swinging kitchen door, carrying heaping bowls of red beans and rice. They were followed by Dolley, struggling under the weight of a platter spilling over with hushpuppies, Madison with a bowl of green tomato relish, and JK carrying two pitchers of iced tea.

As Amelia passed Alex, she whispered, "He is a hunk, isn't he? Wouldn't mind waking up to him every morning."

She groaned. Even her sister was in on her mother's plot to marry her off.

"Please, everyone have a seat." Barbara Boyette lifted her hands like a conductor and everyone scrambled for their seats. She was no exception. Old habits died hard in this family. She pulled out her chair in time for her mother's hands to fall, and sat, as cued, her shoulder brushing Ed's.

She scooted away, glancing down at Molly who had managed to squeeze into the chair beside her. For the first fifteen minutes, most of the conversation centered on passing trays of food and comments praising the chef. She waited for her mother's usual lead-in to her oldest daughter's availability.

Calliope cut Sport's catfish and Sport managed to spear the bites with his fork, cleaning his plate faster than anyone else. He always did like Mom's fried catfish when he was lucky enough to get the leftovers.

Throughout the meal, Alex barely touched her food, her heart lodged in her throat, waiting for Sport to do something that would make her mother ask more than her usual amount of questions.

When everyone filled their plates and eaten a good portion of the food, her mother started the conversation. "Mr. Marceau is a friend of Ben's, up from New Orleans for vacation."

"Please, Mrs. Boyette, call me Ed," he said.

She shoved a forkful of catfish into her mouth with the hope her mother wouldn't ask her a question she'd be expected to answer.

"Are you single, Ed?" her mother didn't waste time.

Alex fumbled with her fork and it fell to the floor between her and Ed.

They both reached for it at once, knocking heads.

Ignoring the pain, she whispered, "Please don't mention this morning."

Ed stared across at her and winked.

"Sorry." She grabbed her fork and sat up quickly, ignoring the scent of Ed's cologne. He smelled really nice. She hoped he was as nice as he smelled and honored her plea.

"Yes, ma'am, I'm single," Ed answered. "I was married once."

"Widowed or divorced?" The matriarch popped a bite of food into her mouth.

"Mom," Alex warned. "You're grilling your guest."

"Not at all." her mother waved her hand. "I'm getting to know him."

Ed's lips twitched. "My wife left me, claiming I was never home. And no, we didn't have any kids."

Alex prayed her mother would end her inquisition. Unfortunately, it was not to be.

"Are you in law enforcement, like my son?" Alex's mom asked.

"No, ma'am." Ed tugged at the collar of his shirt

before answering. "I'm a trained mediator." The tips of his ears turned a little red.

Alex studied him in her peripheral vision. Interesting. Her own ears heated and turned red every time she told a lie. Was Mr. Marceau lying to her mother? "What exactly does a mediator do...Ed?" She hesitated over his name as if by saying the name it brought them even closer than side by side at the dinner table.

Again, his ears reddened. "A mediator is someone people go to in order to help them settle disputes out of court." He turned to her. "Teddy and Roosevelt tell me you own a gym in Morgan City. What does a gym owner do?"

Before she could open her mouth, her mother jumped in. "She helps old ladies like me stay in shape, don't you, honey?"

"Yes, Mom, thank you."

"I bet you work out a lot," he commented. "I like to jog, myself." He popped a bit of catfish in his mouth and chewed.

Alex stewed, waiting for him to out her with her mother.

"The best time to jog around here is early in the mornings," Dolley said. "Right, Alex?"

The tips of her ears burning, she replied. "I wouldn't know. I save my energy for the gym... for the most part." *When I'm not chasing a naked man through the streets.*

"I prefer jogging in the morning." Ed looked up with a challenging smile. "You never know what you might see."

She nudged Ed with her knee and regretted it when a shot of awareness sped through her system at the simple touch.

"Sport, we're so glad you could join us this evening." The consummate host, her mother turned to Sport and Calliope and saved her from the conversation leading to the reveal of her early morning antics.

She clenched her fork and shifted her anxiety from one issue to another, praying for divine intervention.

Her mother smiled. "Sport's an odd name for a man. Alex has a dog named Sport."

"We all had a good laugh over it, didn't we, Alex?" Calliope smiled brightly. "Sport and Alex went to Tulane together."

"You did?" her mom queried politely.

Calliope whispered into Sport's ear and he barked, "Yes!"

"Are you staying in Bayou Miste, Sport?" she asked.

Calliope whispered again and Sport barked, "Yes!"

Alex saw it coming and waited for the next question.

"Really?" her mother asked. "Where?"

Calliope stared pointedly across the table at Alex.

She couldn't let her friend bear all the burden of the charade and jumped in with, "Actually, Mom, he's staying at my house."

"Oh." Her mother looked from Sport to her and back. "Are you two...you know...?" her gaze panned the table of young people. "Maybe we should discuss this later." Her lips pressed together.

"We're friends, Mom," she provided. "And yes, discussing it later would be best."

"Ed, Ben tells me you're an avid fisherman." Her mother drew attention back to her choice of men for Alex.

"I'm hoping to spend my vacation doing a little fishing. I've scheduled a guide for early tomorrow morning."

"Oh, that's too bad. Alex is very familiar with the bayous and knows all the best places to fish, don't you, dear? Perhaps she can take you out in the evenings after she finishes up at the gym."

"Mom, Mr. Marceau would probably rather go with his guide. Besides, I have Sport visiting."

"I could watch Sport while you take Ed out on the bayou," Calliope offered. "I mean, I could keep him company."

She glared at her friend.

Before she could back out of it gracefully, Ed sealed the deal with a smile and, "I'd like that."

The younger children finished their dinners before their older siblings. To avoid further questioning, she jumped up to help Molly, Teddy, Rosie, and Eleanor clear their plates. By the time they ran off to play, the adults had finished. Dolley and Madison gathered the rest of the empty plates and started in on the dishes.

"I'll help," Alex offered.

"No, *ma chère*." Her mother headed her off before she could duck into the kitchen and disappear. "Why don't you give Mr. Marceau a tour of the garden? *C'est magnifique* in the starlight."

She pulled her mother to the side. "Mom, stop playing matchmaker. I know you care about me, but I don't need help finding a man. Besides, like I said, I have Sport staying with me for a little while. Men aren't going to want to go out with me while I have a man staying at my house." There, that lie slipped off her lips a lot easier than the last. And it wasn't totally a lie. Sport *was* a man...for the time being.

Alex's mom touched her arm, her forehead lined with worry. "Sport seems nice and all, though kind of quiet. Are you sure you want to have a man stay with you, alone in your house?"

"I'm twenty-nine, Mom, not nineteen." She patted her mother's hand. "I know what I'm doing."

"Mr. Marceau is such a nice gentleman."

"Yes, I'm sure he is."

Her mother patted her arm again. "Then show him around the garden, and I promise not to bother you anymore."

She knew better than to believe her. "I can't leave Sport alone."

"I don't know why. He and Calliope seemed to have hit it off." Her mother smiled toward her friend and her man-dog. "She's quite taken with him. I saw her whispering to him all through the meal."

Calliope chose that moment to wave at her and called out, "Sport and I are headed back to your house."

"I'm coming," she said.

"Alex, please," her mother begged.

God, she hated it when her mother begged. Since her father had passed, she hadn't been able to say no to her mother.

"Stay and visit," Calliope offered. "I can manage Sport by myself."

"See?" Her mother beamed. "All taken care of."

This is not happening. All the effort to parade Sport in front of her mother as her boyfriend had somehow backfired. Now her mother had it in her head that Sport was Calliope's main man. *If only she knew.* If she had been a good daughter, she'd have been honest with her mother at the start. The opportunity to tell her the truth had come and gone about the time she introduced Sport in the first place.

"Fine." She waved her friend off and turned to find Ed. "One spin around the garden and I'm out of here." She didn't look forward to spending time alone with the man, not when his touch made her skin tingle and his semi-smiles brought on an attacks of butterflies in her belly and a strange ache between her legs. But if it would get her mother off her back, she'd do it and get back to her real issue—finding a way to turn Sport back into a dog.

Chapter Six

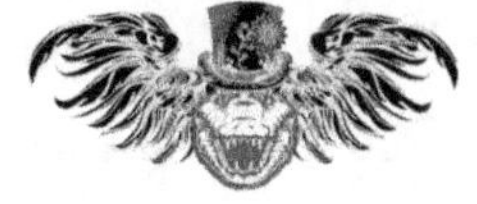

olley and Madison had Ed cornered in the living room, refusing to give him the opportunity to escape through the door and out of the Boyette house. They'd filled him in on their summer job duties of guiding tourists through the Beauregard Sugar Plantation House. Then they'd gone into a discussion of the different classes they were taking toward degrees in Marine Biology at Tulane. Listening to the pretty young girls in stereo was giving him a headache. He glanced around for help getting away and spotted Alex headed toward him.

"Mom said she promised you a tour of the garden. Come on." She grabbed his arm and practically marched him toward the rear of the house.

As they stepped out into the warm, humid night, he breathed in the thick bayou air and let it out.

Alex didn't give him time to absorb the ambience, though, jerking him down the steps of the back porch and onto the lush green lawn.

"In a hurry?" he asked.

"A night tour of the garden won't take long in the dark and you'll be free to go," she said, her tone short, clipped. Something had her panties in a twist.

Remembering a pair of black, lace panties, he wanted to know what had her riled. If it was him, even better. He purposely slowed.

Because she had hold of his arm, she was forced to match his pace or let go. "Do you always run around with your hair on fire?" he asked.

Alex's lips tightened and she glanced across at him, letting go of his arm. "I'm sorry. My mother makes me nuts."

"She obviously cares about her children."

"I know." Alex sighed and walked to the edge of the bayou canal. "Sometimes too much. Thanks for keeping this morning's incident to yourself. I'd never hear the end of it, if my mother found out."

"You're welcome." Ed leaned against a cypress tree and crossed his arms. "I have to admit, I've seen some crazy stuff, but never a man streaking through town followed by a woman in a sexy nightgown." He chuckled, the image still fresh in his mind and equally as tantalizing.

Alex's cheeks grew a deeper shade of pink and her lips twitched into a smile. "Must have seemed pretty strange."

"I was warned they did some crazy things down in the bayous, but what exactly was your friend Sport doing running around town in the altogether?"

"He was..." Alex glanced in all directions and finally stammered, "...he was getting some air." She shrugged as if streakers were an everyday occurrence in Bayou Miste. "Sport is a bit of a free spirit. A nature-lover."

"Are you in love with Sport?"

"We've known each other for a while and I love him dearly...as a friend." Alex blinked. "Not *that* kind of friend. I mean, we're not doing anything. Although he did sleep in my bed last night, but that was before I knew—" She stopped, clapping a hand over her mouth. "I'm sorry. I must sound crazy. It's been a helluva day and I'm having difficulty processing it all."

"You seem to be popular in these parts. Your mother says you're single, but I ran into a guy in Morgan City who said his girlfriend was an Alex Boyette. Is there more than one of you?"

Alex moaned. "For the record, I don't have a

boyfriend. I don't want a boyfriend, and the man you met—"

"Theo," Ed offered.

"—is on the verge of being slapped with a restraining order." Alex dropped onto a nearby stone bench and buried her head in her hands. "All I want to do is run my business and be left alone. Why can't my mother understand?"

He sat on the bench beside her and stared out at the canal in front of him. "You're lucky to have a family who cares."

"I know." She sat back and stared out at the water, too. "My life is too complicated right now."

For a few minutes he said nothing, enjoying the peace of the bayou as the cicadas began their song and frogs croaked. "I take it you're the sister who taught Teddy and Roosevelt all they know about fishing?"

Alex snorted. "It doesn't even touch what my dad taught me, but I'm trying to fill the space."

"When did he pass?"

"Two years ago." She sniffed and touched a finger to the corner of her eye. "I miss him," she whispered, her voice catching.

He slipped an arm around her.

When she stiffened. He assured her, "Don't

worry, I'm not interested in a relationship either. I'm here for a short time, then I'm gone."

After a moment, she leaned into him.

He marveled at how natural and warm and good it felt, her body nestled into his. "Whose idea was it to name all of you after famous people?"

"Dad's." She laughed. "He thought it would be easier to remember our names."

"He had a point," Ed said. The stars laid a blanket of diamonds across the water and the big blossoming flowers all around them gave off a soft, pleasing scent. He could almost see the attraction one might have to bayou living.

But the longer he sat with Alex curled into the crook of his arm, the more uncomfortable he became. His groin tightened, his body heated, and those damned black lace panties flashed through his mind like a persistent neon sign. Finally, he removed his arm and stood. "Well, that should satisfy your mother. I'll just duck in and tell her thank you and be on my way back to my cottage."

Alex stood and laid a hand on his arm. "Ed?"

Her touch lit his blood on fire and it was all he could do not to pull her into his arms. "Yes, Alex?"

"Thanks for not saying anything about...well, you know."

"It'll be our little secret."

Then she leaned up on her toes and pressed a kiss to his lips.

Before she could get away, he captured her around the waist and deepened what was probably meant as a chaste, thank-you kiss into a damn-you-and-your-black-lace-panties bruising kiss that left him breathless.

When he set her back on her feet, he wondered who was more surprised by the kiss, he or she. "In case your mother was watching," he lied and beat a hasty retreat, afraid if he stayed, he'd be in a lot more trouble than he already was.

Now would be a good time to get out on the bayou and check out how his witness was faring. Things had gotten far too dangerous in town.

Alex hurried back to her house on the other end of Bayou Miste, her head in a whirl, a deep ache building at her core. All because of one little ol' soul-defining-curl-a-girl's-toes kiss. What was supposed to have been a quick walk in the garden had turned into something a lot different.

Ed.

What woman in her right mind fell for a guy named Ed? "Not that I'm falling," she muttered aloud. "Not in a million years. I have a house of my own, a business in Morgan City, a family who needs me and a dog..." She clutched her hair, ready to rip it out. "Oh, my God, I have a dog who needs to be returned to his rightful body." She knew she didn't have time in her busy schedule for a romance, no matter how badly she now wanted to get laid. Relationships required time—a commodity she didn't have a lot of. Besides, Ed would be leaving town at the end of his vacation to return to New Orleans.

From what she had observed of friends with long-distance relationships, they didn't work.

Besides, her business and her family were here and took up all of her time. *Get it through your thick head!*

Alex jumped back and screamed as a large, male figure stepped in front of her.

"Hello, Alex."

Pressing a hand to her thundering heart, she funneled all her frustration into the one person she had no desire to see... "Theo Ledet, you scared the begeesus out of me."

"Sorry, I just wanted to see you."

"By slinking around in the dark?" She planted her fists on her hips. "What the hell are you doing in Bayou Miste? I told you, I don't want anything to do with you. That one night at the Raccoon Saloon was a mistake."

"I thought you loved me."

"Read my lips, Theo. I. Don't. Love. You." She'd tried letting him down softly, but nothing had gotten through to him. Not talking to him, not yelling at him. "I had too much to drink. I wasn't thinking clearly. What happened was a *huge* mistake."

"But I want to marry you. Make an honest woman out of you."

She stared at him, realizing she was talking to a very dense brick wall. "Tomorrow, I'm going to march down to the county courthouse and file for a restraining order. Do you know what that is?"

He nodded. "Uh-huh."

"It will mean that if you get anywhere near me, you will be violating the law and they will throw your sorry ass in jail." She inhaled and let it out slowly, trying to bring her pulse rate down. "Theo, leave me alone. Please."

She didn't give him the opportunity to respond. Instead, she pushed past him and jogged the rest of the way home. The entire way she felt as if she was being watched. Twice she almost tripped over her own feet looking back to see if Theo had followed her. The street was clear, but the feeling continued all the way to her house.

The door was locked and she had to knock; a creepy sensation like a spider web floating over the back of her neck made her knock again, louder than she'd meant to.

Calliope yanked open the door. "What's wrong? Where's the emergency? Between you and Sport, you'd think the bayou was on fire."

She fell through the door and slammed it behind her, shooting the bolt home.

Sport stood beside the door, his eyes narrowed, his lips pulled back over his teeth, a rumble building in his chest.

"Is he growling?" she asked.

Calliope stroked Sport's arm. "It was the weirdest thing. Just before you started banging, he rushed to the door and did his human version of barking, then growled. What's out there?"

"Theo, for one."

"That jerk-wad. What did he want?"

"What do you think he wanted?" She pushed the spooky sensation to the back of her mind and kicked off her shoes.

"To marry you and give you a dozen children just as dumb as he is?"

"You got it."

"Well, you said you wanted someone who would love you no matter what."

"Yes, but I also want him to be able to string more than two words together in a sentence and sound halfway intelligent."

Calliope's lips twitched up on the corners. "Like Ed Marceau?"

"I don't know what you're talking about." Her ears burned.

"Ha! So you two did more than smell the roses as you walked through the garden, didn't you?" Calliope pointed a finger in her face. "Don't lie. Your ears are turning red. Fess up. You have the hots for the mediator."

"He's here on vacation. When he leaves, he's gone."

"So?" Calliope spread her arms wide. "What's it hurt to have a little fling? Who knows, you might end up tossing your dirty sweatshirt in the ring and moving to the Big Easy."

"I'm not moving to the Big Easy. My business and my family are here."

"You aren't responsible for raising your siblings. Your mother has a good handle on that and they're growing up."

"Yeah, but they don't have Dad around anymore to teach them the things they need to know that Mom doesn't have the time or inclination to teach."

"Like what?"

"Fishing, karate, self-defense. How to tie a slip knot."

"Honey, they can join the Boy Scouts."

"My love-life is not what's in question at the moment." She stared at Sport curling up on the couch, yawning. "We have to get Sport back to normal." She squared her shoulders and pulled on her mud boots. "Can you stay with him while I pay a visit to Madame LeBieu?"

"At night?" Calliope shivered. "In the dark? Aren't you afraid of getting lost?"

"I know my way around the bayou day or night. Besides there's a sky full of stars and a nearly-full moon rising. Plenty of light to get around. I shouldn't be gone for long."

"Promise me you'll be careful."

"I know the risks." Yeah, but she didn't know why she'd been so spooked minutes earlier. She shrugged it off as a residual effect of her encounter with Theo. "Don't stay up."

"Where do you want Sport to sleep?"

"He seems comfortable where he is. You can have my bed or the futon in the spare bedroom."

"I'll take the lounge chair, just in case Sports wakes in the night."

"Thanks for helping."

"I'm glad I had the night off. Remember, tomorrow night I have to work."

"Oh, yeah. And Mom volunteered me to take Ed out fishing at night. I hope Madame LeBieu has an answer to our Sport problem by then." Alex grabbed a flashlight and let herself out the front door. She glanced right then left, peering into every shadow, that creepy sense of being watched still as strong as when she'd entered.

Theo must have scared her more than she originally thought. Bayou Miste was a quiet little corner of the bayou, free of crime and bad guys. Well, for the most part. There was the time when Ben had come to flush out the man responsible for the attacks on congressional candidate Jason Littington. And the guys who'd tried to kill Craig Thibodeaux's fiancée, Elaine, when she'd discovered them dumping pollutants in the bayou.

Okay, so it wasn't as quiet and safe as she liked to think. But, damn it, she had to get to Madame LeBieu and undo the damage to Sport. She'd be careful and keep her eyes and ears open for bad guys and alligators.

She set off across the road and down the bank to the canal where she kept her skiff tied off to a cypress tree. She stepped in and, with her paddle, pushed away from the bank and pulled the rope to crank the motor. It chugged, spit out a cloud of smoke and engaged. With her hand on the till, she spun the little boat around and skimmed along the still surface of the canal. As she passed the marina, a movement caught her attention and she turned to look back, studying the shadows at the corners. Nothing moved, no one stepped out. Yet, that sense of being watched persisted until she reached a fork in the channel and headed out into the bayou where Madame LeBieu's shack had stood for as long as Alex could remember.

She could find her way with her eyes closed, as many times as she'd visited Lisa and Lucie LeBieu growing up. It still felt strange to know that Lucie wouldn't be there. Having married Ben, they'd moved to Baton Rouge over a year ago. Lisa, her twin, was in and out between her life in Atlanta and her home here in Bayou Miste.

As she skimmed across the water, she let the events of the day slip from her shoulders. To many, the bayou at night might appear spooky, filled with deadly creatures and magic. To Alex, it was the time she remembered her father most. He'd bring her out to fish under the stars. She and Ben had been the oldest and spent more time with him on the occasional weekend he took off from his business of shrimp fishing in the gulf. They'd sit in silence for the most part, hooks in the water, waiting for a nibble.

They had been good times that brought back even better memories.

Alex slid into the little dock in front of Madame LeBieu's house, tied off, and stepped up onto the rickety wooden planks. Before she reached the front porch of the weathered structure with the peeling paint, the old woman flung open the door and filled the entrance. She wore a bright pink, red, and yellow muumuu and a flamboyant red scarf tied around her head and knotted in a big bow. Her light mocha skin glowed in the moonlight, her dark eyes sparkling like the stars above. "Alexandra Belle Boyette, what you be doin' in de bayou dis late at night?"

"Hi, Gran LeBieu." She climbed the steps and hugged the woman who was as much a grandmother to her as she was to her own granddaughters. She'd spent many nights in Lisa and Lucie's room with Calliope going over teen magazines and talking about the boys at school. "I came to see my favorite Voodoo priestess."

The old woman waved her toward the door. "Come in, come in. I have chicory abrewin'."

"Thank you, but I can't stay long." As Alex followed Madame LeBieu into her ancient kitchen, memories washed over her, making her long for the simpler times when her dad was still around, and she and her girlfriends only worried about what to wear and who to gossip about. She ran her hand along the edge of the antique stove where Lucie had concocted a love spell that seemed to have turned the town of Bayou Miste upside down.

"Tinkin' 'bout ol' times?" Madame LeBieu pulled a ceramic mug off a shelf and poured the fragrant chicory-flavored coffee from an old metal pot. "Tell dis ol' woman what be troublin' you."

Alex plopped onto a stool, leaned her elbows on the big butcher block at the center of the kitchen and buried her face in her hands. "Oh, Gran LeBieu, everything's a mess."

"Did not de *gris* help wit' de wishes?" she asked.

Alex dropped her hands and stared across at the Voodoo queen. "That's what I'm talking about. The pouch you helped Lucie make, what kind of magic was in it?"

"A little o' dis, a little o' dat." The woman shrugged. "Did your wishes come true?"

"No!" Alex stood and paced across the room. "That little *gris* bag turned my dog into a man. Mom finally came up with a decent matchmaking candidate who kisses like nobody's business, and I have a man-dog living with me who pees on rose bushes and chases Granny Saulnier's pink poodle. I don't recall wishing for any of that." She flung her hands in the air and faced the Voodoo queen. "Help!"

"Drink." Madame LeBieu filled another cup with chicory-flavored coffee and sipped from hers. "All will be well, if you give de magic time."

"But I don't have time! Poor Sport doesn't have a clue what's happened. Calliope is teaching him how to be a man. What happens when the spell wears off and he goes back to being a dog? He'll be so confused. And I don't have time to keep him out of trouble. He's learning how to open doors and talk, but he's still a dog."

"Dis dog is much smarta dan you tink." Madame LeBieu set her cup on the butcher block and smiled at her. "He learn what he need to know because he loves you. In time, you will be glad o' dat."

"Can you see the future?" She grabbed the old woman's hands and squeezed. "Will this mess clear up before I go insane? Before I have to own up to the whopping lie I told my mother about Sport? I don't know how much more of this I can handle."

Madame LeBieu squeezed her hands. "You be fine, my sweet Alex. All will be well in time."

"Can't you give me something to put things back like they were? A potion. An anti-spell *gris gris* pouch. Anything. I need my life back in order."

"Was you life so great?"

"Yes! I have my own business, I'm close to family. I was happy."

"And alone."

Oh, no. Not Gran LeBieu, too. "I like being alone!"

"Do you?" Madame LeBieu's intense gaze brooked no lies.

"Mostly." She did miss male companionship. Her lips still tingled from that kiss she'd experienced with Ed, leaving her with a whole lot more longing than she'd started the day with. "Okay, so it's been a little lonely lately."

"And you not be gettin' younger."

"Oh, please. You sound like my mother." She pulled her hands free of the old woman's. "Twenty-nine is not over the hill."

"No, but you have so much more love to give, for a man, for children."

"I have enough children in my life."

Madame LeBieu shook her head. "Not you own."

"I don't even have a man in my life, how can I even think of children?" She pushed her shoulders back. "I take it you don't have anything in your bag of tricks to help me out of this colossal mess."

The woman spread her arms wide. "De magic mus' run its course."

Tears welled in Alex's eyes—of frustration and anger. Not so much directed at the Voodoo queen. She couldn't find it in her heart to be mad at this woman who had the best interests of her community at heart. She was angry at her own dissatisfaction that led to her rash wish, and her inability to alter the resulting events. "Thank you anyway." She rounded the butcher block and hugged the woman close, inhaling the scent of perfume that reminded her of her friend. "I miss Lucie."

"She, too, misses you, *ma chère*." Gran LeBieu patted her back. "Give de magic time."

"You don't have a spell that will make me more patient do you?" She leaned back and stared into the woman's dark brown eyes, almost black with her magic.

"Maybe, der is someting dat will help." She shifted Alex away from her, and went to her pantry where she kept everything from sugar and flour to the spit of a tailless raccoon. When she returned, she held something in her hand. "Close you eyes," she commanded.

Alex closed them, laughing nervously. "You aren't going to turn me into a frog, like you did Craig Thibodeaux, are you?"

"No, *ma chère*. Shush and listen to you heart."

Something like powder touched her face. She flinched but kept her eyes closed tight. For a moment, Alex almost wished she'd kept her mouth shut. Madame LeBieu's spells always worked out, but the process sometimes proved tricky.

"Ezili Freda Daome, Goddess of love and all dat is beautiful, listen to our prayers, accept our offerings, and enter into our arms, legs, and hearts."

Alex listened as a soft rumbling like the drums of the ancients thrummed in her head. Her senses sharpened, her thoughts cleared, and her focus centered on the Voodoo queen's softly spoken words.

"Mistress of love, hear my plea,
help dis woman's eyes to see
As troubled times mus' be unfold
to loose de bonds of past dat hold
and know de course when darkness reign
and sacrifice tho gives her pain
help her to embrace de right
for only love will win de fight.
Ezili Freda Daome, Goddess of love and all dat is
beautiful, hear me now."

With a soft touch on her arm, Madame LeBieu broke her trance. "Go, *ma chère*. De hour grows late."

She blinked her eyes open and stumbled toward the door and out to the dock. As she steered her skiff back home, she went over what the Voodoo queen had said, analyzing every word of the old woman's *cunja*. What did she mean troubled times unfolding? Hadn't they already unfolded with Sport turning into a man?

Around the bend in the channel, she went.

Where the water had been smooth as glass from the route she'd come, she noticed the residual waves of a recent disturbance, headed out the opposite direction. Alex spun on her seat and studied the wake in the moonlight until another bend in the path blocked her view.

A chill slithered down the back of her shirt and she revved the throttle, sending her little boat skimming toward the little town of Bayou Miste and home, telling herself that whoever was traversing the swamp this late at night was probably out frog gigging or fishing. Uh-huh. Then why did she hear the sound of drums echoing in her head like a recent memory?

Chapter Seven

Ed held his GPS in front of him as he inched along the waterway, praying he could find the way at night as easily as he had during the day. The bends and forks in the liquid back roads weren't as clear as they'd been before and he wasn't sure, but he thought he'd heard another engine. He'd killed his motor immediately and listened.

Yes, it had been another motor. By the way it gave off a high-pitched, fading whine, it was a small one, headed the opposite direction. When it faded into the distance, Ed restarted his own engine and continued his trek through the bayou for several miles until he came upon what appeared to be an abandoned shack jutting out of the marsh on stilts, tucked into a stand of cypress trees on a rare knoll of land.

He tied off on the ramshackle jetty and climbed out of his boat.

Nothing stirred. No lights shone from the window. As it should be. The Ragsdale woman and her guard were given strict instructions to remain at the rear of the cabin at all times. The windows in the back had been spray painted black to block any light from shining through.

When he pushed the front door open, he waited for someone to challenge him.

Not a sound. His senses on alert, he pulled his Glock from the case on his belt and eased through the door

The cold nose of a rifle pressed into his side.

"You better be Ed," a deep, deadly voice stated, "or you're dead."

"Relax. It's me." Ed pushed the nose of the weapon away, cleared the doorway and closed it behind him before flipping on his flashlight with the red lens cover.

"Well, damn. I'd hoped to get to shoot someone." Marcus Caldwell led the way to the back of the house.

Ed chuckled. "That bad?"

"Worse," he stated. "It's been one of those days.

One lousy day and she's already bored and ready to return to Baton Rouge, hit men be damned."

"I feel your pain." He thought he had it bad in town. It was nothing compared to being stuck in the bayou with a demanding, pain-in-the-ass mob informant. "Any movement?"

"A couple of guys came by in a pirogue rigged with a trolling motor right at sunset." Marcus snorted. "Thought I might get to shoot someone then. Turns out they were frog giggin'."

"Did they nose around or see anything?"

"Nope. It was if they never even saw the old house back here."

"Good. I know you'd rather be where the action's at, but the less people who know anyone's out here, the better."

"Yeah, yeah." Marcus paused in front of a closed door. "Anything going on in the real world?"

"I wouldn't know. I wouldn't consider Bayou Miste the real world."

"Gotta be better than spending time with the informant from hell."

Ed clapped a hand on Marcus's back. "I spoke to Ben earlier. He said Leon isn't talking and from the calls they've monitored, they've gotten nothing."

"So we don't know when he'll have his people make their move."

"No." Ed smiled in the faint glow of the flashlight. "Cheer up. It won't be long. The trial is in three days. Primeaux's thugs have to be looking for their star witness."

Marcus patted his rifle. "I'll be ready." Then he opened the door to the kitchen area at the back of the house.

"About time you got back." Phyllis Ragsdale sat in a folding chair at the collapsible camp table they'd set up in the empty kitchen. She wore shorts and a tank top that didn't quite cover her ample, surgeon-supplied breasts. With her brassy, bleach-blond hair piled on top of her head, she leaned back and propped her bare feet on the ice chest, fresh blue polish gleaming in the light from the Coleman lantern. "Did you bring me the chocolates I asked for?"

Ed reached into the backpack he'd carried up from the boat, pulled out a bag full of every kind of chocolate bar Morgan City's dollar store had to offer and tossed it on the table in front of her.

"Oh, there is a god." She dug into the bag and ripped into the first bar, sinking her teeth into the chocolate caramel and peanuts. "I might survive after all," she said, chewing and talking with her mouth open. "That good fer nothin' louse get fucked in the slammer yet?"

"No, Phyllis," Ed replied. "He's waiting in his very own jail cell until the trial."

"I hope someone jacks him up." She took another bite of gooey chocolate. "He ain't done nothin' but slap me around from the day we met."

"You didn't have to stay with him," Marcus pointed out.

She snorted. "Yeah and I lived in a bed of fuckin' roses? Once ya know somethin', you know somethin'. If he hadn't got caught with his hand in that senator's cookie jar, he'd still be knockin' me around. Between me and the senator, we'll put the bastard away." She smiled up at Ed, chocolate clinging to her teeth. "Then I'll have more time for the likes of you, Eddy."

He hated it when people called him Eddy, especially trash-mouthed women like Phyllis. She'd called him Eddy from the time he'd loaded her into the SUV to the time he'd dropped her off at this Cajun-bubba version of a safe house. If he hadn't needed her testimony so badly, he'd have thrown her to the alligators on the trip out.

"I'd better get back," Ed said. "I have to be fishing out on the bayou early in the morning."

"I don't want to hear your hard luck story, Marceau. While you're sleeping like a baby on a real bed, I get to spend the night in a folding chair, watching over Ms. Pottymouth."

"Oh, you can't leave yet." Phyllis lurched out of her chair and waddled her way over to him, walking on her heels with her wet toenails in the air. "Dontcha wanna stay and play cards? I play a mean strip poker." She draped an arm over his shoulder and ran her fingers along the V of his polo shirt. "Really, I lose, every time," she purred, pressing her boobs against his chest.

He grabbed her wrist and removed her other hand from his shoulder. "I'd rather poke my eyeballs out. But thanks for the offer." He stepped away before she could get her octopus arms around him again. "Why don't you play a hand with Marcus?"

"Thanks, man." Marcus glared at him. "I might just shoot you anyway."

Phyllis pouted. "He's no fun. He keeps threatening to shoot me."

"Yeah, he's like that." Ed chuckled and slipped the straps of his backpack over his shoulders. "He's a trigger-happy son of a gun." He leaned close to Marcus as he passed him on the way to the door and said in a tone loud enough for Phyllis to overhear. "If she gives you any trouble, shoot her in the knee. It'll keep her from moving around and she'll still be able to testify."

"Hey!" Phyllis cried. "I'm not deaf."

"Give the dog a bone." He nodded to Marcus. "If you have any troubles, send up a flare."

"They don't pay me enough for this gig," Marcus groused.

"No, they don't." He opened the door and clicked on his flashlight. "You don't have to walk me out."

"Please. I can use the fresh air after all the nail polish fumes." Marcus walked him to the front door and they stood in the shadows as they scanned the bayou below for movement.

After several long moments Ed whispered, "All clear. See you tomorrow night. Can I bring you anything?"

"A gag for her mouth?"

"You got it." He left, dropping down into the boat and turning on his GPS to get him back. He'd be glad when this assignment ended and Leon Primeaux was safely tucked away in a federal prison for life. He could get back to civilization, away from the bayou and the temptation of kissing a certain bayou princess.

Hell, why did he have to go and think of Alex? Even after visiting the woman from hell, his libido jacked up every time he thought of Alexandra Belle Boyette and that kiss.

That *damn* kiss.

Alex bent to tie her tennis shoe. As it neared the end of her day at the gym, she was so tired, she could barely see straight. She had struggled throughout to keep up with, much less lead, her aerobics classes and had taken a nasty kick to the jaw in her black belt karate class.

That's what lack of sleep got you. She'd tossed and turned after her trip to visit the Voodoo queen. When she did drift into a troubled sleep, she'd dreamed she was running through town in her night-gown. Ed was at the end of the street, waiting for her, his arms open wide.

Joy filled her heart and she tried to run faster, but her feet sank into mud, the suction pulling her back. The sound of Voodoo drums filled her head and a dark presence stared out at her from the shadows of Bayou Miste. Suddenly she was alone on a tuft of land in the deepest, darkest part of the bayou, surrounded by cypress trees whose branches were draped in long swaths of Spanish moss, sweeping low to the ground like arms reaching out to her.

A dark silhouette disengaged from the shadows, stalking her, his eyes glowing red in the moonless night.

She tried to scream but no sound came out of her.

As the fiend steadily advanced on her little island amidst the stagnant water, she saw the flash of a light-colored animal headed her way. It was Sport. Not the man he'd become, but the dog she knew and loved.

Right when the man reached his hands out to clutch her throat, Sport leaped into the air.

"Earth to Alex."

She shook her head and looked up, taking a moment for her eyes and mind to focus on her twenty-seven-year-old sister, Harry. "What's up?"

"You have ten minutes until your next aerobics class. Do you want me to take this one? You look beat."

Alex dropped onto a metal folding chair and sighed. "Would you? I don't know what's wrong with me. I don't have it in me today."

"Could it be you were up all night dreaming?"

"Yes. As a matter of fact, I was."

"About a certain hunky man?" Harry grinned.

Boy did Harry have it wrong, but then if she explained her dream, she'd probably end up spilling her guts about Sport, the Voodoo hex, and her late night trip into the bayou. What was easier, confessing to the insanity or letting her sister believe she'd stayed up all night mooning over a very sexy man and a kiss she wouldn't soon forget?

"I saw you kissing him in the garden. So did Mom

and everyone else. Did she finally strike gold and find you a keeper?"

Alex refused to meet Harry's knowing gaze. "He's all right."

"All right. You were playing tonsil tag long enough that he had to be more than all right."

"Please, Harry. Ed's in Bayou Miste on vacation. When he leaves, he's out of my life. Why get attached?" Alex heaved herself out of the chair and walked over to the punching bag, giving it a light cuff with her fist.

"Because he's nice, good-looking, and apparently a good kisser." Harry grabbed the bag and held it steady.

Alex bounced up on her toes and swung at the bag like a boxer. "So?"

"So? So why don't you see where it goes? He'll be here at least a week. That's plenty of time to find whether or not he's a possibility."

"Harry, he lives in New Orleans. That's two hours from Bayou Miste. He has a job; I have a business. Do the math. It wouldn't work, even if I wanted it to. Long distance relationships don't last.'"

"You don't have to stay in Bayou Miste, you know."

"It's my home."

"So, come home to visit every once in a while.

What would it hurt for you to get out in the big wide world and see more than the stinkin' bayou?"

"Says the one who lives in Morgan City. I never wanted to leave, you did. Speaking of which, why haven't you?"

Harry shrugged. "I don't know. I guess I was waiting for you to go first."

"You'll be waiting a long time."

"Hey, wait a minute. This discussion isn't about me. It's about you and the very distinct possibility of you finding someone to love."

"In Ed?" She chuckled. "The best I can hope for is a quick fling. I'm not moving, and we're back to 'where does he live?'" She bounced again on her toes and threw a side kick at the punching bag. "It won't work."

"But Mom thinks you—"

She kicked the bag again hard enough that Harry staggered back. "Why is it Mom worries about me, when you're just two years younger and don't have a boyfriend?"

"Probably because you're closing in on thirty and your biological clock is ticking." Harry grinned and stepped away from the punching bag as Alex slammed it again with another kick. "How about I take that class for you?" Her sister backed away and made a run for the dance room where the aerobics class was held.

"Did you kick all your frustrations out, or should we go away and come back later?" Calliope led Sport into the gym, keeping out of range of the swinging punching bag.

"It's okay, I don't think I could kick again without falling on my ass."

"Ass," Sport repeated and grinned at Alex.

"No, Sport," Alex said, reaching out to touch his arm. "That's a bad word."

He tipped his head. "Why?"

Alex looked from him to Calliope. "This is new."

"We've been watching TV all day. He's a child-like sponge. You wouldn't believe all he's learned today. He's actually stringing together sentences. Go ahead, ask him something?"

She stared at Sport. "How are you, Sport?"

"Fine, thank you," he said, his words stilted but clear and understandable, not barked like those of the night before. "How are you?"

Alex laughed and clapped her hands. "Very good, thank you." She hugged him and hugged Calliope. "Amazing."

"Yeah, I know. And I hate to leave him, but I have to work tonight and I need to go home and change first."

"Right. You don't know how much I appreciate your staying with him all day."

"It was a pleasure, really. Sport's such a nice guy. A girl could fall for someone like him."

"Calliope..."Alex frowned. "He's a dog. Don't forget it."

She sighed. "I know." Then she stood on her toes and pecked Sport's cheek with a kiss. "But I love him as a man or a dog. Gotta go!" She turned and ran for the door, her eyes suspiciously moist. Before she reached it she stopped and turned. "Oh, and your kitchen sink has a leak. I put a bucket under it and called your mom." Then Calliope was gone.

"Why she leave?" Sport asked.

Alex studied Sport, still shocked that he was speaking so well within such a short amount of time. "She has to work."

"Why?"

"Because she has to make money."

"Why?"

"You need money to pay for things like food and a place to live."

"Do you work?"

She laughed. "Yes, Sport, I do. But right now, we can go home. Harry is taking my last class for the day."

"Calli..." Sport's lips twisted and he started over. "Callipuppy loves Sport?"

"Yes, Sport. Calliope loves you." With a gentle smile, she hooked Sport's arm and led him toward the door. "I love you, too."

"Sport hungry."

"Then let's get you something to eat and get home to see what's going on with my kitchen sink."

They stopped at a barbeque restaurant and got two brisket sandwiches to go. By the time they reached Bayou Miste, Sport had eaten his way through both and was begging for more.

She parked the car in the driveway. Before she switched the engine off, Sport bounded out and ran up the porch steps and into the house.

"Sport, wait!" Had Calliope left her front door unlocked? She hurried after the man-dog. Noises from the kitchen drew her there.

Sport stood by a figure lying on the floor. "What are you doing?"

The man with his head tucked under the kitchen cabinet, answered, "Trying to fix a leak. Where's Alex?"

"Hello?" she called out from the hallway.

"Oh, Alex." The man's head came up fast, banging into the pipe above him.

"Ed?" She entered the room. "What are you doing in my kitchen?"

"Your mother asked if I'd ever fixed a leaky pipe in kitchen sink." He scooted out from under the sink and sat up, rubbing the back of his head. "I didn't know then that she meant *your* sink. She gave me a key and sent me down the street to this house."

Alex crossed her arms. "I'll have a word with my mother. You're on vacation, not here to be her handyman."

"I never was much of a handyman, but I have fixed a leaky kitchen sink before. And I looked it up on the internet." He stood, the width of his shoulders making Alex's kitchen seem much smaller than before.

Her heartbeat stuttered then beat faster, slamming blood through her veins. This man had been in her dreams, in her thoughts, and in her head all day long. Having him in her kitchen was...well...overwhelming.

"Are you done?" she asked, her voice a little breathy, to her dismay.

He wiped his hands on a dishtowel, nodding. "Try it out for yourself."

Alex would rather have stayed across the room from him. Not that she thought he would attack her or anything. More because she didn't want to be attracted to him or risk being close enough to kiss. But he waited for her to test his handiwork.

She eased past him, the scent of his aftershave playing havoc with her senses.

With her attention on him instead of her faucet, she reached for the handle blindly and turned it.

Water poured out of the drain below the sink and sprayed her legs. She jumped back and ran right into his chest.

"Damn." Ed reached around her and turned off the faucet. "Guess I need to try again. Give me a minute, and I'll have it fixed." He dropped down on the floor and slid under the cabinet again, soaking his shirt. "Could you hand me that pipe wrench on the floor beside you?"

She scooped the wet wrench from the puddle of water and handed it to Ed. "Righty tighty, leftie loosey," she said from memory. Her father had taught her that saying, while helping her work on her first car when she was sixteen.

"I knew that." Ed twisted the wrench to the right. "Try it now."

"You sure you don't want me to check it out first?" she asked.

"Well, actually, you might want to."

She dropped to her haunches and ducked into

the cabinet, her chest pressing against his. "What seems to be the problem?"

"This pipe connection is old and had come loose." He pointed to the pipe. "I thought I was tightening it, but I guess I loosened it instead."

She had stopped listening as soon as Ed started talking, the vibrations of his chest rumbling against her breasts, causing her entire body to tingle.

"You want to tighten it yourself?" he asked. When she didn't respond, he said. "Or not." His gaze captured hers. "Maybe we should leave it to a plumber."

Alex straightened and backed away so fast her foot slipped in the water and she fell on her ass beside him.

Ed scooted out from under the cabinet and pulled Alex into his arms. His fingers skimmed along her arms and down her back, sending mini shock-waves into her skin everywhere he touched. "Are you okay? Anything hurt?"

"Only my pride." She moved and winced. "And my tailbone."

"Does that mean our fishing night is off?"

"I don't think I could sit comfortably in a boat after that." What a great excuse to get out of a night alone with Ed.

"Alex?" Calliope's voice called to her from the front of the house. "Why's the front door open?"

"In here." She struggled to stand.

Ed straightened and helped her to her feet as Calliope burst through the door.

"There you are." She stared from Ed to Alex. "Oh, you have company."

"No, I don't." Alex's cheeks heated. "Ed was here fixing my leaky sink." She turned the handle as if to prove it, and the pipe held. "See?" Then she remembered. "I thought you had to work tonight."

"One of the other girls asked to take my place tonight since it's cheap beer night. I thought I'd come back here and hang out. Maybe take Sport for a walk or something."

"Yes, please." Sport pushed through the kitchen door and headed for the front of the house.

"Are you sure you want to?" she asked. "I mean, there are all kinds of distractions."

"It would do us both good after being cooped up in the house all day. Be back in a little while." Calliope ran after Sport, catching up as he darted outside, the door slamming in their wake. With Calliope and Sport gone, she stood in the kitchen, alone with Ed.

Her pulse pounded through her veins as she

turned to face him. "Well, how much do I owe you for your work?"

Ed gripped her elbow in his hand and pulled her against him. "One kiss," he said, his tone deep, rich, and as smooth as melted chocolate dripping over her body.

She pressed her hands against his chest, her gaze slipping from his eyes to his lips. "Just one?"

His mouth crashed down over hers, stealing her breath away. Arms like iron bands clamped around her middle, molding her body against his.

Unable to resist, she sank into him, her arms slipping around his neck, urging him deeper, her teeth parting to allow his tongue access to hers. Her leg slipped around his, the position pressing her aching center to his muscular thigh.

The kiss was so intense, she didn't register that it was her phone jangling until the sixth ring, and it was in the purse she still had hanging on her shoulder.

"You might want to answer that," Ed said, his lips skimming across her cheek and down the long column of her throat.

Fumbling blindly in the jumble of her purse, her hand curled around her cell phone and yanked it out as Ed's fingers slid the strap of her tank top off one shoulder and down her arm. She jammed her finger on the talk button. "What?" her breath caught and held as Ed's lips trailed to the swell of her breasts.

"Alex?"

Even the jarring sound of her mother's voice didn't yank Alex out of the spell Ed's hands and lips were weaving over her body. "Uh-huh."

"Are you home?"

Big, warm fingers hooked the hem of her shirt and dragged it up over her head, forcing her to take the phone away from her ear before replacing it and replying, "Uh huh."

"I asked Ed to fix your leaky sink. Is he still there?

At that moment Ed flicked the catch on her bra and her breasts spilled free. "Oh, yeah."

"Let me talk to him, please."

Past cognitive thought, she handed Ed the phone and reached for the hem of his shirt.

Chapter Eight

Ed held his arms up as Alex slid his wet shirt up over his head and tossed it across the room. Then he pressed the phone to his ear. "Ed speaking." He bent to take one lush nipple between his lips and pulled it into his mouth.

Alex moaned softly, her fingers threading through his hair.

"Oh, Ed, how'd it go?" Mrs. Boyette asked. "Did you fix the leak?"

Letting the breast slide out of his mouth, he nipped the tip before answering, "It's fixed."

He brushed his lips across the other nipple and it beaded into a tight little, tasty bud.

"Thank you so much for doing that for her," Mrs. Boyette droned on.

"You're welcome." He nipped the bud and rolled it across his tongue.

Alex's leg slid up the back of his calf and she straddled his thigh, rubbing her crotch against him.

Molten heat shot to his groin and he nearly came.

"Now, make sure my daughter thanks you properly."

"Oh, she is. Sorry, Mrs. Boyette, gotta go." He hit the end call button and tossed the phone onto the counter. When he turned his attention back to Alex, a frown was pressing her brows together.

"Maybe we shouldn't..."

"Oh, I know we shouldn't." He growled low in his chest, the most primal instinct urging him on. "If you want to stop, say so now, otherwise..." Ed cupped her bottom and lifted her, shoving her up against the wall.

She wrapped her legs around his waist and pressed her full, luscious breasts against his naked chest. "What if Calliope and Sport return?"

"Then we'll make this quick."

She breathed in and then let out a long stream of warm air that brushed across his neck. Leaning forward, she whispered, "Then hurry."

He didn't need a second invitation. Ed bent to claim her lips, thrusting his tongue between her teeth, stroking hers in a sensual dance.

When he broke off for air, he lifted her. "Which way?"

"Down the hall, first door on the left," she said, her words clipped, her breathing coming in short gasps.

His dick swelled against the confines of his jeans, aching to be free. Blinded by lust, he marched down the hall and kicked the door to her bedroom open, carried her through, and shut it with his foot.

Though her bedroom was a study in femininity with a pink and yellow floral comforter and light cherry furniture, all he could see was the bed.

"Put me down," Alex said. Her legs slid to the ground and she stood in front of him, ripped the buckle loose on his belt, and stopped. "Are you packing?" She pointed to the holster attached to his belt where he kept his Glock.

He shrugged. "I hear there are really big alligators in these parts." He tweaked her nipple, rolling it between his thumbs. "Does it bother you?"

"No, my brother carries." She reached for the button on his jeans. "Besides it makes you seem more dangerous." When she couldn't get the button free, she slid her fingers into his waistband.

"Dangerous, huh?" He brushed her hands aside and yanked her bicycle shorts down to her ankles, where he noted her bright pink toenail polish gleaming up at him.

She stepped free of the garment and kicked it to the side.

He groaned.

Instead of black lace panties, she wore a neon green thong, the tiny patch of fabric covering the apex of her thighs and nothing else. With a grin, she hooked the thin elastic band and slipped them off.

Quicker than he could say *orgasm*, he pulled his wallet from his back pocket, and fished out a small foil packet. He tossed it to her and she caught it. While she tore it open, he kicked off his shoes and peeled his wet jeans off, laying them, gun and all, across a chair. "Last chance to change your mind."

Her gaze slid over him, catching on his erection. "No way you're backing out now. Show me what this handyman can do." She slid the condom over his cock and circled her hand around him, leading him by his staff toward the bed.

"Just so you know," she said as she scooted her butt onto the mattress and spread her legs wide. "I'm not interested in a long-term relationship."

"How long is long?" He captured her face between his palms and tipped her head back. "I'm here for a week. Two tops."

"I like my independence." She wrapped her legs

around his middle and pressed her heels into his buttocks.

"I hope that's not all you like." He slid into her slick entrance and her channel tightened around him, drawing him deeper.

Alex fell back against the mattress, her head tipped back, her fingers pinching her nipples as he drove into her again and again.

Long, black hair worked free of her loose braid and spread across the pale pink and yellow comforter. Her gorgeous curves made him want to bury himself inside her. Her heels dug into him, urging him faster, deeper, harder until he was hammering, the intensity of his thrusts driving him to the edge far sooner than he'd expected.

One last time and he pulled free and dropped to his knees between her legs.

Alex leaned up on her elbows, her face flushed, her eyes glazed. "Why did you stop?"

"I want you to feel it, too."

"Oh, hon, I am."

"Not like you're going to." He spread her thighs and kissed a path up to her damp core and thrust his tongue into her.

"Okay. I'm beginning to see what you mean." She dropped to her back her fingers clutching his hair. "Please, continue."

He chuckled and parted her folds, moving in to take the sweet spot by storm.

One flick and she moaned. Another and her back arched off the bed, her fingernails digging into his scalp.

His cock swelled even more as he sucked her clit between his lips and pulled hard.

"Oh, my, don't."

He let go and blew a warm stream of air over her heated sex. "Want me to stop?"

"Oh, my, don't...stop!" She dragged him by the hair back to where he'd been. "Please!"

He swiped his tongue over her in a long steady stroke, then flicked the tip, again and again until her body tensed, her hips rising, pumping. When he had her where he wanted her, he stood and scooted her up on the mattress and climbed between her legs.

In one long forceful thrust, he drove into her as deep as he could and held for a moment to gather himself. He leaned over her and captured her mouth with his as he withdrew and slid back into her, settling into a steady rhythm, the pace increasing with the pressure inside him. He held tight to his control for a full minute then let go, allowing the sensations to catapult him into the heavens. Buried deep inside her, he dropped down onto her, breathing hard.

When he could think again, he rolled to his side, taking her with him.

Alex wrapped her arms around his neck and pressed her face into his neck. She didn't say a word.

He brushed the hair out of her face and tipped her chin up. "Are you okay?"

For a long moment, her face remained pressed to his neck and she didn't speak, then she slapped her hand on his chest and pushed up. "No. I'm not all right." Alex glared at him and rolled off the bed.

"I'm sorry. How did I hurt you?"

"Damn it." She stood in front of him, her hair curling around her naked breasts, her shoulders back and fire flashing from her eyes. She was so beautiful it took his breath away.

Alex pointed to her door. "Get out."

"I must have misunderstood." He eased off the bed. "When you said please continue..."

"Just leave." Her voice caught and if he wasn't mistaken, those were tears trembling on her lashes.

He pulled up his damp jeans and zipped.

Her bottom lip trembled and one lonely tear made a shiny trail down her face.

Up to that point he had been ready to leave. But this...

"Oh, hell, Alex." He reached out and yanked her into his arms, crushing her to him.

Her body shook against him, her tears wetting his chest. "It wasn't supposed to be like that."

"If you'd tell me what it was supposed to be like, maybe I could do better." He tipped her chin up and stared into blue eyes swimming with tears.

"You don't understand." She shook her head, more tears slipping down her cheeks. "You're supposed to be a fling. I'm not supposed to be that impressed. You're leaving!" She flung her hand in the air, catching him on the chin.

He flinched and drew back without loosening his hold around her middle.

Alex's eyes rounded. "Oh, Ed, I'm sorry. I didn't mean to hit you." She leaned up and pressed a kiss to the spot she'd hit him. Her mouth moved along his jaw line to his lips where she seared her mark on him.

His hands slipped down to the swell of her bottom and he tightened his hold as heat flowed south, swelling his cock yet again, where it nestled against her belly. When she broke off the kiss, she leaned her forehead against his chest. "This was a mistake."

"Didn't feel like one to me." He tugged her closer, rubbing the ridge of his jeans into her soft skin. "Let me get this straight. You're disappointed because you weren't disappointed?"

"Yes!" She palmed his chest, the sound like a slap. "Now I need you to go and never come back."

He chuckled. "Problem is, I'm having a hard time leaving." Again, he pulled her into his arms and held her, enjoying the feel of her breasts, the taut muscles beneath satiny-smooth skin, and the curve of her narrow waist right before the sensuous flair of her hips. "Yeah, a really hard time."

Alex pushed away and sighed. "Thanks anyway, but we can't do that again." She turned and gathered her clothes, slipping into her stretchy bicycle shorts and grabbing a baggy T-shirt from a drawer. When she had pulled the shirt over her head, she faced Ed.

He frowned and slid his feet into his shoes. "That's it?"

"I told you. I don't believe in long-term relationships, especially long-distance relationships.

Why he felt the need to argue, he didn't know. But when he opened his mouth to tell her he wanted to see her again, he didn't get the chance.

"Alex, we're home!" Calliope's voice cut through the tension-thick air.

Alex's eyes widened and she ran for her bedroom door. "Stay here until I get your shirt. And don't say a word."

"Why?" Then a thought hit him. "Hey, you and Sport aren't together, are you?"

"Huh? He's my—" She clamped her lips shut and stared at him then turned toward the door. "Just stay."

Before she could sneak out, her door flew open and two faces peered in.

"Alex?" Calliope's eyes grew as wide as saucers and her mouth dropped open.

Sport's eyes narrowed, his lip curled back in a snarl, and he actually growled.

"I think that's my cue." Ed eased past the pair, ducked into the kitchen, grabbed his shirt, and escaped through the back door. Instead of walking straight back to his cottage where he stood a chance of running into more of the nutty Boyette clan, he pulled on his shirt and headed the opposite direction, passing by the marina.

The sun was well on its way to the horizon, painting the sky in brilliant shades of orange, purple, and mauve. He couldn't see past the anger simmering just beneath the surface.

His phone vibrated in his pocket and he yanked it out. The caller ID indicated yet another Boyette to torment him. One he was obligated to answer. "What?"

"Ed?"

"Yeah, who did you think it was?"

"What's wrong?"

I just screwed your sister, she threw me out, and I'm not sure why, although I have my suspicions. "Nothing."

"Good, got something for you. Not much to go on, but thought I'd pass it on." He paused. "You sure you're all right?"

"Just spit it out, will ya?"

"Okay, okay. Although I'd like to know what's got your shorts in knot."

I really don't think you do, buddy.

"Word on the street is that Leon's put a bounty on our girl's head."

"We figured he'd hire a hit man, but a bounty?" He stopped walking, a heavy weight settling in his gut. "Damn. If that gets advertised far and wide, we'll have every thug in the lower forty-eight gunning for her."

"Yeah. It's a rumor we can't substantiate, but I thought it was worth warning you."

"Thanks."

"Anything I can do for you?"

"Got an army of bodyguards you can spare? If the rumor is true, my job here just got a whole lot more complicated." *Even above and beyond your sister.*

"You, me, and Marcus are the only ones who know where we've stashed the witness. Not even

Gordon Dean knows where she is," Ben said. "Every so often he tests me by asking, but I haven't told him or anyone else. We have to keep it that way."

"Understood." He didn't much care for Gordon. As his supervisor, he had to take orders from the guy, but he didn't have to like him. Tall and cocky, he thought a lot of himself. Ed always walked the other way when he spotted his boss's shock of neatly combed white hair headed his way. The man was annoying, flashy, and too politically oriented for his tastes.

"Ed, remember, it's important for you to blend in with the locals, let them know you're really there on vacation. We can't have someone poking around asking questions about you and watching your every move. The more believable you are as a tourist, the less likely they'll follow you out to the safe house. Have you met some of the residents yet?"

"Your family seems to comprise eighty percent of the population of Bayou Miste."

Ben chuckled. "Seems that way, doesn't it? Has Mom tried to set you up with one of my sisters?"

"Oh, yeah. First night at dinner."

"Which one? Alex?"

"You got it."

"Take it all with a grain of salt. My mom is determined to get her married off before she's thirty and

Alex is equally determined to retain her independence."

"I've noticed that. Besides, she'd got a man living with her." *And he growled at me when he caught me in your sister's bedroom.*

"What?"

"I take it that's news to you."

"Yeah. And here I thought she was a confirmed bachelorette. She must really care about this guy to let him move in with her. I'll have to call Mom for the scoop. In the meantime, keep your head low."

"Will do."

"Hey, Ed, if you want all the latest gossip on the comings and goings in Bayou Miste, pay a visit to Mozelle Reneau, or spend some time talking with my mother or Joe Thibodeaux."

"Got it. How's that trial going? Are you gonna free up anytime soon to help out down here?"

"Doesn't look like it. I've had some of the guys here volunteer to help babysit our witness, even Dean."

"He'd lower himself to play bodyguard to our diva?"

"I think he wants a piece of the limelight when we bring her in to testify."

Ed snorted. "I could do without that kind of help."

"Exactly the reason I chose you for the job."

"Thanks. Send the city dude to the bayou to wrestle the alligators. I see how it is."

Ben laughed. "You can handle it, as long as you don't take the plunge. Alligators love things that make a big splash."

Nice. He pocketed his smartphone and continued his stroll along the streets of Bayou Miste, keeping a close eye out for two-legged snakes and four-legged alligators. A desk job was looking better every minute.

"I can't believe you did the nasty with Ed." Calliope kneeled in front of Alex, holding her ankles while she did a set of fifty crunches on a mat.

Some local businessmen played a game of three-on-three on the basketball court at the other end of the building. Sport sat on a pile of mats nearby, watching as the men played, ready to jump up and chase the ball every time it rolled his direction.

Alex had pushed herself and her aerobics classes hard today and she couldn't let up now. Every time she gave herself downtime, she thought of Ed and she couldn't afford to dwell on what couldn't be. Her abs burned with each repetition until she fell back against the mat. "It was a mistake. Can we not talk about it?"

"Are you kidding me?" Calliope let go of her ankles and rolled back on her heels. "I want all the details."

"Your turn."

"I'm not the one needing to burn off my sexual frustrations."

Alex rose to a kneeling position and pointed to the mat. "Get down and give me at least thirty."

Calliope dropped onto her back, bending her knees. "You don't have to be bitchy."

"If you're doing sit-ups," she grabbed her friend's ankles and leaned into them, "you won't have the breath to grill me with questions."

"You used to be fun." Calliope groused and, huffing and puffing, gave her a half-hearted attempt at crunches. After twenty-five reps, she collapsed against the mat. "So how was he?"

Alex sat back and drew her heels in, dropping her knees to the side and bent over until her forehead touched the floor. "Freakin' incredible."

Calliope jumped to her feet. "What did you say?"

"Freakin' incredible. He was freakin' incredible." She looked up, her heart pinching in her chest. "I told you, I didn't want to get involved with someone who wasn't going to stick around. I'm not cut out for long-distance relationships, and my life is here." Alex rose and folded the mat, stacking it in the pile beside Sport. "It's just as well. He's not into long-term relationships, either."

Calliope darted in front of her. "He said so?"

"No, but he didn't protest when I told him I wasn't into them." She dodged around Calliope and headed for the room she'd set aside for karate classes. "Come, Sport."

Sport hopped off the mats and followed.

Running to keep up, Calliope pointed out, "Those are two entirely different things. He might be looking for his perfect match. And that could be you, *couyon*."

"I'm not stupid. Don't you and Sport need to go for a walk, or something?"

Sport grinned and grabbed Calliope's hand. "Callipuppy take Sport for walk."

Calliope frowned at her. "Fine. But don't think you're getting out of talking this easily." She slipped her arm around Sport and stared into his eyes. "You're so cute. I can't resist."

Alex frowned. "Calliope."

"Don't think you can give me advice on love. *You're* the one who's all messed up." She turned and marched Sport out of the room, calling out over her shoulder, "I'll bring Sport home later."

With a sigh, Alex bowed, stepped onto the mat, braced her feet slightly apart, and bent her knees. She balled her fist and struck out at the air, pulling her arm back sharply.

"This where you take out all your frustrations?"

She spun and dropped into a defensive position, her arms drawn into her sides, ready to strike.

Ed leaned against the door, no hint of a smile tugging at the corners of his lips, his face poker-straight, his brown eyes near black with intensity.

"How did you find me?" She shook her head. "No, don't tell me. Mom." She turned away and resumed her stance, this time throwing a double punch. "Why are you here?"

He slipped out of his shoes, bowed, then advanced on her, closing the distance until he stood so close she could smell his aftershave. "What happened last night?"

She shook her head. "Nothing." Her stomach clenched. She balanced on one foot and kicked the air as if she could kick her emotions into outer space. Damn this man for coming into her world and making her question her life. "I told you it was a mistake."

"No, it wasn't. Look at me and tell me it was a mistake."

When she didn't, he laid a hand on her arm. "Alex."

Something snapped inside, and she swept out her leg, planted her palm on Ed's chest and shoved.

Ed landed on his back and she came down on him, pressing her knee into his chest. "Why can't you leave me alone?"

He lay there for a moment, staring up into her eyes. "Because I can't." Then he erupted beneath her, flipped her onto her back, and pinned her to the mat with the full length of his body, trapping her wrists above her head. "Your words are telling me one thing, but your body language has an entirely different story."

"I told you, I don't want to see you anymore."

He shook his head. "Now, see? There you go again." He leaned close, his lips hovering over hers. "Look into my eyes and tell me you don't want to kiss me."

She struggled beneath him, refusing to face him. When she couldn't break his hold on her, she made the error of locking gazes with him. All the fight seeped out of her.

"Tell me," he repeated.

"I don't..." She bit her lip, her body burning everywhere his touched hers and she wanted his lips to claim hers so badly she could taste it. "Damn you."

Glaring up at him, she whispered, "Kiss me, already."

His mouth came down on hers, crushingly possessive.

When he released her hands, she threaded her fingers through his hair and dragged him closer, deepening their connection, her tongue thrusting through to slide along his.

Time seemed to suspend as they lay on the mat, locked in a kiss that rocked her world and scattered all her well-laid plans for her life and future to the four winds.

At last, Ed raised his head, his eyes glazed, his cock nudging against her. "Told you."

"Why did you come here, today?"

"I needed a work out."

"Alex?" A voice sounded outside the room.

She squirmed beneath him. "Let me up."

Ed rolled to the side and she jumped to her feet as Harry ducked through the door.

"Oh, there you are—" Harry's gaze bounced from her to Ed, who was rising from the floor, straightening his shirt. "Sorry, did I interrupt something?" She grinned. "I can come back later."

"No. You didn't interrupt anything. Ed was just leaving."

"Actually, I came to see if I could get in some

time on the weights." He turned the full wattage of his killer smile onto Harry.

Alex groaned, her tummy tightened, and her core ached. How was she supposed to concentrate on her business with Ed in the building?

Harry fell for Ed's charm. "Of course. I can show you the weight room, if you like." She darted a glance at Alex. "Unless you'd rather have Alex show you."

She waved her hand. "No, please. Show him. I have errands to run, then I'm headed back to Bayou Miste. Can you take my afternoon classes?" She didn't really have anything pressing, but she had to get out of the same room with Ed to regain some sense of self-control. Every time she was around him, she couldn't think straight. Her structured existence fell to pieces.

"You could use a little time off, sis. You've been tense the past couple days. Why don't you go out for lunch, go shopping, or get a manicure? I'll cover for you." Harry hooked Ed's elbow and led him away, smiling up at him.

She loved her sister, but at that moment, she wanted to scratch her eyes out.

Ed is mine.

Whoa. Where had that thought come from? Ed was no more hers than the moon. He was temporary.

She was firmly rooted in her life here in the bayou, near a family who needed her.

With a blunt reality check, she reminded herself that Ed hadn't made any declarations with his kiss or making love the previous evening. He'd bought into the short-term quickie idea and probably wanted to add it to his list of vacation activities to be enjoyed while in Bayou Miste.

She slapped a hand to her forehead. Of course. He only wanted the fling she'd offered in the beginning. Except, where she'd wanted to end it after one amazing hop in the sack, he wanted to take it through the rest of his stay.

Then what?

Then life would return to normal. The spell on Sport would wear off and Alex's structured, predictable life would resume.

She tugged her shirt in place, bowed at the corner of the mat, and left the karate room, realizing she was deluding herself. Never again would she look at those mats the same way.

Crap. Why did Ed Marceau have to pick Bayou Miste as his choice for a vacation in the first place?

Chapter Nine

Ed really hadn't had time to work out that morning and he wasn't exactly sure why he'd headed for Morgan City when his job was to keep his eyes open in Bayou Miste. But after his early fishing date with Joe, he'd made a pass through town in his Jeep and headed to Morgan City.

What he'd hoped to accomplish with that kiss was another mystery.

Alex Boyette wasn't part of his plan. Bayou Miste was a detour on his road to a promotion in the Criminal Investigations Division of the Louisiana State Police Department. He knew what life as an officer of the law did to marriages. His ex-wife had left him after three years of sitting at home alone more nights than he'd been there.

Then why had he gone back for more, when Alex had told him to get out and stay out of her life?

Because she was beautiful.

No, that wasn't all. She cared about others, not just herself, and she wouldn't abandon family.

But she had a man living with her. One she'd admitted caring for.

After a quick tour of the weight room with Harry, he made his excuses and headed back to Bayou Miste and back to work. With a bounty on Phyllis Ragsdale's head, he didn't have time to play with the locals, no matter how tempting.

As he cruised through Bayou Miste, his stomach rumbled. The town was so small, it couldn't justify the usual fast-food chains. His choices were limited to the Pancake House and the Cajun Kettle. He pulled into the Cajun Kettle's lot and parked.

The outside of the building didn't inspire great confidence in what lay within. Weathered white paint peeled from the sides, mildew gave the entire building a greenish tinge, and the wrought iron tables and chairs sitting on a concrete pad had long since lost their umbrellas meant to shade customers from the hot Louisiana sun.

He pushed through the screen door and a bell jingled over his head. Inside the lighting was dim and it took a moment for his eyesight to adjust. Red and white checkered vinyl tablecloths covered the mish-mash of tables and booths in the interior. The black and white linoleum tiles shouted the fifties and probably dated back to then based on their worn appearance. The order counter was so old, it looked gnawed-on by local wildlife. But the Cajun seasonings scenting the room promised better fare than ambience and made his stomach rumble even louder.

An older woman with coppery red hair and gray roots collected a paper bag from the counter and turned. When she spotted him, she smiled. "You must be Mr. Marceau. Joe's been tellin' me all about you."

"I'm sorry, should I know you?" He held out his hand.

"Mozelle Reneau, but you can call me Mozelle or Miz Mozelle." She turned to the chalkboard listing the menu items. "Clovis makes the best shrimp-okra gumbo in the parish. It is *très bon,* and the blackened catfish is fresh. Joe caught them this morning. But you know that."

Knowing what Joe used to catch the catfish, he opted for the gumbo. He placed his order with the big man behind the counter, who would better fit the role of a bouncer at the Raccoon Saloon.

While he waited, Mozelle continued to talk.

"We don't get too many folks come to visit in

Bayou Miste. Seems like we've had more than our share just this week."

His ears perked. "Is that right? I thought I was the only visitor."

"Oh, no." She laid her hand on his arm. "A retired gentleman rented Joe's cottage the same day as you rented Barb Boyette's. Funny, you two coming in the same day." She shifted her bag of food to her other hand. "Interesting man, Mr. Mills. Goes out every day in his boat for hours and comes back without any fish. Wonder what he does out there all day long." Mozelle stared into the distance then shrugged. "Who knows? We've had stranger visitors than that. Take the *couyon* who came in this morning, asking about airboat rentals. *Dis-moi la verité!* No one rents their airboats. Anyone who's been out in the bayou knows you have to have experience handling one of them and they aren't cheap."

"Did he give you his name?"

Mozelle's brows wrinkled. "No, as a matter of fact, he didn't." The bell over the door jangled and Mozelle started. "*Coo Wee!* Look at the time. I promised I'd be back in ten minutes. Joe's bound to be growlin' for his lunch. Nice to talk with you, *ma chère*. Stop by after fishin' for some beignets tomorrow morning. I make a fresh batch every other day." She scooted out the door, leaving blessed silence in her wake.

Ed took a seat by the window where he could watch the town's main street. Before long, the burly man emerged from the kitchen carrying a huge, steaming bowl of gumbo and a plate of crackers. The scent of shrimp and spices wafted up, making his stomach rumble in anticipation. As he dug his spoon into the thick liquid, the bell over the door rang again and Alex sailed in.

"My usual, Clovis, please." Alex turned to find a seat, spotted him, and rolled her eyes. "Are you following me?"

"Seems I was here first." He lifted his spoon. "Look, you might as well join me. I promise not to attack you or your food."

She frowned at him.

"Come on, Alex. Relax. What's having lunch with me going to hurt?"

"*Mais, oui.* I guess it won't." Her feet dragging, she walked across the floor and dropped into the seat across from him, letting out a huge sigh. "How long did you say you'd be in town?"

"Counting the days already?" His lips twisted. "A week, maybe two. Then I'll be gone and you won't have to bump into me anymore." That thought made a hard knot twist in the pit of his belly. Having only known Alex for a whole day, he found he liked her company and might miss it when he left.

Clovis set a bowl of gumbo in front Alex with the requisite plate of crackers.

"Thanks, Clovis." She lifted her spoon and nodded. *"Bon Appetit."*

They ate in silence until most of the food in their bowls had all but disappeared.

"I'm glad you're not one of those women who picks at her food." Ed set his spoon in the bowl and leaned back.

"I own a gym, teaching several aerobics classes every day. I burn calories."

"Have you always been in this great of shape?" His gaze raked over her, admiring the curves, clearly defined by the skin-tight exercise outfit she wore.

Her cheeks reddened. "No. I grew up chubby. In case you didn't notice, Cajun food can be fattening. When I went to college, I learned how to control my diet."

"And your life?"

"Yes."

"So you went to college to learn how to become a control freak, huh?"

Her lips thinned. "If that's what you want to call it. I like structure. So sue me."

"And relationships are too messy?" He lifted a

cracker and broke it in half, dunking it into the remaining soup at the bottom of his bowl.

"I didn't say that."

"I consider it implied."

She scraped the last bit of rice from her bowl with her spoon and stuck it in her mouth, then sat back, her eyes narrowing. "You're a mediator. I bet you have to deal with a lot of divorce cases, don't you?"

He nodded, on edge to give the right answers that fit with his cover.

"With all those divorces, I'd think you'd be the last one to believe in long-term relationships." She leveled a direct stare at him. "Have you ever been married?"

Ed's chest tightened, that knot in his gut growing. "Yes."

Alex's eyes widened and she sat up straighter. "Oh, please tell me we didn't...I didn't...with a married man."

He raised his hands. "No. I'm not married anymore. Divorced three years ago."

"Why?" This time she raised her hands. "Sorry, that's personal. You don't have to answer."

For a long moment he didn't. "It's okay. My job was too demanding. She wanted more...of me...of my time." As soon as the words were out of his mouth, her brows wrinkled into a frown and Ed realized his mistake.

"Your job? I didn't think a mediator's job was that demanding. Isn't it strictly an eight to five commitment?"

He tossed the other half of his cracker in the bowl. "The point is, she needed me around more, and I wasn't there."

Alex sat across from him for an extended, silent moment, then asked, "Did you love her?"

Ed looked down at his empty bowl. "I don't know. I've never been sure what love is, or if I've ever loved anyone before."

"I know it's a different kind of love, but what about your parents?"

"Died when I was four," he stated, his voice flat.

Alex leaned forward "Your adoptive parents?"

"Foster homes." The more she questioned, the more the gumbo in his gut churned.

When her brows furrowed and she reached out to lay a hand on his arm, he jerked away. "Look, I don't need anyone's pity. You don't miss what you don't have."

Alex shook her head. "I can't imagine having grown up without the love of my parents. Even now, I miss my dad so badly, it hurts every time I think of him."

"That's the beauty of never having loved your parents." He snorted. "I never knew mine. I feel no pain." He pushed to his feet. "Look. I don't need you or anyone else. What happened last night was nothing more than good sex."

"And that's why you came looking for me today?" she asked.

"Yes." He walked to the door without looking back into Alex's sad eyes.

Anger, he could stomach. Pity? Never.

He stepped out into the bright sunshine, dragging his shades from his pocket.

"Ed!" Calliope waved from across the street.

"Ed!" Sport echoed and waved as well.

"Wait up." Calliope glanced both ways and waited for traffic to pass.

In no mood to talk, but not wanting to be rude, he waited for Calliope and Sport.

A tractor-trailer rig rumbled past from one direction. As it passed, Calliope and Sport stepped into the road.

With their attention on the big rig, they didn't hear or see the dark, four-door sedan racing down the middle of the street from the opposite direction.

Ed edged out into the street, his hand up. "Wait," he called out to Calliope and Sport.

The car swerved toward him and accelerated.

He didn't have time to get out of the way and braced himself for the impact.

At the last moment, Sport leaped across the road and pushed him out of the way. He fell back against the curb and rolled out of range of the car's tires.

Sport wasn't so lucky. The car clipped him in the side, sending him flying into the outdoor tables and chairs in front of the Cajun Kettle.

Ed rolled to his feet, but not in time to catch the license plate. The vehicle had peeled out, leaving a trail of smoke.

Behind him, a scream rent the air and the door to the restaurant slammed open. Alex rushed forward, dropping to her knees beside Sport.

The man whimpered, a gash in the side of his face, bleeding onto the concrete.

Ed jerked his phone out of his pocket and tossed it to Calliope. "Call 9-1-1." Then he bent over the man who'd saved his life. The man Alex loved.

Sport lay sprawled across Alex's bed, sound asleep after swallowing three pain killers and a tall glass of water. The trauma of being hit by a car had taken its toll on him, and his old canine habit of sleeping the day away kicked in.

Alex stood on one side of the bed holding his hand. "I should never have wished him to be a man."

Calliope sat in a chair on the other side, petting his arm. "He could have as easily been hit by a car as a dog, and might not have survived." She lifted his hand to her cheek, a tear trailing down her cheek. "He's been so good about everything that's happened to him so far."

"Poor Sport." Alex rubbed the masculine arm. Damn the Voodoo magic that put him in that position. "I want my dog back."

"I want Sport to be okay."

She stared across at her friend. "Oh, Calliope, you can't fall in love with Sport. You don't know how long he'll be a man."

"It's too late, Alex." Calliope brushed the hair from his forehead, careful not to disturb the bandage on his cheek. "He's gentle, he's kind, and he's everything a man should be."

"He is, isn't he? He's like another member of my family." She thought of Ed, her heart aching even more for a man who'd never known the love of a family. He'd even admitted he wasn't sure he'd loved his wife. How sad.

At that moment a knock sounded on the door.

She didn't have the heart to get up and answer it.

After a moment the front door squeaked open and footsteps echoed down the hallway.

Ed poked his head into her bedroom, then entered, carrying a box of chocolates. He laid it on the table beside the bed. "Calliope told me Sport likes chocolate. How's he doing?"

"Better."

"I still think we should have called 9-1-1. He could have internal injuries."

She had done her best with butterfly bandages, pulling the edges of the gash on Sport's cheek together. She too would rather have taken him to the hospital in Morgan City, but Calliope had reminded her he had no insurance and worse, no name to give the administration at the regional hospital in St. Mary Parish. Ed had helped them get him back to her house and into her bed where he'd promptly fallen to sleep.

"I owe him my life," Ed said simply. "Chocolates seem inadequate thanks for taking a hit for me."

"I'm sure he'll love them." Calliope sniffed. "He loves chocolate."

Not for the first time, frustration led Alex to pace. She left her bedroom and crossed the hall to the living room where she marched from end to end, going over and over in her mind the events of the day.

"You're going to wear a hole in the carpet," Ed said from the entrance to the living room.

"I can't stand around and do nothing. I saw what happened through the window of the Kettle. That driver was purposely trying to hit you." She stopped in front of Ed. "Are you sure you didn't get a license plate? Not even a part of it? Can't they run a plate with a partial?"

"The police can, but I got nothing. By the time I pulled myself out of the gutter, it was gone."

"Damn." She ran her hand over his chest, reliving the horror of what she'd witnessed. "What if Sport hadn't been there? What if that car had hit you?" Her hand stopped and she gazed up into his eyes through the mist of tears in her own. "That could be you banged up, or worse."

His mouth quirked upward on one side and he captured her hand in his. "Feeling sorry for me again?" He shook his head. "Don't. I can take care of myself."

"I nearly had a heart attack." She leaned her forehead against him. "That car coming so fast. You standing in its path." She wrapped her arms around his middle and buried her face in his shirt. "And then Sport, throwing himself in front of the car."

Ed stiffened beneath her. "You love him, don't you?"

"Sport?" She sniffed into his shirt. "Of course, I love him, and he loves me. He's been a part of my life for the past eight years. He helped me through the death of my father. I don't know what I'd do without him."

"Was he upset about last night?"

Alex sniffed again and looked up. "Upset? Why?" As his question sank in, her eyes widened. "Oh, you mean about us?"

"Well, yes." He set her at arm's length. "If you love him, why did you fool around with me?"

With the truth poised on the tip of her tongue, she hesitated. As good as it felt to have Ed's arms around her after what she'd witnessed, she couldn't continue down this path—no matter how wonderfully solid and warm he was against her. Until she resolved her issues with Sport, she couldn't consider any kind of relationship at all. Long-distance or short-distance. And Ed would be leaving soon. She'd be smart to end it now. Although she hadn't been too smart lately.

"Sport is very special to me," she said at last. "He understands me."

Ed's arms fell to his sides.

Cold that had nothing to do with the AC unit blasting in the window washed over Alex.

He backed away until his legs bumped into the couch. "Tell him thank you for saving my life."

When Ed turned to walk away, she caught something in his expression that made her chest tighten. Was that hurt in his eyes?

She raised her hand to stop him, and let it fall. It would be best for both of them to stop this craziness before it went any further.

Before he reached the door, Ed spun back, stalked across the floor, and grabbed her arm, yanking her against his chest. His lips crashed down over hers in a breath-stealing kiss, slanting over her mouth, his tongue diving in to claim hers.

She melted into Ed, her hands sliding around his neck, urging him closer, knowing she shouldn't.

He backed her against the wall and scooped his hands beneath her thighs, wrapping her legs around his waist. When his lips left hers, he seared a path down her neck. "Does he make you feel like this?" he asked.

She couldn't lie. "No." Her body was on fire, blood raging through her veins. A deep, wrenching ache built at her core, spreading outward. She wanted him more than anyone she'd ever wanted in her life.

Then he untangled her legs from his waist and let her legs drop to the ground before he stepped back, his eyes cold. "Think of that when you're with him."

Her heart pounding, tears welling in her eyes, she watched as Ed left her house, the screen door slamming closed behind him.

She walked back to her bedroom to find Sport wide awake and perky.

Calliope sat on the bed with him, a deck of cards laid out across the sheets. "Sport woke up and seems to be feeling fine." Calliope leaned over and pointed at his cards. "That's a pair. See? Two queens. "

Alex scrubbed a hand across her face and sank into the chair beside the bed. "Tell me you're not teaching Sport to play poker."

"Of course, I am. He's learning fast. He already plays better than you."

"Great."

Calliope scooted off the bed. "What's wrong?"

"Ed left."

"Is he coming back?"

"Probably not."

"Alex." Calliope shook her head. "What did you say to him?"

"He thinks I'm in love with Sport."

"Why would he think that?"

"Because I implied as much."

Calliope rolled her eyes. "Why do you push men away?"

"The timing is not right for me to be in any relationship. I'm finally getting my business off the ground—"

Her friend pressed her fingers to her ears. "Blah, blah, blah. You sound like a broken record. You really need to get over yourself and live a little."

Her cell phone rang and she pulled it out of her pocket, glad, for once, to see her mother's picture in the display screen. Anything to avoid another lecture from Calliope. "Hello, Mom."

"Dinner will be at six tonight. Don't be late."

"Mom, I can't make dinner. I have Calliope and Sport at my house."

Calliope snatched the phone from her. "Mrs. Boyette, Alex can make it to dinner, after all."

She groaned and reached for the phone, but her friend danced out of reach.

"No, no, don't worry about us," she was saying. "I'm taking Sport out for dinner in Morgan City. I'll take a rain check on that gumbo though. You know how I love it. Yes, we should be back in time for the festival. Yes, it was good talking to you, too. Bye now, *ma chère*." Calliope clicked the phone off and tossed it back to Alex.

"Thanks a lot." She nodded toward Sport. "You

shouldn't take Sport out after being hit by a car earlier today, he needs rest."

Sport rose from the bed, stretched, and winced, pressing his fingers to the bandage on his face. "Sport okay." He smiled and winced again. "Ow."

"He'll feel better after we stop at his favorite barbeque place." Calliope slipped an arm around Sport's waist. "Right, Sport?"

"Right. Want barbeque."

"I'd rather go with you two than to my mother's house. You know she's going to throw Ed at me again."

"Is that so bad?"

"The way he left out of here? Yes."

"You have got to learn to loosen up." Calliope ducked around her. "I'll be back in a few minutes. I need to run to my house and freshen up." She pointed at Sport. "Stay. I'll be back shortly."

"Sport stay."

After Calliope left, Alex straightened the bed and stacked the deck of cards on the nightstand.

Sport's gaze followed her around the room. As a dog, that didn't bother her. As a man, it made her more self-conscious.

"What wrong, Alex?"

"Nothing you would understand, unfortunately." She sighed and left the bedroom to straighten the living room. She had to keep moving. Whenever she slowed down, she thought. About Ed. *Damn it.*

"Ed love Alex?"

She spun to face Sport. "Where did you get that idea. From Calliope?"

He shook his head like a dog shakes his coat and sniffed. "Sport smell it."

"You can smell love?"

Her man-dog nodded. "Alex love Ed."

Her laugh caught on a sob. "I barely know Ed. I met him yesterday. You can't fall in love in a day."

Sport tipped his head. "Why?"

"You just can't." She ran past Sport and into her bathroom where she stripped out of her clothes and ducked beneath the cold spray of her shower, hoping it would shock her back into reality.

All it did was make her wet and cold.

As she toweled dry and slipped into a clean cotton sun dress and sandals, Sport's question echoed in her mind. *Why?*

Why can't you fall in love in a day? At the ripe old age of twenty-nine, had she discovered for the first time that love at first sight actually existed?

Chapter Ten

Ed sat on the porch steps, replacing the spinner with the buzz bait on his fishing line. Joe hadn't judged him when he'd first thrown his line out in the bayou and immediately snagged a cypress knee.

The older man had untangled the snag and retied his line before casting his own line, thus showing him the proper technique. The two mornings he'd been on the bayou had been the most peaceful times he'd ever experienced. Even when an alligator drifted by, he'd been calm, accepting that the bayou might be serene and beautiful, but it held its own dangers. Being aware of his surroundings was key.

When he finished tying the lure, Ed sat back and

stared out across the small town of Bayou Miste. Through the late afternoon, residents could be seen stringing lights on their houses and fences, draping colorful beads on the bushes, and hanging garish flags in the yard. A small carnival had moved in the night before and set up in the community park. Carnie music drifted toward him, bringing back memories of the few times his foster families had taken him to the fair in Baton Rouge. He could almost smell the funnel cakes from where he sat.

He'd been cornered by Barbara Boyette an hour ago and coerced into coming to dinner at the Boyette house, yet again. Not looking forward to it, but realizing how much more difficult it would be to say no to the woman, he'd agreed, praying Alex wouldn't be there. Knowing Barbara Boyette, she would play her hand at matchmaking again.

Ed chuckled.

"Whatcha laughing about?" a tiny voice asked from beside him.

He spun toward the sound and shook his head at the smallest of the Boyette brood, Molly B. "I'm laughing at how funny people can be."

"What people?"

"Everyone." He gazed down at the pretty little girl with the dark ringlets hanging down from her two ponytails perched high on her head. "How are you today, Miz Molly B.?"

"Fine, thank you," she responded politely.

"What does the B stand for?"

"Brown," she answered promptly. Her chest swelled out and she tipped her chin up. "I'm unsinkable."

"Well, Miz Molly Brown Boyette, what can I do for you today?"

"Mamma sent me to get you." She held out her hand with all the trust of the five-year-old child she was.

Ed wondered how anyone could let their small child wander so far from their own front door with so many pedophiles stalking the streets, looking for their next victim. That had been only one of his reasons he'd never wanted children. And the fact his own childhood had been less than wonderful and he wouldn't wish that on a kid.

He glanced toward the Boyette house and could see Mrs. Boyette, peering through the window. Okay, so Molly B wasn't alone, but being watched over by a loving mother.

He lifted a hand in greeting and Mrs. Boyette waved back.

"Guess that's our cue." He stepped down off the porch, Molly B.'s hand in his. A warm feeling tugged at his heart. Maybe if he'd been inclined to have children, his wife wouldn't have left him. Hell, he'd heard she'd already had one baby with her new husband and had a second on the way.

Maybe kids weren't such a bad idea, with the right parents. If he could have kids like Molly B., Teddy and Rosie, it couldn't be too bad. They'd grown on him.

Inside, the Boyette house was every bit as chaotic as it was the night before. Children of all ages and a few of the grown ones crisscrossed each other's paths setting the table, icing the glasses, and carrying trays of food into the dining room.

A dozen "Hello, Mr. Marceaus" crossed with a few "Hi, Eds" made him feel welcome and wanted there.

Mrs. Boyette backed through the swinging kitchen door, carrying a heaping plate of dirty rice.

"Oh, there you are Mr. Marceau. We're so happy you could make it."

"Here, let me." He grabbed the heavy platter from her and set it in the middle of the table, marveling at how strong she was. "I'm renting your cottage, you don't have to feed me, too, you know."

She laughed. "*Mais, oui.* But what's one more mouth when you have so many? Sit, Mr. Marceau."

He obeyed the command with a smile. "Yes, ma'am. Please, call me Ed."

"I do feel as if you're too young to be called Mr. Marceau. You're the same age as my son, Ben, I believe."

The family gathered around the table, a few missing from the night before. Ed couldn't remember which ones, but he only counted fourteen of the siblings.

As if in answer to his unspoken question, Mrs. Boyette said, "Harry and Truman had other plans tonight, Amelia had to head back to New Orleans sooner than she'd expected, and Alex—ah, there she is." Barbara Boyette smiled as her oldest daughter stepped into the room.

His hand tightened on the napkin in his lap.

Alex wore a dress for the first time since he'd met her, the soft cotton molding to her shapely figure like a glove. Her legs were bare and she had strappy sandals on her feet that displayed her pretty little toes with the bright pink polish he'd admired last night as he'd stripped her bicycle shorts down her legs.

His groin tightened and he reined in his thoughts. Now was not the time to think of Alex naked. Not in a room full of Boyettes. He nodded. "Alex."

She gave him a cool nod in return. "Mr. Marceau."

So it was *Mr. Marceau,* now. He supposed it was appropriate, given they weren't going to see each other anywhere but at her mother's dinner table.

He'd like to think he choked down the shrimp *etouffee* and dirty rice Mrs. Boyette had prepared, but it slid right down his throat, despite the heavy tension brewing between him and Alex. "Mrs. Boyette, you could open your own restaurant." He sat back and patted his belly. "Best *etouffee* I've ever eaten."

Barbara Boyette smiled and blushed. "Thank you, but I have ulterior motives. I'm just buttering you up."

He sat forward. "Need a sink fixed? You got it."

"Better off hiring a plumber," Alex muttered.

Her mother scowled at her and shined a smile at him. "As a matter of fact, I do have a favor to ask of you, Ed."

"Name it." He'd figure out whatever mechanical puzzle she had for him, just to prove to Alex he was up for the challenge.

"Tonight is the local Crawfish Festival, and I'm too tired to take the children. Would you and Alex be dears and take them?"

A cacophony of cheers rose from the younger Boyettes.

"We'll help," Dolley and Madison volunteered, in unison.

"George and I had plans to hit a movie in Morgan City, but we can cancel if you need us to," Abe offered.

Their mother waved them off. "No need. Between Ed, Alex, Dolley, and Madison they'll have it covered. You two go on."

He almost laughed out loud at the stricken expression on Alex's face. It was that look that made him say, "Alex and I would be happy to help. Wouldn't we?" He raised his brows in challenge.

Alex's jaw twitched, but she managed a nod. "We'd love to," she said through clenched teeth.

"Since that's settled, you better get going. Molly B. won't last too long and she's been looking forward to going all week. She even saved her allowance for cotton candy."

"*Pink* cotton candy," Molly piped up.

"Then pink cotton candy it will be." He pushed back from the table and helped carry dishes to the sink.

Alex caught him coming out the swinging door as she was going in. "What are you trying to prove?"

He held the door for her. "Nothing. Your mother

has been kind enough to feed me and I want to return the favor." He leaned close. "Not everything is about you, Ms. Boyette." He let go of the swinging door and it smacked Alex in the butt.

Her voice carried through the wood paneling. "Oh! That man!"

The children gathered in the hallway, Teddy, Rosie, and Molly hopping up and down, too excited to stand still. Woodrow and Susan B. grinned and laughed, but refrained from the exuberance shown by their younger siblings while Paul, Thomas, Edison, and JK waited outside, teenagers and therefore too cool to be associated with the rest.

Alex counted heads. "There are fourteen of us. Dolley and Madison, you take the teens. Mr. Marceau and I will take the subteens."

Molly tugged on his finger. "Am I a subteen, Mr. Ed?"

He scooped her up in his arms. "Yes, ma'am, you are."

"Can I ride piggy back?" she asked, crawling across his arm and onto his back like a monkey.

"I can do better than that." He hiked her up, settling her little legs around his neck and ducked low as they headed out the door for the four-block walk to the park.

Alex wondered how she'd been conned into

spending another evening with the man whose kisses made her forget everything she'd worked so hard to build.

And damned if he didn't look right surrounded by the often overwhelming Boyette family. She would never have guessed he'd grown up a foster child. And damned if he wasn't the first man that hadn't run screaming from her raucous gaggle of siblings.

He'd make a great father.

Mon Dieu! She had to quit thinking that way. It would merely lead to heartache.

Ed was good at his word, keeping a close eye on the little ones, attentive to their every need, even taking the boys to the portable potties when they'd had too much soda. He marched Molly over to the stand selling pink cotton candy, and held it for her when she rode the spinning rides.

Teddy and Rosie squealed with delight when Ed made three basketball tosses in a row, winning a pretty purple unicorn, which he promptly handed over to Teddy.

Calliope and Sport found them in front of the shooting stall where Paul, J.K., Thomas, and Edison went up against Ed for the grand prize of a toy Daisy BB gun. It took five rounds of games before Ed worked his way up to the grand prize. He insisted on carrying it home to present to their mother for her approval first.

Rosie tapped Ed's arm and the big man bent toward him. When he straightened he headed toward Alex, Rosie beside him. "We're going to make a quick trip to the bathroom. Can you handle them while we're gone?"

She nodded, admiring Ed's trim waist and narrow hips as he walked away. The man made jeans look sexy.

"Nice ass." Calliope leaned close to her. "And he's so good with the kids."

"Yeah," she said, wiping all enthusiasm from her voice, not wanting to encourage Calliope to continue.

Her friend swatted her shoulder. "Don't be so grumpy. How often do you find a man who fits in with your family?"

Never. "I have too much going on in my life right now. I can't even think about this...this...thing."

"That *thing* is feelings."

Ed returned with a smiling Rosie, running alongside him.

They looked so natural together, smiling and laughing. Alex's heart squeezed. The man needed a family of his own.

Calliope stood back as Sport watched Ed helping Teddy and Rosie toss rings over the necks of bottles.

"He's perfect for you. Sometimes you have to take a chance."

"I told him I didn't want a relationship." Alex raised her hands. "And I have a man living with me."

"Speaking of whom." Calliope turned to Alex. "I'd like to take Sport over to my house. I promised we'd watch all the *Homeward Bound* movies together."

Alex captured Calliope's hands. "At the risk of sounding like a broken record, don't fall in love with Sport. The spell might not last."

Calliope cast a soft glance at the man-dog trying his hand at throwing rings. "I'll try not to, but I'm afraid it's far too late. Besides, I'll take all the love I can get, as long as it lasts."

Her friend had a point. When you had a chance to love, you had to go for it. How did the old saying go? *Better to have loved and lost than to never have loved.* "I guess it's okay." Unfortunately, that would leave her alone and being alone wasn't all that great anymore, not when she'd sampled what being with someone felt like. "What time are you bringing him home?"

"Rather than wake you, he can sleep on my couch." She raised her hand. "Honest. Just sleep."

"Okay," she agreed, reluctantly. Her friend was grabbing for every minute she could spend with the man she was falling in love with, knowing it probably wouldn't last. Being in love with a man who turned back into a dog was a much bigger hurdle to overcome than being in love with a man who lived in a different city. So what was her problem?

Throughout the evening, Ed remained attentive to the children, not letting the little ones out of his sight for a moment. At the same time, he looked around for unfamiliar faces. The entire time he was at the festival, he felt as if someone was watching him. With the trial date approaching, paranoia was bound to surface, not to mention Leon Primeaux's hired hit men.

Twice he thought he'd seen someone lurking in between tents. One tall man wore a hoodie that obscured his face. Ed never got a close look at him before he turned away and disappeared behind a booth. Molly chose that time to trip and fall. He couldn't excuse himself and go after the man without leaving the kids or Alex alone for a few minutes. When he'd taken Rosie to the portable bathrooms on the edge of the border of the carnival and the parking lot, he could have sworn they'd been followed, but when he turned around, no one was behind them.

Alex and Calliope had their backs to him and

were talking with two strangers when Ed glanced away from the kids playing games. Both men were big and tall. One wore overalls and a faded T-shirt that had a five-year-old advertisement for the crawfish festival.

The other man was a little bigger and wore old army camouflage pants and a ripped black T-shirt with the words *I'm with stupid* written in bold white letters. "She got away from Granny 'bout thirty minutes ago. Cain't find her nowhere."

"I haven't seen FeFe since earlier this afternoon," Alex was saying.

"Sport and I just walked up from my house a little while ago and didn't see her along the way," Calliope said.

"*Mais*, if you do, give ol' Mo a call." The man backhanded the other guy in the gut. "Come on, Larry."

Larry stuck his hands in his pockets and rocked back on his mud boots. "Maybe T-Rex done her in, or she got runned over by some *couyon* what ain't got a lick 'o sense runnin' ova a pink poodle."

"Shut jo mout' ya ol' coonass. Granny'd be bawlin' her eyes out iffn' someting happens to dat danged mutt."

"Something wrong?" Ed interrupted.

Alex turned to him. "Ed Marceau, this is Maurice

Saulnier and Larry Ezelle, friends of ours. They're looking for Mo's grandmother's poodle, FeFe. She went missing a little while ago."

"She be pink today," Larry took his hands out of his pocket and shook Ed's hand.

Mo shook Ed's hand next, his brows furrowed. "You de fella fishin' in the mornin' with Joe?"

He nodded. "That would be me."

"Catch anyting?" Mo asked.

"Joe caught a couple of catfish. I'm angling for bass, but no luck so far."

"Bayou Black's good for de largemouth bass," Larry offered.

"Iffn' you're inta frog giggin', de swamp over by de ol' trapper shack is chalk full of dem. But ya gotta go at night to get de bigguns."

He tensed. The trapper shack was where they'd hidden the witness. "Do many people go giggin' at night?"

"Mostly me 'n Larry," Mo said. "But der be some mo' boats out late at night in de past coupla days. Not sure what dey be after, but dey be movin' too fast to gig frogs."

Was someone searching the swamps for something more than frogs and fish? He needed to get out to the shack and make sure Marcus was ready, in case whoever it was meant to hunt stool pigeons. He'd have to go later, when no one was around to see him head down the canal. He couldn't risk being followed.

Mo backhanded Larry in the gut again. "We best be goin'."

Mo and Larry lumbered off, muttering as they went about pink poodles and alligators.

Molly B. tugged on Ed's shirt and raised her arms.

He lifted her and laid her head on his shoulder, where she went right to sleep.

"I think it's time to head home." Alex patted her sister's back and gathered the others.

The walk back was a combination of bursts of laughter and tired silence, the night proclaimed great fun by all. Except for Alex, who looked none too thrilled to be in his company.

Alex had tried to be mad at Ed for his earlier parting kiss and for volunteering them to take the little ones to the festival, but couldn't stay that way. He'd displayed a side of himself that she found hard to resist. A softer, caring side that raised him up several notches in her estimation.

Well, damn. If he wasn't from New Orleans and

planning on returning there soon, she could fall for guy like Ed.

As they arrived in front of the Boyette house, Calliope and Sport said their goodbyes and continued on to Calliope's house, hand in hand.

She shook her head, but what could she do? For the time being, Sport was a man.

Once inside, Ed and Alex tucked Molly B. in bed, each pressing a kiss to her soft forehead. Alex moved down the hallway giving each of her siblings a goodnight hug and kiss, working her way back to the front door where she watched as the little ones all hugged Ed and the teens shook his hand.

He bent to return their hugs and laughed at J.K.'s attempt at a joke.

How did he do it? He'd charmed his way into their lives. He even kissed her mother's cheek and thanked her for letting him take the kids to the festival.

She ducked out the front door, intent on making her escape before she fell for the man all over again. She was halfway down the driveway when the front screen door slammed.

"Alex, wait."

She pretended she hadn't heard him, ducked her head, and walked faster.

Footsteps sounded behind her, coming fast.

She wasn't ready to be alone with Ed again. She increased her pace until she was running. A block from her house, he caught up to her, grabbed her arm and spun her around.

"Damn it, Alex. I just wanted to give you this." He lifted her hand and placed a miniature version of the stuffed unicorn he'd given Teddy into her palm.

Her pulse pounded and her heart squeezed hard in her chest as Alex stared at the stupid little purple unicorn. Tears welled in her eyes and slid down her cheeks. "Damn you."

"I thought you could use some cheering up since Calliope and Sport took off without you." He tipped her chin up and brushed the tears from her cheeks. "Hey. What's this?"

"Why do you have to be you?" She flung her arms around his neck, leaned up on her toes and kissed him hard on the mouth.

His hand slid around her waist and he pulled her against him, drawing away from her mouth to whisper, "I don't understand you."

"I don't understand me either." She laughed and kissed him again.

His hands slipped down over her bottom and he lifted her, wrapping her bare legs around him.

"Not here," she said and sucked his bottom lip

into her mouth, then let go to press kisses to his cheek, his ear.

"Your place." Ed carried her toward her little house, refusing to put her down.

"Go around back, I have noisy neighbors that report to my mother."

Ed crossed a yard and slipped around the house to her back door where he set her on her feet. She pulled the key from the pocket of her sundress and slid it into the lock. Past caring what she was doing, she shoved the door open and they fell through. All she wanted was to feel.

Ed grabbed the hem of her dress, ripped it up over her head, and groaned, staring down at her with an expression so hot it made her knees melt.

Then he hooked the thin strap of her string bikini panties and slid them slowly down her legs, his knuckles skimming her skin all the way to her ankles.

Naked and on fire, she combed her fingers through his thick brown hair and backed up until her bottom bumped into the kitchen dinette table. Then she hoisted herself onto the edge and parted her thighs, already wet and ready for him. "Come here."

His hands rose to his belt buckle and he hesitated. "What about Sport?"

"We have an understanding."

"What if I'm not comfortable with that under-standing?"

"You're not staying. Why should you care?"

He stepped between her legs, still fully dressed, his hands cupping her cheeks. "Because, despite what you might think, I do care." Then he kissed her again, the caress a connection that seared a path all the way to her heart. "I care too damned much."

"It's not meant to be anything beyond tonight," she whispered against his lips.

"Then let's make tonight count." His fingers wove through her hair, tugging until her head dropped back, exposing her throat to his lips, his teeth, and his tongue. He branded her with his heat as he pressed his lips to the pulse beating wildly at the base of her throat. He moved to the ridge of her collarbone and downward to capture one puckered nipple between his teeth.

"*Mon Dieu*, I'm on fire." She reached for his shirt, tugging it up over his head and dropping it to the floor.

He unbuckled his belt and flicked the button to his jeans open.

Alex ran the zipper down, freed his erection into her palm and guided him to her entrance.

His body stiffened and he held back, the velvety

tip of his cock nudging, but not entering her. "I have protection in my wallet."

Alex reached around him, removing his wallet from his back pocket.

He snatched it from her and held it out of her reach. "I'll do that."

A little shaken by the force with which he'd grabbed for the wallet, her lust cooled. "I only wanted to help."

"I know." After a quick kiss to the tip of her nose, he held the wallet away from her, opened it just wide enough to remove a foil package, then slid it into his back pocket. He tore the packet open and rolled the condom down over his cock before curling his fingers around the back of her neck. "Did I tell you how pretty you were in the dress you wore tonight?"

"The one you threw across the room?" She tried to hold onto her irritation at his handling of the condom, but the way his fingers kneaded the back of her neck, she was quickly becoming putty in his hands.

"You should wear dresses more often. They show off your legs."

She warmed to his compliment. "It's not practical to work out in a dress."

"It's a shame." He skimmed her lips with his,

sliding his tongue in to stroke the length of hers. "You really have great legs."

She shrugged off her misgivings as he started the assault on her senses all over, this time taking one breast into his mouth and sucking hard enough her body responded with an answering tug at her center. She wrapped her legs around his hips, wanting him inside her.

He held back, unlocking her ankles from behind him and dropping to his knees in front of her, kissing her belly and moving lower. His big hands spread her thighs wider, skimming fingers along the sensitive skin, angling closer to that aching place, begging for consummation.

She leaned back on her hands, caught in the magic of his touch, eager for what came next as his thumbs parted her folds, exposing her to him.

He flicked her with his tongue, moistening the little bundle of nerves and flesh.

Alex's breathing grew ragged and she her body tensed. "Please."

He tongued her again, this time in a long, sensuous glide, circling back to do it again. He slid a finger into her channel, then two, then three, swirling around the juices, while his mouth worked that nubbin of intense desire.

"Mon Dieu!" Her hips rocked, pressing closer to

the wonder of his tongue, his hands, his mouth. "You make me come undone," she gasped.

He chuckled and rose to his feet. "That was the plan. Now," He wrapped her legs around his waist, pressing the tip of his cock to her entrance. "Make magic with me." With one, swift thrust, he entered her, sliding all the way in.

She cried out and clutched his shoulders, digging her nails into his skin.

He pulled halfway out. "Am I hurting you?"

"No! Do it again." Her inner muscles tightened, refusing to release him. "Faster."

He pumped in and out of her, hard and swift, his face tense as he held her hips.

As the sensations intensified, her legs tightened around him and she flew over the edge in a fire burst. Tingling started at her core and flooded her body, spreading outward all the way to her toes.

Ed slammed in one more time, his body stiffening as he held her hips, pressing deep inside, the width and depth of his member filling her completely. When his hold loosened, he gathered her in his arms. "You are incredible."

"You're not so bad yourself." Replete, yet exhausted, she leaned into him her face nestling against his muscular chest. "What is it you didn't want me to see in your wallet? A picture of an old girlfriend?"

"No." He tipped her head back and gazed into her eyes, still connected to her in the most intimate way. "There are no other women in my life." He didn't say it, but she could swear the words *Only You* lingered in the air. With his thumb, he skimmed her bottom lip, then followed it with a gentle kiss.

She sighed and wrapped her arms around him. "What is it about you that keeps me coming back for more?"

He chuckled. "My magnetic personality?"

Though his words were true, she snorted. "Nah. Must be the incredible sex."

He leaned back and brushed the hair from her cheek. "What's next?"

A loud crash saved Alex from answering as a rock sailed through her kitchen window.

Ed ducked, dragging her with him, but not fast enough.

The rock clipped her chin and she fell off the table into Ed's arms.

Silence settled over them.

Ed tilted her face and studied the gash in her chin. "Are you okay?"

"Yes, but what happened?" She pressed her

fingers to the wound and felt warm, sticky liquid. "*Mon Dieu*, I'm bleeding."

"It doesn't look bad. Just—"

"A flesh wound." She glanced around. "Still have that gun on you?"

"Yes, why?"

"Can I borrow it? I'm going after that son of a bitch who broke my window."

"If it's all the same to you and you're sure you're all right, I'll go." He winked at her, his gaze skimming across her naked body. "You're not exactly dressed for the occasion."

"Fine. You go." She gave him a shove, then grabbed his sleeve and yanked him back and kissed him full on the mouth. "But zip it and be careful."

Chapter Eleven

Anger sent Ed through the door like a rocket blasting off the launch pad. Based on the trajectory of the rock, whoever had thrown it had been standing in Alex's backyard. He peered into the darkness broken only by moonlight filtering through the overhanging trees. Nothing moved but the branches of the trees swaying in the breeze, no silhouette shifted in the gloom, lurking, waiting to pick a fight.

Gun drawn, he ducked low and slipped into the shadows, listening for the sound of footsteps running away. Who the hell would have targeted Alex's house? Had someone figured out he was part of the detail protecting the Ragsdale woman? Hell, he hadn't been doing much of a job by jumping Alex's bones every chance he got.

Granted, the festival had been a great opportunity for strangers to mix and mingle with the locals. If anyone had spotted Marcus and Phyllis at the old shack in the bayou, they might run off at the mouth without realizing they were giving away the location of a protected witness.

He had enjoyed his time with the Boyette children, all the while keeping an eye open for strangers. He'd spotted the retiree, Oscar Mills, wandering amongst the crowd. Alone.

They'd sized each other up from a distance, but moved on.

Other than that one encounter, he hadn't gotten any vibes from any of the other passersby. But that didn't mean someone wasn't watching him, waiting for him to make his next visit to the witness.

He searched through backyards and then headed out to the main road.

Mo and Larry were headed his way, Mo carrying a puff of pink.

Larry raised a hand. "We found FeFe."

"Glad to hear it," Ed said.

"She be scarfin' up hotdogs de kids done dropped at de festival." Mo shook his head. "Gonna have her one helluva bellyache."

The pink poodle was nestled in the crook of the man's arm, listless, her head hanging low.

"Did you two happen to pass anyone on the street a few moments ago?"

Larry and Mo both shook their heads.

Mo shifted the poodle to his other arm. "Dint see no one runnin' but saw a car take off."

"Which way was it headed?"

"Toward Morgan City, I be guessin'." Mo patted the dog. "Better get FeFe home before Granny calls out de National Guard." The two men went on their way.

Ed continued the search of a two-block radius from Alex's cottage, finally admitting defeat. Whoever had thrown the rock had gotten clean away, probably in the car Mo had mentioned, headed for Morgan City.

Two attacks in one day and the common denominator seemed to be him. The rock would have hit him in the head had he not ducked. Alex had been hit instead.

The reckless driver on the street today had made a determined attempt to run him over, not Sport. Sport had taken the brunt of that attack.

Perhaps Alex was right. Their relationship would end badly, but not for the reasons she'd listed.

With his gun still held in the palm of his hand, he headed back to Alex.

She met him at the back door, pushing it open

with one hand, while holding a dish towel to her chin with the other.

"He got away."

"I'm glad." Dressed in a T-shirt and shorts, she hugged him around the middle. "I was worried you'd be hurt. I bet it was some random teen getting a little rowdy after the fair."

He disengaged her arms and made a circle around her kitchen, lowering the blinds over the windows. When he finished, he crossed to her and pulled out a chair at the dinette. "Sit."

Alex smiled crookedly at him. "Giving orders now?"

"Damn right." He softened his words with, "Let me see." Gently, he pulled the dish towel away from her face and studied the damage the rock had made.

"I think it'll bruise more than anything." She smiled up at him. "It just ticks me off that someone broke my window."

"I'm more worried about you than a damned window." He carried the towel to the sink and ran clean, cold water over it, returning to dab the blood away. "Do you have a first aid kit?"

"In the bathroom cabinet." She started to rise, but he laid a hand on her shoulder.

"Stay here. I'll get it." He hurried into the bathroom and rifled through the well-organized contents of the cabinet until he found a small plastic container with First Aid written on the outside.

"It's not that bad, just a bruise, really," Alex called out.

Ed returned and dabbed antibiotic ointment on the cut, then spread a bandage over it. When he was done, he kissed her lips. "Come on, you can shower while I clean up the glass."

She frowned. "I can do this."

"I know. You take care of everybody else, and you're capable of taking care of yourself." He lifted her hands and squeezed them. "But this once, let me." Before she could protest further, he scooped her up and carried her to her bedroom, setting her on her feet with a pat on her behind. "Now go."

"Will you still be here when I'm done?" she asked.

"I'm staying." His jaw clenched. "At least until you go to sleep. You really should get a dog."

"I know." Her eyes glazed with unshed tears and she turned away.

Hadn't her mother said something about her having one called Sport? Probably named after the man she lived with.

He wondered if the dog had run away, thus the reason for the sudden tears.

After sweeping up the broken glass, he made a pass around the exterior of the cottage and reentered as Alex emerged from her bedroom, dressed in the baby-doll nightgown she'd worn the first morning he'd seen her running through Bayou Miste.

Had it only been two days ago?

Her eyelids dropped to half-mast and she smiled. "You can sleep in here."

"I'll sleep on the couch." If he lay down with her, he'd once again lose focus on why the hell he'd come to town in the first place.

"Really?" She glanced down at her nightgown. "I don't tempt you in the least?"

He closed his eyes and drew in a deep breath to slow his pulse and tamp down his libido. "Darlin', you'd tempt the devil to sell his soul. But it's best if I don't get too close to you. There's only one way it could end."

She twirled the end of her long, black hair, hanging in loose, damp ringlets around her face. "Is that a bad thing?"

"Got to bed, Alex."

She huffed and turned, the hem of her nightgown flouncing, revealing a pair of black lace panties.

He groaned and turned his back on her, his hands clenched in fists and shoved into his pockets to keep from reaching out and grabbing her. He strode to the window and peered out on the street where a light shined down from the lampposts at the corner of each block. Nothing moved except the cars and trucks headed away from the festival. Soon even those thinned to a trickle.

After much bed-squeaking and sheet-rustling, the house grew silent.

He crept into Alex's room.

She'd gone to sleep with her back to the door, her arm around the spare pillow, and clutched in her fingers, the little purple unicorn. A frown dimpled her forehead and he wondered what she was dreaming about. Was it him, her attacker, or maybe Sport and Calliope? She was keeping something from him about Sport. He couldn't believe for a moment that they had an open relationship. Alex wasn't the kind of woman who tolerated a mess. Open relationships smelled of disorder. The bandage on her chin stood out in the dim light shining from the hallway. The more Ed stared at it, the angrier he grew. After one last trip around the house, securing windows and checking the locks on the doors, he dialed Ben.

"Ed?" a groggy Ben answered. "Anything wrong?"

"I'm not sure." He paced the kitchen keeping his voice to a low whisper.

"Talk to me," Ben's voice snapped like a whip across the line.

He filled him in on the hit-and-run and the

rock through Alex's window while he'd been there, but skipped the part about the great sex with his sister.

"You're right to be worried. I wonder if we need to bring her in early. Sounds like having her there could make it dangerous for the people of Bayou Miste."

"That's what I'm afraid of." Ed's chest tightened. The folks around here might end up being collateral damage in an all-out war between Primeaux's army and the Louisiana State Police. "I'm headed out to check on our pigeon and make sure everything's still good out there. I'll let you know."

"I think it's time for me to pay a visit."

"No," he said, a little too forcefully. "If anyone links you to Ragsdale, they'll follow you here."

"Okay, no visit."

"Anything on Oscar Mills?" he asked.

"Nothing yet. But then I've been busy at the courthouse. I'll check in the morning. We're still on board to bring Ragsdale in day after tomorrow. Wait, that would be tomorrow since it's already today. Are you and Marcus up to it? Need me to send reinforcements?"

"We can play it by ear today and see what unfolds. If I think it's risky, I'll give you a shout."

"I'm concerned about using my cell phone to talk

to you. I might call you on one of those burner phones next time I call."

"Understood."

Ed hung up, checked once more on Alex, then slipped out the back, locking the door behind him.

Time to get serious. The clock was ticking, Leon Primeaux's trial would begin the following day. If someone was after him to get the location of Phyllis Ragsdale, he had to stay on his toes. No more playing around with the local attraction.

He laid a hand on her shoulder and shook her. "Alex."

She yawned and stretched, her eyes opening, a smile curving her lips. "Hey."

"I have to go, now, but I don't want to leave you alone."

"I'll be fine."

"I'd feel better if you went to your mother's house and stayed there until I get back."

"Where are you going?"

"I have some things to check on. Please, go to your mother's house."

"Okay. But don't be gone long." Her hand slipped across his face and she pressed a kiss to his lips.

He wanted to slide under the sheets and continue where they'd left off before she'd fallen to sleep. But he had work to do. He kissed her one last time and left, slipping out the backdoor, praying she'd do as he'd asked and go to the Boyette house.

After Ed left, Alex climbed out of bed and padded barefoot through the house to the kitchen and peered around the corner of the blinds out into the darkness of night. She would have missed him, had he not slipped from the corner of her house to the shadow of a tree at that moment. A thrill of fear skittered over her until she recognized the way he moved and his dark profile briefly illuminated by the stars.

Why would Ed sneak around like a crook or spy in the night rather than walk down the street? The incident of him snatching his wallet from her hands popped up in her mind and she wondered again, what was he hiding? Was he really there on vacation? Sure, he'd been fishing with Joe every morning, but what else was he doing while she was in Morgan City working? Something wasn't right and his surreptitious behavior didn't appear to be the kind to keep the neighbors from talking. Not when he carried the kind of gun he did.

Alex smacked a palm to her forehead when she thought of how she'd bought his line about carrying a gun in the bayou because of the alligators. Granted, she'd been surprised on more than one occasion by Maurice Saulnier's pet alligator, T-Rex. The creature stretched to over eight feet long now. He needed to transfer him to an alligator farm before he hurt someone or ate his grandmother's poodle.

In the meantime, Alex had a dilemma. She was falling for a guy who probably wasn't being truthful with her, while she hadn't been completely honest with him. Then again, how did one tell the guy she'd made love to twice that the man living with her was really a dog?

If Madame LeBieu wasn't going to help her, she'd have to make a run to Baton Rouge and get Lucie to undo the magic that made Sport a man.

Damn. Tomorrow she had an important meeting with the administrator from the hospital at Morgan City dropping by to negotiate a contract to provide services to their employees. And it would have to be late in the afternoon. That wouldn't leave time for her to make it to Baton Rouge before rush hour and would put her back later than she liked.

Alex watched for a little while longer, but didn't catch sight of Ed again, though the shadows near the corner of her house seemed to shift several times. She shivered and crossed her arms. Without Sport in the house as a dog, she didn't have that same comfort level living alone. And she didn't own a gun like Ed's.

She scrounged through her kitchen drawers and unearthed her favorite butcher knife and carried it to her bedroom, laying it on the nightstand before settling beneath the sheets. How much nicer would it have been had Ed stayed. With his arms around her, holding her cocooned against his body and his gun lying on the nightstand instead of the butcher knife, she'd have slept a whole lot better. Or not.

With a groan, Alex rolled over, tucking the spare pillow against her. It wasn't a muscular chest by far, but it was better than the emptiness of being totally alone. Ah, hell, who was she kidding? Nothing was better than a muscular chest attached to a warm body.

She wondered how Calliope and Sport were doing. Had they watched the movies and then gone to sleep...in separate locations? Deep down, she suspected those two were headed for heartbreak, and she was well on her way there herself.

Keeping to the shadows, Ed slipped away from Alex's house, hugging the edge of the bayou, moving from bush to tree to boathouse until he made his way back to the little boat he'd rented from Mrs. Boyette. The

GPS was hidden in the leg of an old pair of hip wader boots that had seen much better days.

Ed crouched low to the ground in the shadows and waited, listening for any sounds of movement. After a while, the crickets, cicadas, and frogs sang again, the dissonant sound blocking out everything but the rumble of trucks on the highway or the occasional bark of a lonely dog.

With the stealth of a ghost in the night, Ed slipped over the rim of the boat and pushed away from the bank, using the wooden oar. For the first fifty yards, he paddled the small craft through the mirror-smooth water until he came to the first fork in the bayou that would lead him away from the canal that paralleled the highway and out into the maze of the bayou. When he'd rounded a bend and the town disappeared from sight, he cranked the engine and guided the skiff to the little shack in the bayou where Marcus and the Ragsdale woman waited for news from the outside world.

Rather than tie off to the rickety dock, he ran the boat up into the shore beneath the overhanging Spanish moss. Halfway up the bank to the back porch of the shack, he tripped over a line, landing on his hands and knees, cursing to the rattle of tin cans. He grinned and stayed down until a figure emerged from the back of the shack and slipped silently toward him.

"I know, I better be Ed, or I'll be dead." Ed called out when Marcus came within range of his whispered call. "I like the early warning system."

"I put The Mouth to work stringing cans. Kept her busy for most of the afternoon."

"Good thinkin'." Ed stood and brushed the moss from his hands and jeans.

"She wanted to help me string them out there. Threatened to shoot her if she stepped one foot out of the building."

"That trigger finger gettin' itchier?" Ed led the way up the hill. Marcus followed, walking backward, his automatic rifle aimed toward the bayou.

"Been more traffic today than the past two."

Ed's head jerked toward him. "Anyone suspicious?"

Marcus snorted. "Hard to say. They all look the same. Most of them had fishing poles. One boat came by with a man in it that didn't have a fishing pole. He did have a camera and was takin' pictures."

"Of the shack?" Ed climbed the steps of the back porch, his hand on the doorknob.

"Yeah."

"Not good."

"You tellin' me. I had him in my sights."

"I'm surprised you didn't shoot him."

"I coulda," Marcus said. "Alligators round here would have cleaned him up. Counted two in the lagoon across the channel. Don't think the water's quite deep enough here to have hidden their boat for long, though."

"You scare me the way you think, you know that?" Ed chuckled and pushed the door open.

"Not much to do out here, but think."

"No shit." Phyllis Ragsdale sat at the card table, a mirror propped between cans of beans, the Coleman lantern beside the mirror as she plucked her eyebrows. "I won't have any brows by the time we leave this shithole."

"Nice to see you too, Ms. Ragsdale."

"Fuck you."

"Had to put up with that all day." Marcus thumbed the safety on his rifle as if he'd like to put a bullet in the witness and end everyone's misery.

Ed really had it easy in town compared to what Marcus was dealing with.

"What do you hear on the outside?" Marcus asked.

"Need to maintain your nonexistence here in the bayou. I think things are heating up in Bayou Miste." He filled them in on the two attacks.

"What, no bullets?" Marcus kicked a chair out

into the middle of the floor and sat, then pulled the magazine from his weapon and ejected the round from the bolt. In less time than it took to say *laissez les bon temps rouler*, he'd stripped the weapon down, laying the parts on the floor in front of him. "Wouldn't mind someone trying to make a run at this place. Beats the boredom and spending time with The Mouth."

"Yeah, maybe someone will shoot your dumb ass," Phyllis said, shifting her plucking from her eyebrows to the whiskers on her chin.

"Being on high ground, you're in a better position to defend, if you see them coming." Ed glanced around at the gaudy, peeling wall paper that had probably been glued back in the sixties. "Another thing to consider is that this shack is a prime candidate for a Molotov cocktail, served hot and wet. As old as the wood is, it would burn before you got your painted toenails out."

"That's one thing Trigger Happy Marcus and I agree on. We're ready for a little action."

"Well, you're going to get it tomorrow. We're making a trip to Baton Rouge for the first day of the trial."

Marcus looked up from cleaning his weapon. "About time."

"Thank God," Phyllis said. "I could do with a real night's sleep in a real bed."

"Sorry. It might only be a preliminary hearing and you'll be back here by the end of the night."

"Shit." She threw her tweezers on the table. "Tell me something I *want* to hear."

"You're still alive and Leon's still in jail," Ed said.

"Big fuckin' whoop." She stood and stretched, the tube top she wore sliding dangerously down over her huge breasts while her shorter than short shorts rose up displaying more than Ed ever wanted to see of her ass.

"I'm usually good for a piece of ass," Marcus said, squirting oil onto a cotton rag. "But not that."

"Oh shut up, you know you want it." Phyllis plumped her boobs, then refocused her attention on Ed. "Did you bring me chocolate today?"

"I brought you enough to last a week, the day before yesterday."

"I got bored." She shrugged. "I'll take that as a no. No chocolate, no TV, not even a radio in this godforsaken rat trap."

"Sorry. It was this or risk being nailed by one of your ex-boyfriend's mercenaries."

The woman snorted. "I'm beginning to think I should have taken my chances."

"I better go. I'm due to go fishing in a little under an hour. The diehards will be stirring."

"You wouldn't want to take her with you, would you?" Marcus slid the bolt in place, reassembled the rest of the weapon, and stood. "This place would be a whole lot nicer without her mouth."

"Hang tight. It won't be much longer." He rested a hand on Marcus's shoulder.

"I'll walk you out."

He stepped out on the back porch, followed by Marcus. "Stay here. I can find my way back without your help."

"Watch out for the—"

"Booby trap? I think I can find it this time."

"You managed to step over the first one. Look out for it as well."

"Will do." He nodded toward the shack. "Try not to kill her, even if she deserves it."

"I'll do my best." Marcus stood on the corner of the porch as Ed stepped off into the brush. Before Marcus had pointed out there were two alligators in the area, he hadn't considered that he might run into one there. Now he was on the lookout for them. Between the alligators, mad drivers, rock launchers, and the bitchy witness, and making love to a beautiful woman and then leaving her to defend herself—

guilt formed a knot in his chest—he wasn't getting much sleep.

But then he could sleep when this was over. Or when he was dead.

Chapter Twelve

Alex didn't see Ed all day. He didn't show up at the gym and he hadn't called. After the first two nights of great sex, she'd practically come to expect more.

The meeting with the Hospital Administrator netted a contract that would put her in the black and make her a tidy profit she could use to reinvest in additional equipment and resources. But a successful business coup didn't have the same thrill as it had a week ago. Not when all she could think about was Ed and how great he'd been with the kids the night before, not to mention how incredible it had been making love on her kitchen table. She'd never eat another meal there without thinking about it.

"Wow, you really have it bad." Harry waved a hand in front of her face. "I've been talking to you for two whole minutes and you haven't heard a word I've said."

"Sorry." She pulled her ponytail out and ran her fingers through her hair. "I guess I'm tired."

"Late night with Mr. Marceau?" Harry's grin was sly. "Did you get that bruise performing mattress gymnastics?"

"Harry!"

Harry laughed, then her smile faded. "You haven't told me how you got that bruise. Did he hit you? Because if he did, he'll have me and the rest of our family to answer to."

Alex smiled, touching her chin. "No, he didn't hit me. Some teen lobbed a rock through my window. I just happened to catch it with my chin."

"*Coo Wee!* The little jerk-wad." Harry tipped her face to the light. "What's with kids these days? Mom made note of the fact Ed didn't return to his cabin all night. Was he staying to protect you from the creep?"

"Great. The woman's too nosey for her own good. Mom's going to get her hopes all built up and for what?" She rolled her eyes. "A big fat nothing. He's only into me for a vacation fling. And I'm not interested in anything more than that."

"So you keep saying. But are you sure? You've been more distracted than I've ever seen you since he showed up."

"It's this hospital deal. I've been keyed up over it."

"Yeah, right. You didn't even stutter or hesitate when you gave your pitch. I was so proud of you."

"I internalized the nerves." In fact, her head had barely been in the game. If she hadn't had the gym in top shape with the help of her team, they might have walked away.

"No, you were thinking about Ed." Harry raised a hand. "Don't try to feed me another line."

"Are we eating lines, now? Is it some kind of new diet? I could use one, I've put on a pound or two in the last couple of days."

Calliope entered the gym office, Sport in tow. "Leapin' lily pads, what happened to you?"

With a sigh, Alex touched her chin. "It's a long story. The bigger question is where the heck have you two been?" She glared at her friend. "Have you decided to move Sport into your place permanently?"

"I would, if you'd let me." Calliope grinned and hugged Sport's arm. "We had the best time watching movies into the wee hours." She yawned. "I'll be worthless at work. Speaking of which, I promised Sport you'd bring him to the Raccoon Saloon tonight."

She groaned. "Why did you do that? I'm too tired to think, much less go out."

"Please." Calliope grabbed Alex's hand. "Sport's

never been there and we don't know when or if he'll get another chance. He isn't going to be in town for long." She hoped.

Sport looked at her with a hint of the sad dog look in his brown eyes. "Please."

"Guess who's going out tonight?" Harry laughed and headed for the door.

"Oh, no you don't. If I have to go, you're coming with me!" Alex called out.

"I'll dust off my cowboy boots." Harry waved without turning back.

Calliope pressed a kiss to Sport's cheek before heading out to go home and get ready for work.

Alex had promised her mother she'd bring pizza home for the family. She placed her order and picked it up before leaving Morgan City. Looking forward to a quiet drive back to Bayou Miste, Alex was instead bombarded with one question after another. It seemed Sport wanted to know everything as fast as he could think to ask.

"What is blue? How do cars work? Where do babies come from?"

By the time they pulled up in front of her mother's house, Alex's patience had been exhausted.

Her mother opened the front door for her and Sport. "Oh, Alex, thank you for bringing dinner. The kids were about ready to gnaw on the furniture."

Alex carried in four large boxes while Sport carried the other four, and they set them in the middle of the table.

"Who's not coming?" Alex asked after counting the number of settings at the table. Harry had called her before she'd gotten to Bayou Miste and said she'd had to take the late shift at the gym for a sick employee. Truman had his own place in Morgan City and didn't come to dinner often.

"Abe and GW called and said they had other plans and Dolley and Madison are staying late at the plantation for a special event."

"Will Ed be eating with us?" Teddy asked, saving Alex from letting her mother know she cared.

"No, *ma chère*," she patted her young daughter's hair. "He said he had plans, but thanks anyway."

"I wonder what plans he had," Alex said absently.

"Interested?" Her mother smiled. When she frowned in return, her mother went on to say, "He mentioned something about heading to Baton Rouge tomorrow and needing to take care of some business before going." Her mother sighed. "It's too bad, I was getting used to having him at the dinner table, and the kids like him, too." She glanced across the table at her. "You two didn't have a fight, did you?"

"Why would we have a fight? It's not like we're dating or anything." She didn't look her mother in the eye and her ears burned. *Mais, it was the truth.* They weren't dating. You couldn't call a night of plumbing and taking a herd of kids to the festival anything like a date.

"Oh, Alex, you did, didn't you?"

"No, Mom. We didn't argue." She glanced at her watch. "I have to go. Calliope made me promise to take Sport out to the Saloon tonight. I want to get there before the crowd to get a seat."

Her mother kissed her cheek. "Ed's a good guy. You should give him a chance, honey."

She sighed and hugged her mother. "I know. But he's not here tonight and I have to go."

"At least you're not saying no. *Mais,* have a good time, *ma chère.*" Before she left the room, her mother had pizza on the plates of the youngest Boyettes and was taking her seat. The woman could have run an army, she was so efficient.

As she stepped out the door, Granny Saulnier's poodle, FeFe, ran by, the hot pink supplanted by day-glo orange.

Sport tensed and leaped off the porch after the poodle.

"Sport!" Alex ran after him and waited until she'd gotten out of hearing range of her mother's house before yelling, "Sport! Heel!"

He ground to a halt, his entire body quivering.

"Come," she said, using all the commands her mother had taught by example.

Sport's head dipped and he turned toward her. "Sport bad?"

"Yes," she said, but couldn't stay mad at him. Not when he looked so forlorn with those sad, puppy dog eyes. "What are we going to do with you, *mon cher?*"

"Sport like FeFe."

"I know." She hooked his arm with hers. "Do you miss being a dog?"

"Sport love Callipuppy."

"Oh, dear. No, Sport, you can't. Even though you're a man now, you'll go back to being a dog when the spell wears off."

He tipped his head. "Sport not understand."

"Never mind. Let's go have some fun. It might be the first and last time you get to go to a saloon."

He perked up. "Callipuppy there?"

Alex could almost imagine his floppy reddish-brown ears rising. Her heart wrenched. She missed having her golden retriever greet her when she arrived home, all happy and excited, begging for a treat.

She led Sport back to her car and drove to her house, where she unloaded a medium-sized pizza she'd bought to put in the freezer and eat the next day. Since she hadn't had the heart to sit at her mother's dinner table without Ed being there, she opened the box, pulled out two plates, and ate with Sport.

When they were finished, she changed, straightened her hair, applied a bit of makeup to her bare face, and helped Sport choose from a selection of three outfits Calliope had bought for him to wear out that night.

They arrived at the Raccoon Saloon a little after nine o'clock. Music vibrated through the building, into the night.

Sport was bobbing his head to the beat like he'd done as dog. Even then, he'd enjoyed music. She grabbed his arm and pasted a smile on her face. Tomorrow she'd head into Baton Rouge if she had to in order to get Lucie to undo the spell. Sport might as well have fun on his last night as a human.

The place was hopping with a Zydeco Band playing traditional Cajun music, upbeat and crazy. She tried to get in the mood, but fell short.

Sport spotted Calliope as she carried a tray of empty beer mugs. She was as beautiful as ever, wearing a pretty pink halter top and a long floral skirt, with her wild red curls pulled over one shoulder in a loose ponytail.

Breaking free of Alex's hold, Sport made a beeline for her. She dropped her tray on the counter and wrapped her arms around his neck as he hugged her around the middle and swung her around.

Alex sighed. She wished she could find that carefree exuberance that Calliope and Sport seemed to own. Their happiness to see each other made her want to go back home and crawl into a gallon of Rocky Road ice cream.

Calliope guided Sport to an empty stool at the bar and set a beer mug in front of him.

Alex groaned, wondering what reaction his new man-body would have to alcohol. She hoped he wouldn't turn out to be an angry drunk. She glanced around as the bar filled with locals stopping by for a little beer and fun after a hard day's work. Most of the men worked at Littington Industries and still wore their work overalls with Littington embroidered on the chest.

She half-hoped she'd see Ed there amongst the familiar faces. But then her mother had said he had business to take care of before he headed to Baton Rouge the following day. Hadn't he said he was from New Orleans? What business would have in Baton Rouge? Unless he'd been called in to mediate a special case. But in the middle of his vacation?

She still couldn't help but think that some things about Ed Marceau didn't add up. Next time she saw him—if there was a next time—she'd try to get her questions answered. Like why did a mediator need to carry a gun? And last night, why had he slipped away from her house like a special agent in a spy movie?

She slid onto the stool beside Sport and lifted the long-neck beer Calliope set on the counter in front of her. "What if I'd wanted draft tonight?"

Calliope shook her head. "You always get the long-neck. Face it, Alex, you're predictable."

Predictable? "You say that like it's a bad thing." She couldn't help being defensive. She prided herself on her orderly existence. It had earned her a degree in marketing, a business, and a house she was paying for, all by herself. "Predictable gets results."

Calliope rolled her eyes. "Haven't you ever wanted to do something rash? Something you hadn't thought through completely?"

Like making love to Ed? "I have. A couple times." *Lately.*

"I'll bet you thought it to death afterward and talked yourself out of doing it again." Calliope flipped her long, loose ponytail over her other shoulder and smiled. "You really need to let go and go with the flow. Let your spirit guide you. Listen to what's inside your heart, not your head."

"And fall in love with a dog?" She snorted.

Calliope frowned. "At least I *let* myself fall in love." She flicked her skirt with as much anger as her happy spirit could muster, grabbed a full tray of drinks, and went back to work.

"Why you make Callipuppy mad?"

Already regretting her words, Alex lifted her beer to her lips. "I know I shouldn't be ugly. Calliope's my friend. *You're* my friend. I should be happy you two have found each other." She turned around on her stool and stared out at the crowd.

"Alex sad?"

"Maybe."

"Why?"

"I don't know."

"Alex love Ed?"

She turned to Sport. "Why would you say that?" she raised her finger. "And don't tell me you smelled it."

Sport's brows wrinkled and he tipped his head like he did when he was trying to figure something out. "Alex and Ed are like Callipuppy and Sport." He smiled, his open, how-easy-is-this grin. "Love."

"It isn't that simple."

"Why?"

"Alex can't have Ed." She shook her head. Now she was talking like Sport. "When he leaves, he won't come back."

"Why?"

"He doesn't live in Bayou Miste."

"Then be with Ed where Ed lives."

"I can't." Alex sighed. "I live here."

"Why?"

Why indeed?

Calliope sailed over to the bar, her cheerful face glowing brighter every time she looked at Sport. "I'm on break." She set her tray down and grabbed Sport's hand. "Come dance with me."

Sport let her drag him to the dance floor where she taught him how to two-step. The band took a break and the jukebox took over. Within five minutes they were circling the floor to a country song. They looked like they belonged together. Happy and in love.

Another sigh escaped her, and as much as it hurt to witness their happiness, she couldn't drag her gaze away. The music slowed and Calliope wrapped her arms around Sport's neck and leaned her cheek against his chest. He held her around her middle and rested his face against the side of her hair, closing his eyes. When the song ended, Calliope leaned up on her toes, cupped Sport's face and kissed him. From where she sat, it appeared Sport was kissing her back. Another song started up and the couple resumed swaying, oblivious to everyone else dancing by them in a flowing waltz.

"Dance wit' me, Alex," a voice said next to her. "Or be you too good for ol' Theo?"

A chunk of lead hit the pit of her belly. She turned to stare up into Theo's eyes. The man reeked of too much alcohol and sweat.

Way to put the kibosh on dreams of love and happiness.

"Go away, Theo." She turned away from the dance floor and lifted her bottle to her lips.

Ed spent the afternoon preparing for the next day's transportation of the witness to the courthouse in Baton Rouge. He cleaned his rifle and handgun, filled the rental car's gas tank, checked the tires, and charged his smartphone. He even went to Morgan City to purchase a burner phone in case he needed an untraceable number, should the mission go south.

The plan was to move the Ragsdale woman under the cover of night, late enough that everyone would be in bed asleep. Until then he had to cool his heels and wait. He'd declined Mrs. Boyette's dinner invitation, claiming he had things to do. Truth was, he didn't want to see Alex when all he wanted to do was hold her and kiss her and...well, lose sight of the reason he was there. If the rock through her window last night was meant for him, he might already have put her and her family in danger.

At nine that evening, darkness had settled over the bayou, but it was still too early to make his move. He'd paced the length of the house and back a hundred times, working through every scenario he could imagine and his potential response. Between him and Marcus, they had to get Phyllis out alive and deliver her to the courthouse without incident.

His phone vibrated in his pocket and he jerked it out. Caller ID indicated a blocked number. He pressed the talk button. "Yeah."

"Ed, it's Ben."

"You on a burner?'"

"Yes. As close as we are to D-day, I didn't want to risk your phone being traced from mine."

"Great minds think alike." He gave him the number of the burner he'd purchased earlier. "What's happening on your end?"

"Primeaux has had someone observing him twenty-four-seven and he hasn't seemed to make a move to have our witness terminated."

"What are the chances he'll let her live to testify against him?"

"Everyone at this end is betting a hundred to one."

"Right."

"Tomorrow's going to be hectic. Have her wear a bullet-proof vest, you and Marcus, too. If he really has a bounty out on her, you know there will be bullets flying." Ben heaved a tense breath. "Any other attacks on your end?"

"Not today, but then I haven't been outside much, other than to jog this morning and once this afternoon."

"Oh, I did get something on Oscar Mills."

He tensed. "Shoot."

"Retired DEA sharpshooter."

"Retired DEA sharpshooter?" He shook his head. "What's a guy like that doing here in the bayou?" Unless he was hired by Leon. "Anything in his background show he's gone dirty? Any foreclosures? Owe a ton of money? Default on his loans or taxes? Cousins in the Primeaux family? Anything?"

"No. The man was highly decorated in the DEA, retired early after twenty-five years of service. He's only forty-three."

"Hell, he could be on his second career as Leon's hit man." Ed ran a hand through his hair. "I don't like it."

"You have a couple hours to kill. Sorry, poor choice of words." Ben chuckled. "You have a couple hours before the extraction—get out there and get a bead on Mills."

"Will do."

"And Ed?"

"Yeah."

"Be careful."

"I think I'll be more in danger of crossfire from Marcus shooting at Ragsdale than anything else. Have you heard the mouth on that woman?"

Ben hung up, laughing.

He tucked his weapons into their cases, locked them, and shoved them under the bed. With his keys in hand, he locked up, jumped in his car, and drove slowly along the main street through town, checking out any movement. Before he reached the cabin where Oscar Mills was staying, the Ford Fusion Mills had been driving pulled out of his drive and headed north.

Falling in behind him, but keeping a reasonable distance back, Ed followed the retired sharpshooter, all the way to the Raccoon Saloon. Was he stopping there for a drink or to meet with one of Primeaux's men?

Only one way to find out.

He passed the saloon and gave Mills enough time to park and enter, before he made a U-turn on the highway and returned to the bar, parking in the rear.

He slipped in through the back door the employees used. With no one there to question him, he managed to enter the saloon unnoticed, emerging near the hallway leading to the bathrooms. For the next few minutes, he panned the interior of the saloon, until he found Oscar Mills sitting at one end of the bar, nursing a beer, by himself, while staring out at the room full of natives line dancing or drinking pitchers of beer and downing oyster shooters.

At the other end of the bar, closest to Ed, a big man stood with his back to him. By the breadth of his shoulders and the way he stood, he guessed it was Theo Ledet.

The man swayed and spoke loud enough that Ed could hear his words over the music. "What, are you too good ta dance wit' me now dat you got de hot shot from Naw-lins to screw?" The man leaned into whoever he was talking to, swaying.

The woman to whom he spoke reached up a slim hand and slapped the crap out of him.

He staggered a step backward and braced his feet. "You shoulda not done dat." He reached out and grabbed her.

A flurry of movement and flying arms resulted, and, within seconds, Alex Boyette had Theo Ledet face down on the sticky barroom floor with his arm twisted up behind him. She stepped into the middle of his back and said, loud enough for everyone in the joint to hear, "Theo Ledet, for the last time. Leave. Me. Alone."

Ed chuckled. She hadn't been kidding when she said she knew karate. Then again, the man had been stone drunk.

Alex stepped over the guy and started toward the dance floor. She'd only gone two steps when the dumbass on the floor grabbed her ankle. She toppled like a statue, hit the ground hard and lay there stunned long enough for Theo to haul himself to his feet and grab her by her hair.

Every protective instinct inside him erupted into bottled-up rocket fuel and Ed launched himself across the room, plowing over chairs, legs, and people scrambling to get out of his way.

As Theo pulled Alex up by the hair, he flung a right hook into the side of his face.

Theo barely recoiled, but he did let go of Alex's hair and turn the full force of his inebriated anger on him.

"Back off, Ed, I've got this," Alex said as she rolled over and staggered to her feet, pushing her hair out of her face. "The man has a jaw of iron; you won't faze him—"

Theo threw a punch aimed at his nose.

Ed dodged to the side, but wasn't fast enough to

miss the second swing. He took it in the jaw and jerked back, pain radiating through his head.

The next punch, he was ready for. He dodged, hooked Theo's arm, and yanked it up behind his back between his shoulder blades. "You gonna act nice or am I gonna break it?" he demanded.

Theo whimpered. "I'll be nice. Promise."

"You gonna quit following Miz Alex and leave her alone?"

"Yes sir, I be leavin' dat gal alone."

Alex focused on the bartender. "Call the sheriff, this man needs help getting home." Once he had Theo loaded into a patrol car, Ed returned to the saloon. Oscar still sat at the end of the bar. His gaze met Ed's, a smile curling the corners of his lips. He tipped his mug at him and nodded.

When he looked around, Ed noted Calliope and Sport locked in an embrace on the dance floor, but Alex was gone.

Face it, buddy, you have to move on. Mills didn't appear to be a threat, and looked like he'd be at the saloon for a while.

Having already wasted enough time in town, it was time to get out to the bayou and collect the package to be delivered.

Chapter Thirteen

The extraction went smoothly. Marcus and Ed got Phyllis out of the swamp with no problem other than trying to keep the harpy quiet when they'd reached Bayou Miste. Marcus looked ready to pull the trigger. If not on her, then on himself.

After spending four days with the witch, he was certain Marcus would get off on an insanity plea.

To burn time, they sat in the car on a deserted road west of Baton Rouge for a couple hours. They weren't expected to arrive at the courthouse until nine in the morning. He and Ben had planned a circuitous route so they could throw a tail or see if anyone was following them.

Phyllis whined and complained about wearing

the bulletproof vest, claiming it wasn't her color and it made her look fat. In the end she put it on for fear Marcus would be the one to shoot her.

On the drive through Baton Rouge, the occupants of the Jeep grew tense. Even Phyllis shut up as they got closer to the courthouse where she was to testify against one of the most ruthless mobsters south of the Mason Dixon line.

Twice Marcus thought he'd spotted a tail. Twice Ed rerouted and took another turn to confuse any would-be hit man. As the clock neared nine, they rolled up to the steps of the courthouse. Marcus got out first, his hand on his gun inside his suit jacket, and held the door for Phyllis to alight.

Ben met them with two other plainclothes cops. Ed circled the car and blocked the view as Phyllis stepped out.

Some members of the press, who'd gathered around the prosecuting attorney at the top of the steps of the East Baton Rouge Parish Courthouse, spied the vehicle and moved as one to get an interview with the next arrival from the trial of the century.

As Phyllis stepped up on the sidewalk, her heel caught on the curb and she lurched forward.

One of the plainclothes cops jerked backward and landed on his ass on the concrete, groaning.

"Gunshot fired!" Ed yelled, planted his hand on Phyllis's head and shoved her into the back seat on the floorboard, folded her legs in after her, and slammed the door. "Get in!" he shouted to Marcus.

The back windshield exploded in a spray of glass fragments.

While he ran around to the driver's side, reporters screamed and uniforms herded bystanders into the courthouse. Marcus dove into the passenger seat and Ed gunned the accelerator, sending the damaged rental flying away from the crime scene.

He tossed the burner to Marcus. "Call Ben, tell him we're going to stash the loot and wait for an all-clear before we attempt this again."

"What the fuck?" Phyllis raged from the back floorboard. "I'll sue the state of Louisiana on assault charges. Did you have to be so goddamn rough? Shit, I broke a nail!"

As planned, if the transfer got botched, they ditched the Jeep in a parking garage and picked up the replacement and headed back to the bayou, taking a long route to make sure no one followed. They'd decided the bayou was the best location since they could see danger coming, and if it came to an all-out war, fewer people would be hurt in the crossfire, than if they hid her in town.

Frankly, he couldn't wait to get back. Number

one, to get rid of the witness from hell whose mouth should be exiled to a deserted island. Although he wouldn't wish that on the fish and the palm trees.

Number two, he wanted to see Alex and make sure she was all right. Hell, and to admit to her that he was falling for her.

Alex had called in sick to her gym for the first time in the three years she'd owned it. After seeing Ed last night take a hit for her, she'd wanted to go to him, melt into his arms, and tell him she loved him. But the feelings were so raw and uncontrolled, she'd run from them, from Ed, from what she really wanted. Once she'd gotten into her car, she realized her mistake. She should have gone back in and told Ed how she felt. Instead, she'd gone home in a funk so blue she couldn't focus.

Sport had spent the night at Calliope's again. Which meant Alex had been alone throughout the night. She'd tossed and turned, her body alternating between cold and lonely and raging heat from memories of what she and Ed had shared in her bed, on her kitchen table, and all the places they hadn't had the opportunity to try out.

Sometime during the night, she'd fallen into a deep, dreamless sleep and slept past her alarm. When she finally woke, it was past nine o'clock and the sun peeked through her blinds. Too wound up to focus on work, she'd called Harry and asked her to pull a double, taking the early and the late shift that day. With energy to burn, she pulled on her jogging shorts, sport bra and sneakers, and hit the road.

Joe Thibodeaux was out in front of the marina painting the exterior wall as high up as he could reach without a ladder.

Too curious to pass him by, she slowed to jog in place. "What happened to your morning fishing buddy?"

"Cancelled. Said he had business to take care of today."

She jogged a few more steps in place. "Did he say when he'd be back?"

"Nope. Said not to expect him back in. He'd call if he wanted to schedule another morning." Joe shook his head. "He was comin' along pretty good for a man who'd never put a hook in the water."

Alex stopped jogging. He'd said he'd come to Bayou Miste to get some fishing in on vacation. "He'd never been fishing?"

"Couldn't have. Not the way he handled the rod."

Joe scratched his beard, smearing white paint on his face. "What he lacked in experience, though, he made up for in enthusiasm."

Interesting. A man on vacation in a bayou town who'd never been fishing. "Have a nice day, Joe."

"You, too."

She jogged past her mother's house, almost tripping over her own feet as she passed the little rental cottage where Ed stayed, craning her neck to see if he was home. Disappointment flooded her. His car was gone and the place looked empty. If he never came back, that's how it would remain.

A lump the size of a wadded up tube sock lodged in her throat and she had to blink to clear her vision. Pushing harder, she ran faster and faster, until she was a mile out of town and feeling no better. She turned and headed back, passing her home once again.

"Alex!" Her mother waved at her from her porch. "Care for a cup of coffee?"

Tired and sweating, she shook her head. "No, thanks, Mom. But I'll take a glass of iced tea if you have some."

Her mother smiled. "I even have some fresh beignets—Miz Mozelle brought them by this morning. She wanted to give them to Ed, but he hasn't been home all night. I thought he wasn't heading into

Baton Rouge until this morning, but I guess he left under the cover of darkness." She shrugged. "Our benefit. We get the beignets."

Alex bypassed the large dining room table, opting for the dinette that seated six in the Boyette kitchen. "Kids off to school?"

"Left a couple hours ago." Her mother poured two glasses of iced tea and set them on the table, sinking into the seat. "This is one of my favorite times of the day."

"Morning calm?"

"Umhmm." She sipped from her glass and smiled. "My other favorite time of day is dinner when everyone's here and talking at once."

"Don't you get lonely?"

"Oh, no, *ma chère*. I like my time alone. Much as I love my children, I look forward to the day when I can leave Bayou Miste."

Her heart skipped several beats and then hammered away. "What?"

Her mother patted her hand. "To travel, *ma chère*. This will always be my home, but when I was young, before I met your father, I used to dream of seeing other places, other countries. I still have those dreams." The light in her mother's eyes made her appear younger, more vibrant.

She could almost visualize the young woman

she'd once been, before nineteen children had tied her down. "Why did I never know that about you?"

Her mother smiled. "Your father loved Bayou Miste, it was his home and he never wanted to leave. I was happy with that, as long as I had him or my children." Her eyes glazed with tears. "But once my work is done raising all of you, I want to spread my wings, before I get too old to do it."

Alex swallowed on the knot in her throat that the memories of her father always brought. "Did you ever regret having so many of us?"

She smiled, shaking her head. "Never. I can't imagine life without every one of you." Her mother reached out and caressed her cheek. "My one regret was that you had to grow up too soon. Now, I'm afraid you feel responsible for all of us, and that's not at all what I wished for you, my first daughter. I dreamed of you spreading your wings, getting out of Bayou Miste, and experiencing the world."

"And here I am." A tear pushed out of the corner of her eye and slipped down her cheek. "I couldn't leave you to handle everything by yourself."

Her mother smiled. "I'm pretty tough. I can handle things." She leaned forward as if imparting a secret. "And in case you didn't notice...I'm not all by myself. Your brothers and sisters are quite capable of helping out, just like you did growing up. It builds character." She covered Alex's hand with hers. "If there's another life you want to lead or were afraid to dream, don't let it pass you by. Reach out, run toward it. You have my blessing. Not that you need it."

"Oh, yes, I do." More tears trickled down Alex's face and she squeezed her mother's hands.

"If that young man comes back, don't you push him away like you always do. Give him a chance."

"What if he doesn't want me?"

Her mother shook her head. "Who wouldn't want you?"

She laughed, the sound catching on a sob. "From Mom's mouth to God's ears."

"Now go to work. The day will pass much more quickly."

She left her mother's house, her heart much lighter, her feet barely touching the ground.

When she entered her house, she shed her workout clothes, grabbed a towel, and headed for the bathroom while dialing Lucie's number.

"Alex, did you hear?" Lucie asked, her voice shaking.

She had reached to turn on the shower, but paused. "Hear what?"

"About the shooting." Lucie sobbed into the

phone. "At the courthouse. Someone tried to kill the witness in the case against the mobster, Leon Primeaux. One of the cops escorting her was hit."

She gripped the phone, her heart clenching so tightly she could barely breathe. "Where's Ben? Was he there? Is he all right?"

"He was there!" Lisa cried some more while Alex held her breath. "But he's okay. He wasn't hurt."

The air rushed out of Alex's lungs and she sagged against the sink. "Don't scare me like that!"

"I'm sorry. I was shaking so badly, I thought I'd miscarry this baby. I'd heard it over the news and I tried to get Ben on the phone and...and...I was so scared, Alex. I'm not cut out to be the wife of a cop."

"Yes you are. You know you love him." She did her best to soothe her friend when her own hands were shaking. "Can you imagine being with anyone else?"

"No. But if something should happen to him, I couldn't stand the idea of living without him."

She envied Lucie. She'd found someone she cared about so much she would sacrifice everything to be with him, even her life. And she couldn't be with a better man than Ben. "*Ma chère,* we never know how much time we have with the ones we love. Be thankful for every day you have with him."

"I know. I know. I'm being hormonal, but I love him so much."

"Honey, he's okay. You're going to be okay. Take a deep breath and pull yourself together. The baby needs you to be strong."

After a few sniffles and a loud snort as if Lucie was blowing her nose, she said, "Thanks, Alex, I needed to hear that. Now, I *know* you didn't call for me to have a nervous breakdown in your ear. Why *did* you call?"

Figuring it would take Lucie's mind off Ben's near-miss, she drew in a deep breath and launched into the reason for her call. "Is the Voodoo that made Sport human permanent?"

"Oh, Alex, I have no idea. Whatever Gran LeBieu put in that *gris gris* bag had to have been some powerful stuff to have done what it did."

"I need to know if it will stick."

"*Mais*, the spell she put on Craig Thibodeaux lasted over a week. I'm not even sure my grand-mother knows how long her spells will last. She always says something like *they'll last as long as they're needed* or something vague like that. Why? Are things pretty bad down there?"

Alex sighed. "No. But I wonder if it's possible for the spell to be made permanent."

"You'll have to run that by my grandmother."

Lucie paused. "Are you falling in love with Sport as a man?"

She laughed and then sobered. "No, I'm not falling for Sport, but Calliope is. And he's in love with her."

"*Coo wee!* I can't say I miss the craziness of Bayou Miste." Lucie clucked her tongue. "That's so like Calliope. She has such a big heart."

"I know, and I'd hate to see it broken."

"Wish I could help."

"You can help by taking care of yourself, my godchild, and my big brother."

"I'll do my best. What about you, Alex?" Lucie asked. "Is there someone special in your life? I always dreamed we'd have babies at the same time so that our children could grow up together. Anything on that front?"

She cringed when she heard the sound of her biological clock ticking for the first time. Immediately Ed's face appeared in her mind. "No, nothing yet."

"I'll burn a red candle for you," Lucie offered. "Maybe it will bring you luck on the love front."

"Thanks, but don't burn the house down doing it." She hung up, jumped in the shower, and got ready for work, after all. Staying home left her way too much time to think. She needed the day to go by quickly like her mother had promised. Her heart beat faster in anticipation of seeing Ed that evening. *Please let him come back.*

"I'm sick and tired of being in this car. I'm hot, I'm thirsty, and I have to pee like nobody's goddamn business."

Marcus and Ed chimed together, "Shut up!"

Phyllis Ragsdale sniffed. "I'm the one being shot at. You could be a little more sympathetic to the lady present."

Marcus glared at the woman in the back seat. "You are no lady. You're a—"

"As soon as it's dark," Ed cut in, "we'll take you back out to the bayou and you can stretch, drink, and pee to your heart's content."

"I don't want to go back to the bayou. It's dirty, buggy and...and...unairconditioned!"

"And you might stay alive a day longer there than in the city," Ed said, his voice a little less strained. The sun was setting and they had been driving down back roads with grass growing up so close to the edges, the roads appeared as if they hadn't been used in decades. Every once in a while, they stopped in a pullout or overgrown driveway to cool the engine and find a bush to urinate behind. The last stop had been over an hour ago, and even he was ready to get the hell out of the car.

As the sun set and the stars started popping out against the black backdrop of sky, he turned the car toward Bayou Miste, slipped onto the first side street, and parked behind an empty building. "Tighten your vests."

Phyllis shrank against the back seat, showing the first signs of fear since leaving Baton Rouge. "You think they'll be gunnin' for me here?"

"We don't know, but there's only one way to find out." Marcus climbed out and held the door for her. "Let's go."

Ed and Marcus flanked her as they hurried across the street and down the bank of the canal to where they'd tied off the pirogue.

The trip back to the shack in the swamp passed without incident and very little talking. Phyllis insisted on sitting at the bottom of the boat, as low to the water as she could get without getting wet. When they arrived at the shack, Marcus took the lead and cleared the building before they stepped one foot inside.

By the time Ed returned to Bayou Miste, collected the car, and drove to the rental cottage beside the Boyette house, he was tired and ready to hit the sack for some much-needed rest. He glanced down the street, wishing he could see all the way to Alex's house. Was she awake? Would she let him in, if he were to knock on her door? After all that had happened that day, all he wanted was to feel her in his arms.

He climbed out of his car and headed for the little house that had become more of a home to him than his apartment back in Baton Rouge.

A movement on the porch made him reach for his gun, setting his senses on alert.

"Is that a gun in your hand, or are you happy to see me?" Alex's chuckle drifted to him on the warm, moist night air, wrapping around him like the scent of honeysuckle.

"What are you doing here, sitting alone in the dark?"

"Waiting for you to come back."

"What if I hadn't?"

"I guess I'd have gone home." She rose from the steps and waited for him to close the distance. "You look tired."

"It's been a rough day."

"Wanna tell me about it?"

"No, I want to know why you left the saloon last night without saying anything to me."

"I wished I hadn't as soon as I did. Too many

things hit me all at once and...and..." she shrugged, "I ran."

"What things?"

"Things like realizing I was beginning to care too much about you." She smiled, tears trembling on her lashes. "I was scared."

"That would make two of us, then." He stood in front of her wanting to take her into his arms, but realized that if she was scared of her feelings, she had to make the first move.

Alex held her arms open.

He walked into them and hugged her for a long time. Her body melted against his, fitting perfectly. He would have stayed that way much longer, but the events of the day kept coming back to him, like a car's factory-installed warning light that couldn't be turned off. "Let's go inside."

She didn't resist, taking his hand as they climbed the steps. "I know we haven't known each other that long, but I missed you today."

Ed unlocked the door, pulled her through, and locked it behind her, then pressed her against the door and kissed her.

Her hands locked behind his head and she leaned into him, opening to the thrust of his tongue, sliding her leg alongside his.

When he had to come up for air, he peppered

tiny kisses along her cheekbone to her ear and down the side of her neck. He couldn't get enough.

She laughed and feathered her fingers through his hair. "I've wanted to do this all day long. I'd been counting the minutes until you came back."

He leaned back and gazed into her blue eyes. "After you left the saloon last night without saying anything, I thought you were done with me. What made you change your mind?"

"A very wise woman told me not to let life pass me by out of some mistaken sense of duty." Alex shrugged. "I decided it was time to start living for me."

"And how do I fit in this picture?"

Her face shined up at him. "I feel alive when I'm with you. More alive than I've felt in a long time."

He cupped her cheeks, his heart melting at what the sparkle in her eyes. "You don't know me."

"But I want to." Alex turned her face to his palm and kissed it.

"What if you don't like me when you *do* get to know who I am?"

"I'll take that risk."

"That's pretty bold for someone who craves structure in her life."

"I'm turning over a new leaf. I even rearranged

the towels in my bathroom so that nothing is stacked according to the color."

"Big step for a control freak."

"Hey." She slapped him on the shoulder, playfully. "It is, for me."

Ed leaned his forehead against hers. "Like I said, this has been a rough day."

Alex stiffened beneath him. "If you'd rather I left and let you get some rest, I will."

"No. Please, stay and let me finish." He brushed his thumb across her cheek, loving how soft and silky her skin was. "Even during the worst parts of my day, I couldn't stop thinking about you."

Alex's brows wrinkled. "In a good way or a bad way?"

He chuckled. "Definitely in a good way." His smile faded. "The problem is that right now, I can't afford to think about you."

"What do you mean?" She gazed into his eyes, her light blue ones darkening to gray. "What aren't you telling me?"

"There are things you don't know about me and I can't tell you right now."

"I was right." She pushed against him. "You're married."

"No. I'm single. In fact, some, including your brother, would call me a confirmed bachelor."

She stopped struggling and rested her palms against his chest. "And are you? Confirmed?"

"Until I met you." He kissed the tip of her nose and she stood on her toes to kiss his lips.

He returned the kiss then gripped her arms and set her at arm's length. "Give me time. I have something to take care of before I can think of us."

"If you told me what it was, maybe I could help."

"No." He wanted to tell her the truth, but the more she knew the more she would become a target of Leon's band of murderers. "I can't. You have to trust me."

She sucked in a breath and let it out slowly. "Okay. We'll do this your way." Her fingers tightened in his shirt and she pulled him close until they were nose to nose. "But know this—When I want something badly enough, I don't give up easily."

He laughed and brushed his lips across her full, sensuous mouth. "Baby, I'm counting on it."

This time when they kissed, he let himself believe there would be another time for them. After the trial. After his job here was done.

Tires squealed outside and a loud crash put his senses on alert. He shoved Alex to the floor and crouched there with her.

"What the hell was that?" Alex cried.

The scent of gasoline filled the air and then

smoke filtered in with it. "Fire." Ed leaped to his feet and ran into the living room of the little house. The front window had a gaping, jagged hole and the old sofa was drenched in gasoline and fire. And the fire was spreading quickly. He grabbed a throw pillow and beat at the flames, but the gasoline had soaked into the cushions and no amount of beating was going to stop the fire from spreading. It swept to the filmy curtains beside the window and licked at the ancient wallpaper.

"Leave it." Alex grabbed his arm and dragged him toward the door.

He couldn't let her go out the front for fear it was a trap and someone could be out there waiting to shoot at them as they made a run for it. He turned her toward the rear of the house and ran for the back-door as smoke filled the interior.

As they fell through the back door, Ed tucked Alex into the curve of his arm and ran with her to her mother's house.

Barbara Boyette met them at the back door, her phone in her hand, the children gathered behind her, eyes wide and scared. "I called nine-one-one, they're sending a fire truck from Morgan city. They'll be here as soon as they can."

Ed shoved Alex into her mother's arms. "Keep her

here and stay inside until I come back. Don't follow me. Do you understand?"

Alex and her mother nodded.

He made a wide circle around the two houses, checking all the shadowy bushes and dark corners of buildings for anyone lurking, ready to take a shot at him or anyone else. When he felt comfortably sure whoever had thrown the homemade fire bomb at the house had gone, he ran into the Boyette house. "It's okay, whoever did it is gone. But if that fire spreads to the trees, it could put your house in danger. We need to gather all the hoses you have."

Alex led him to the burning house and located the hoses on the outside, while Mrs. Boyette put her army of children to work collecting buckets and hoses around her house.

They sprayed the exterior of the Boyette house and fought back any burning embers that strayed in their direction. Calliope and Sport joined them.

"We were awake, watching old reruns when we saw that the sky light up." Calliope swept a hand out, taking in the disaster. "*Coo wee!* We never thought it was your mom's house. We came to help." She and Sport started a bucket brigade. Joe Thibodeaux, Mozelle Reneau and Oscar Mills, the retired DEA agent, joined the fight, along with other neighbors. It seemed as if the inhabitants of Bayou Miste all teamed up to save the Boyette house from destruction.

By the time the fire engine arrived, the rental cottage was too far gone to save, but the Boyette house stood as strong and intact as ever. Firefighters hooked up giant hoses to the hydrants and sprayed a steady stream of water at the core of the fire, pumping hundreds of gallons of water onto the flames.

Alex and her mother herded the children away from both houses, maintaining a strict headcount throughout. Friends and neighbors stood by, watching as the house burned and the firemen fought the blaze.

Ed glanced around at the throng, knowing that arsonists like to lurk on the fringes and witness the destruction. It gave them a sense of power. He scanned the faces in the crowd of neighbors and onlookers, searching for anyone who looked different. It was then that he spotted someone he recognized that didn't fit in with the other residents of Bayou Miste. "Alex," he whispered into her ear and laid a hand on her shoulder. "Is that Theo Ledet standing in the shadow of the house down the street?"

Alex turned the way he directed and scanned the street. "Yes, it is."

"If I remember correctly, he doesn't live in Bayou Miste, does he?"

"No, but he likes to come down from Morgan City to the Raccoon Saloon." She stiffened. "You think he did this?"

His hand dropped to his side. "I don't know, but I'm going to find out." He slipped behind the crowd and walked along the other side of the street that paralleled the bayou until he was across from the house where Theo hid.

As he crossed the street, Theo spotted him, his eyes widened, and he ran.

Ed took off after him. In his peripheral vision, he saw Oscar Mills leap from the front porch of his rental, and run straight for Theo.

Theo dodged the former agent and Ed tackled the younger man to the ground, yanked his arm up behind him, and pinned it between his shoulder blades.

"You got him?" Mills asked.

"Got 'em," he answered. "Thanks."

"Good, 'cause I couldn't have done much more than that." Mills bent over his knees and sucked air into his lungs. "Damn, I'm out of shape."

Alex caught up with them, breathing fast. She stood with her fists on her hips, looking like a warrior ready to rip into the man on the ground. With her eyes burning bright and twin flashes of color in her cheeks, she was so beautiful, Ed almost let go of his captive to kiss her.

"Theo Ledet, did you burn my mamma's rent house down?"

"No." Theo grunted as Ed pushed his arm up higher. "No, I didn't."

"If you didn't do it, why the hell did you run?" Alex crossed her arms. "Stinks like guilt to me."

Ed pushed the arm even higher. "Tell the truth. They can pull prints off the bottle you threw. You won't get away with it."

The man strained beneath him, his face streaked with sweat. "Okay, okay. I did it."

He jerked the man's arm, anger burning in his gut. That fire could have killed Alex. It could have spread to her family's home, maybe injured one of her siblings, like Teddy or Molly. "I told you to leave Alex alone."

"I was a gonna, but dat man paid me damn good money to do it."

His heart skipped a beat and he leaned closer to Theo. "What man?"

"The one at the Raccoon Saloon. He paid me to start de fi-yuh."

"What'd he look like?" Ed demanded.

"Like a business man, wearing pressed pants and

de polo shirt. Older. White hair." Theo groaned. "Let up on de arm and I'll tell ya more."

He eased the man's arm down a fraction. "Talk."

"He wanted me to distract you."

"Why?"

"I dôn know. He asked 'bout airboats and guides to get out in de bayou."

"What did you tell him?" Ed demanded, his hand tightening on the man's arm.

"I tol' him 'bout Thibodeaux. He wanted a different guide, someone not from Bayou Miste. So I tol' him 'bout my cousin what live up de road toward Morgan City. He dôn have no airboat, but knows someone what do."

"When did you tell him this?"

"Afore I come to set de fire. Couple hours ago."

Alex glared down at Theo. "You almost burned my family home to the ground."

"I dint want dat. Only to get rid of de man what took my gal."

Alex leaned toward Theo. "When are you going to get it through your thick head. I'm not your girl, never was and never...I repeat...*never* will be."

"You wit' dis man now?" Theo jerked his head toward Ed.

"As far as you're concerned, yes." She challenged Ed with a glare that made his heart kick over and warmed his insides. "Now, if you'll excuse me, I'm going to get the sheriff."

She was back in moments, dragging the sheriff and two of his deputies who'd come to help direct traffic around the emergency personnel handling the fire.

They loaded Theo into their vehicle and took him to Morgan City's jail house on suspicion of arson.

By the time they finished with Theo and returned to the fire and the diminishing crowd, the firemen declared it safe to go back to their homes. It was nearing morning, and the first streaks of gray lit the eastern sky. Joe and Miz Mozelle had helped Mrs. Boyette and the older children get the younger ones inside and put to bed.

Then Miz Mozelle, Joe, and Oscar Mills stood outside with Mrs. Boyette, overlooking the smoldering hulk of the rental. Once the last fire engines had left along with all the emergency personnel, quiet finally descended on Bayou Miste.

Ed approached an exhausted Mrs. Boyette and took her hands in his. "I'm sorry."

"*Mon cher*, what have you to be sorry about?" She gave him a weak smile, the wrinkles around her eyes deeper, and the shadows beneath her eyes darker.

She had enough to worry about without him being there.

"I'm afraid my being here has put your family in danger."

"Don't be silly." Mrs. Boyette hugged his arm. "How could that be?"

"I can't say now, but I won't be staying in Bayou Miste much longer." He met Alex's gaze over her mother's head.

Confusion warred with hurt in her expression. "Do you want to stay at my house until you have to leave?"

"No." Every moment he spent with this family put them deeper and deeper in the danger that was Leon Primeaux's doing. "I have to go."

Before he'd taken two steps away from Alex and her family, he paused to listen to the sound of a speeding vehicle, headed their way.

The car raced down the street and skidded into the driveway, spewing gravel.

He reached for his gun. "Stay back."

Mrs. Boyette leaned around him, peering at the car in the driveway. "It's Ben and Lucie!" She pushed past him and ran toward the driver emerging from the car, landing in her oldest son's strong embrace.

Alex and Calliope followed, pulling Lucie into a group hug.

"Oh, Lucie, why are you two here, when you should be home with your feet up?" Alex asked.

"I came with Ben." Lucie rubbed her hand over the mound of her belly. "He said he needed to get to Bayou Miste ASAP, but he wouldn't tell me why and I wouldn't let him leave me. Not after today's shooting at the courthouse." She wrinkled her nose and glanced at the damp, smoking remains of the rental. "I'd say we're a little late."

Ben shook his head "I hope not." His gaze caught Ed's over the top of his mother's head. "Heard from or street informant. Word's out. They know she's here."

Chapter Fourteen

Alex glanced from her brother to Ed. "What are you talking about?"

Ed's focus remained on Ben, his face tense, his hand still resting on the gun attached to his belt. "How? No one else should know."

"You two work together?" Alex touched Ed's arm.

"Yes," Ed answered, the word clipped, not inviting more questions from her.

She refused to be ignored. "You weren't here on vacation to fish?"

"No." His lips twisted. "Although I did fish as part of my cover."

"Which would explain why you didn't know how." Anger burned inside, and disappointment. He'd lied to her from day one.

Ben's mouth tightened. "There's a mole on the

force. Someone must have leaked it that you and I were hiding her. A person on the inside could have put a trace on my cell phone usage or contacted the phone company for a records search. Whatever happened, Primeaux's thugs know she's in the area."

"She who?" Lucie's face had gone white. "The witness who was shot at this morning?" She gripped Ben's arm. "Tell me she's not here—she's not in Bayou Miste."

"Sorry, darlin'. But Phyllis Ragsdale, the key witness in Leon Primeaux's trial has been hiding out on the bayou for the past three days."

Her chest tightened. No wonder Ed had come to Bayou Miste. And that would explain why he'd disappeared on occasion.

"Ed's been undercover watching for signs of Primeaux's hit squad, while Marcus, our other man, has been babysitting the Ragsdale woman out in the bayou."

"I'm sorry I had to lie to you," Ed said to Mrs. Boyette, his gaze shifting to Alex. "I couldn't say anything to anyone. We didn't know who to trust and couldn't risk word getting out."

"Now that they know she's here, all hell's gonna break lose." Ben's jaw tightened. "Ed and I have to get out there and make sure she survives the day." He turned to his mother. "Keep Lucie inside and safe."

Their mother nodded, her face tired, but determined. "I will."

"If you have a gun, get it out and use it if anyone approaches any member of your family," Ed said.

Alex swallowed her anger. "If they're hiring someone to drive an airboat, you'll need something faster that will go where an airboat goes and get you there before them."

Ben's head dipped as if he was thinking hard. "If they could get someone out this early without a reservation, it would still take time to travel the distance along the canals and tributaries. We need an airboat."

"Sorry, we've been getting by with your mother's jon boat." Ed shook his head. "Top speed is about twenty knots."

Oscar Mills stepped forward, his face smeared with soot from helping with the fire. "Joe's got one."

Joe grinned. "That's right. I do."

Ben and Ed faced the man and spoke simultaneously. "Since when?"

Joe's grin widened. "Yesterday. Had it in the shop, rebuildin' the engine. Was about to start advertising bayou tours. Oscar, here, was gonna be my first customer."

"What are we waiting for?" Ben headed for the marina.

"Wait," Ed called out. "If we go out on the bayou

now, and they see us, the chances of getting back unharmed are slim. We need a plan."

Oscar Mills raised his hand. "I'd like to help."

"I don't know you." Ben frowned. "How do I know you're not one of Leon's men?"

"I spent twenty-five years as a DEA agent before I was medically retired."

"Seems kinda strange, you showing up at the same time I did," Ed said.

"That was pure coincidence." Mills's smile faded.

"Joe says you've been out on the bayou every day and that you weren't taking any fishing gear."

Oscar shot a glance at Joe. "I didn't come to the bayou to fish."

Ed and Ben crossed their arms across their chests at the same time.

"Then why did you come?" Ed asked.

"I came to see Madame LeBieu." Mills ducked his head. "I heard she was a good healer."

Lucie giggled. "Seems my grandmother has a following that extends beyond Bayou Miste. What did you need healing for?"

Mills's back straightened and he held his head high. "I was diagnosed with brain cancer."

Alex gasped, a band tightening around her chest. "Brain cancer? Isn't that terminal?"

The agent nodded. "All the doctors gave up on me. I was ready to try anything, even Voodoo."

For the first time since she'd met the man, Alex noted how deep the lines were around his eyes and how pale his face was. "How long did the doctors give you to live?"

"Anywhere from four months to two years."

Silence fell on the folks gathered. She couldn't think of anything to say that wouldn't sound trite. Her heart went out to the man who'd been desperate enough to seek help from a bayou legend.

Oscar raised his hands. "It's okay. Whatever Madame LeBieu has been giving me is working. The tumor has been shrinking. My doctors are calling it a miracle."

"Can you still shoot straight?" Ed asked.

Mills nodded. "I have my own guns, too."

"Ammo?" Ben asked.

"Two magazines each," Mills responded.

"You can ride with Ben in the jon boat," Ed said. He turned to Alex. "Sorry, babe. Duty calls. Stay with your mother until we know Bayou Miste is safe." He cupped her face, brushing a thumb along her cheek. "We'll talk when this blows over."

Her heart pounding against her ribs, she stared up into his eyes. "Promise?"

"You bet." Then he kissed her. Although brief

and hard, it left her feeling as if it wouldn't be the last, should he survive the day.

Joe kissed Miz Mozelle and Ben kissed Lucie and his mother then the men were gone, headed toward the marina.

Alex stood with Calliope and Lucie, but her heart and her mind went with the guys.

"I want to go. Okay?" Sport's gaze followed the men. "Maybe help?"

Trust Sport to voice exactly what she had been thinking. She'd give anything to be out there, helping make sure no one got killed.

Calliope held his hand. "No, Sport. They have training."

"Sport—I have training." His chest puffed out, his brows dipping low and menacing.

Alex laughed and said softly, "Obedience school isn't enough, sweetie."

"I want to help." Sport stared after the men, his face tense.

She patted his arm. "You can, by helping protect the family."

Her mother stepped up beside her. "I should have known Ed was a cop or something. He had that look about him."

"What look is that, Mom?" She could have kicked herself for not seeing it sooner.

"That need to protect look." She winked. "He's pretty sexy when he takes charge, don't you think?"

"Oh, yeah," Alex whispered. "He's sexy all right. I just hope he comes back alive so I can tell him what I think about all the lies he fed us."

"*Ma chère*, he had reason."

"Yeah, Alex," Lucie said. "Cut him a little slack. It's part of the job and part of yours as a significant other to be supportive."

"Who said I was his significant other?" she demanded, wishing it could be true.

"You really are blind, you know." Calliope grinned and spun to face Lucie. "We've been so caught up, I haven't had a chance to admire your baby bump."

Lucie smiled. "I'd wondered when you were going to say something."

Alex forced her attention away from the marina and the fear running through her that everything was not all right and wouldn't be until Ed returned unharmed.

It had been three months since she had been to Baton Rouge to have lunch with Lucie and she looked so different, it brought tears to her eyes, along with a twinge of envy. "You look wonderful."

Lucie's lips twisted. "Fat is more like it."

"No. You're radiant and more beautiful than I've ever seen you."

Calliope hugged Lucie, "Pregnancy suits you."

"Yes, it does." Mrs. Boyette took her arm. "And I'm sure you haven't slept all night. Let's get you inside and your feet up."

Alex hung back. "Mom, I'm going to head home for a shower and change of clothes."

Mrs. Boyette stopped on her way into the house. "You heard Ed, he wanted you to stay with us until they were sure all was clear."

"I'll only be little while. I don't have clothes here and I need to check on...on...my dog."

"Don't be long, or I'll worry," her mother called out.

"We'll come with you." Calliope grabbed Sport's arm. "Won't we?"

"Yes, we will," Sport said, sounding more and more like a man than a child learning to talk for the first time.

Alex prayed for Calliope and Sport's sake the Voodoo spell would last. Sport made a wonderful man and Calliope deserved to be loved so unconditionally.

The three of them walked to her house as the sun popped up over the horizon in glorious shades of mauve, orange, and yellow. Birds sang, flowers bloomed, and nature continued unimpeded by the danger looming in the bayou. Alex didn't let it fool her for one moment.

Ed and Joe took the airboat, while Ben and Oscar followed behind in the jon boat, moving much slower and staying low and as close to the vegetation as possible to avoid detection. Loud and rising high above the water, the airboat was the decoy to draw attention to them and away from the small boat.

They made it to the shack without spotting another vessel.

Marcus rose from the grass, his AR15 pointed squarely at Ed's chest. "You here of your own free will, or is that man holding a gun on you?"

Joe chuckled. "I'm the chauffeur. No weapons on me? See?" He held up his arms, then his shirt, displaying a rounded white belly and beltless jeans. Then he patted his pockets and was about to pat his legs.

Ed interrupted, "He's with me and we've got trouble."

The little jon boat putted in behind the airboat.

He hurried down and helped Ben and Mills out, then he jumped in and pulled the little boat beneath the cypress tree with the thick overhang of Spanish moss. He stepped ashore, climbed up the hill and looked back. The boat was completely concealed from the hill and from the water.

Ben nodded. "Good thinking."

"You and Mills will escort the witness while Marcus, Joe and I provide a distraction."

"Does that mean I get to shoot someone?" Marcus grinned. "About damned time. I was ready to put a bullet through my head as soon as you left last night."

"That bad?" he asked, hurrying toward the shack.

"Worse." Marcus got there before they did and flung open the door. "Get off your ass, we're movin' out."

"Thank gawd." Phyllis Ragsdale leaned out the door, blinking at the sunlight. "I'll be glad to see the last of this shit hole. I hope you're taking me to a hotel where I can get a shower and a fuckin' massage."

Ben's brows rose. "Is she kidding me?"

Ed and Marcus shook their heads. "You have no idea the trash that comes out of this woman's mouth."

Ben grinned. "We might have a cure for that." He held out his hand. "Ms. Ragsdale, if you'll come with me, we'll get you to safety."

"That's more like it." She shot a glare at Ed and

Marcus. "At least *he's* a gentleman." She picked her way down the bank and stared at the airboat. "And that is more like the transportation I expect."

"Sorry, Ms. Ragsdale. We're not going in that." Ben led her toward the curtain of Spanish moss.

"You're kidding me, right?" She ducked beneath the moss. "Well, goddamn. You can't expect me to get in that toy boat those two baboons have been haulin' me around in. I'm not goin'."

The whine of engines in the distance alerted Ed to trouble. "Get her quiet and keep low until we're out and away from here," he called out as he jumped onto the airboat.

Joe followed. "Hope this damned thing starts," he muttered as he cranked the engine. It fired up the first time.

Marcus, loaded with every weapon he could sling across his shoulders or clip to his bullet-proof vest, leaped aboard as Joe pulled out into the channel and spun around. He handed Joe a similar vest. "Put it on."

Ed held the helm while Joe shrugged into the vest. "Gonna get crazy out here?"

"You want me to drive?" Ed asked.

"Oh, hell no. I'm game, just watch my back while I drive this baby."

"You got it. And keep as low as you can." He took

one side of the airboat and Marcus hung off the other, a smile on his face as the wind blew the last four days of babysitting Ragsdale out of his hair.

As they turned onto the main channel leading away from Bayou Miste, another airboat skimmed up over a man-made earthen berm and splashed into the water a hundred yards behind them.

"Here we go!" Joe hit the throttle and the airboat sped across the water, the fan blowing air out the back at upwards of two hundred miles an hour, the sound loud enough to blow Ed's eardrums.

Marcus lifted a set of binoculars to his eyes, leaned out as far as he could, and studied the boat behind them. "They're loaded for bear!" he shouted above the noise. "Get ready!" He hooked his arm around a metal handrail, slung his high-powered rifle up to ready position, and waited for the first shot to be fired.

He didn't have to wait long. Soon bullets spit water up beside the boat and pinged against the giant fan blade.

Joe headed straight for a cypress forest, gunning the engine. "Hold on!" he shouted.

At the last moment he turned left, the boat skidding sideways across the water and shooting forward.

Ed had the side toward the oncoming boat and let loose with all thirty rounds in his magazine, zeroing in on at the men aiming at him. One jerked back and fell out of the boat. The other hunkered lower and kept firing. Ed hit the magazine release, dropped the empty, and slid another in place. Shifting his aim to the driver of the other craft, he did his best, the swaying of the boat making it more of a challenge. In the second five-round burst, he hit the driver and the vessel swerved to the right, the gunmen up front, scrambling to hang on.

Joe shouted, "Going airborne!"

Ed gripped the handrail and bent his knees.

Thibodeaux hit the throttle hard and sent the airboat over a mound of dirt and crashing into another area of the swamp covered in giant lily pads.

The boat behind them flew over the mound and landed with a huge splash.

Joe swerved to the right, giving Marcus a clear shot of the slowed boat, and headed for a stand of cypress.

Marcus fired off a burst of bullets, hitting two of the four men left on the trailing boat. The attackers swerved left.

Joe cocked the craft to the left and Ed opened fire.

The approaching boat dropped back and turned around.

"Joe!" Ed yelled, and waved at the Joe to get his attention, then pointed behind them.

They'd figured out the witness was not aboard their boat and were headed back the way they'd come.

Joe spun the airboat to follow them, pushing the vehicle as fast as it would go. Slowly, they gained on the other craft cutting through a stand of tall marsh grass, until they pulled alongside it. Marcus fired on the remaining gunmen, wounding one. The other threw himself overboard. The driver maintained his speed, and glanced over at their boat. He pulled a hand gun and aimed it at Joe.

Joe swerved at the last moment, missing an alligator nesting mound.

The other boat hit it on one side, tipping the craft enough that the driver lost control and crashed into a cypress tree.

Joe kept going. "Where to?"

Ed scanned the bayou. No other boats could be seen anywhere around them. "Rendezvous point."

Joe nodded and turned, taking them into a darker, denser part of the bayou, where cypress trees towered over the water, Spanish moss hung low enough to touch the surface, and sunlight barely reached within.

Ed shivered, wondering what he'd gotten himself

into. He had to trust in Joe to get them where they needed to go and hope Ben and his boat had arrived safely at their destination. And he prayed they bad guys didn't head back to Bayou Miste and cause more trouble for Alex and her family.

Chapter Fifteen

Alex emerged from her bathroom, wearing clean jeans, a baby blue tank top, and her hair pulled back in a ponytail, too impatient to blow it dry and straighten the curls. Her heartbeat hadn't slowed since Ed and the guys had headed out into the swamp. She needed to jog, sprint, or work out to burn off the nervous energy, but didn't want to get too far from home in case they came back soon. "Heard anything?"

"Nothing." Calliope sat with Sport on the couch, his arm over her shoulder, holding her close.

"You two look good together," Alex admitted.

"I love Calliope," Sport said.

Calliope squeezed his hand. "I love you, too."

Alex didn't comment on their mushy comments, but instead wished she and Ed were sitting there saying the same things. "You're getting the hang of talking normally, Sport. I thought it would take you longer."

"Television is great." He grinned and stood, extending a hand to Calliope. "We go back to Alex Mamma's house?"

Calliope let him pull her to her feet. "You bet."

"When this is all over, we should take Lucie and Sport out to see Madame LeBieu," Alex said.

"No!" Calliope stepped in front of Sport. "You can't turn him back into a dog."

She smiled. "Relax, I want to ask her for something to make him a human permanently."

Her friend's shoulders relaxed. "Well, then I'm all for it."

"Are you sure you want to stay human, Sport?" Alex gazed at his soft brown eyes. "I have to admit, I miss my dog, but it's been great getting to know you as a person."

Sport reached out and touched her face. "I miss you, too. And sometimes I miss chasing FeFe." He grinned. "But not T-Rex."

She laughed at the memories of Sport chasing FeFe only to be brought up short by Maurice Saulnier's pet alligator. "I hope Madame LeBieu can help."

"Me, too." Calliope slipped an arm around Sport's

waist and leaned into him. "He's everything a girl could ask for."

"We should get going. Mom will be worrying if we take much longer." She led the way to the door. Heeding Ed's warning, she checked outside for any suspicious movements, then held the door for the two lovebirds. As she fit her key into the lock, she remembered her cell phone on her nightstand. "Looks safe enough. You guys go on ahead. I need to place a call to the gym and make sure my staff opened it on time."

"Don't be long," Calliope called out, already halfway down the driveway, her hand in Sport's.

"I won't. Tell Mom I'll be there in fifteen minutes, tops."

"Will do."

Alex entered the house, went straight for her bedroom, and snatched up her cell phone. As she paged down through her contacts, the front door creaked.

"Did you decide to wait for me?" she called out, her hand poised over the number to the gym as she stepped into the hallway.

Instead of Calliope, a tall man wearing a ski mask stood in her hall with a wicked looking handgun pointed at her chest. "Alexandra Belle Boyette?"

Her heart nearly leapt out of her chest, and all her karate training scrambled in her brain. "W-who wants to know?" she answered, her thumb pressing the number on her phone, praying whoever was on the other end would answer immediately instead of letting it ring ten times like usual.

"We're going for a walk." The man motioned toward the rear of the house.

"Wow, you've got a gun. Where are we going?" She spoke in a loud, clear voice. If someone was on the other end of the line, hopefully they'd hear and call the police. Her gaze darted from the man in her hall toward the front door, praying Calliope and Sport would return. But at the same time she prayed they wouldn't or they'd be in danger, too.

"Turn around and walk. Make a sound and I'll shoot you."

"Please don't shoot me," she said as loud as she could without being too obvious. Willing her mind to calm, she weighed her options. Turn the way he'd indicated or take a bullet. Now wasn't the time to be a fool.

When she turned away from him, he slipped up behind her and pressed the gun into her side. Then he grabbed her cell phone, threw it to the floor, and stomped on it, killing any chance of someone finding her by tracing her phone.

Before she could drop into a ready stance and use her training in karate, the man clamped her arms to her sides and stepped in close enough that she could smell his cologne. What murderer wore cologne to a killing?

Then he jerked her wrist up between her shoulder blades.

Pain shot down her arm, bringing tears to her eyes. She rose up on her toes to alleviate it, but he pushed harder. Then she felt a thin strap of plastic rub against her wrist, and he pulled her other arm behind her and zip-tied her wrists together.

Again, he brought her close enough so that she couldn't kick out. With her hands tied behind her back, she was in a heap of trouble with no way to fight free. She opened her mouth to scream, but he shoved a wadded up sock into it. Big enough to fill her mouth and absorb all her spit, but small enough not to be noticed by someone from a distance. Clever on his part. Really bad on hers.

"Move." He pushed her to the back of the house and through the rear exit into the back yard. His hand left her side for a moment as he yanked his ski mask off his head and tossed it to the ground. "Keep walking."

Like she had a choice. All her self-defense classes had taught her to fight no matter what. Even if her attacker shot or stabbed her. Most attackers killed their victims anyway.

He crossed to the street behind hers, cutting through the yards, working his way to the far edges of town where some of the houses had been abandoned, their owners relocating to the city to find work. The farther away they got from her house, the deeper she sank into despair.

No one was expecting her for another ten minutes. Plenty of time for this man to kill her or shove her into a car and leave town undetected and then dump her body in the bayou. No one would know where to look. No one would find her before the alligators stripped her bones.

Her pulse pounding, her eyes shifting left and right, Alex had to make a move before she ran out of options.

He shoved her toward an abandoned mechanic's shop on the farthest edge of town. No one ever came back here and what few yards they'd passed through, the owners had already left for work or school.

If she wanted to get out of this mess, she had to do something soon. She threw herself to the ground, landing hard on her arm. She twisted around, caught her attacker's legs in a sweep and brought him down.

"Damn!" he muttered, hitting the ground hard, his gun flying from his hand.

Struggling to stand without the use of her hands and arms, she lurched to her feet and ran as fast as she could. She'd gone less than a block when she was hit from behind in a flying tackle. With no way to brace for her fall, her head hit the curb. Pain blinded her, then everything went black.

Joe pulled the airboat up to the dock at the marina and shut down the engine. Ed leaped out and pulled out his burner phone, punched in the number to Ben's, and waited for it to ring, hoping they had reception where they were in the bayou.

"We made it," Ben's voice came across.

"I'm calling in the local sheriff to get out there and clean up the mess."

"Do that. We're good for the time being, although our witness is in a flap. If Madame LeBieu doesn't have something to cure her trash mouth, I might shoot her before Marcus gets the chance."

Ed grinned. Hang tight. We'll be out to pick you up as soon as we're sure we got them all."

"Will do."

Joe stepped onto the dock. "Don't look now, but here comes trouble."

He glanced down the street. The entire Boyette clan was moving his way en masse. He scanned the faces and didn't see the one he wanted to see the most. His heart thumping hard against his ribs, he ran to meet them. "Where's Alex?"

Calliope spoke first, tears streaming from her eyes. "She went back for her cell phone. We went ahead of her. We'd only been gone fifteen minutes. When she didn't show up, Sport and I went back looking for her. She wasn't there and all we found was this." Calliope held up a broken cell phone.

He gripped Calliope's arms and forced her to look at him. "Where did you find that? How long ago?"

"In her house, on the floor. She's been gone twenty minutes." Calliope crumpled into sobs.

Mrs. Boyette touched his arm, her face pale, her tired blue eyes gray with worry. "There's more." She glanced back at the little ones, already crying in their older siblings' arms, and lowered her voice, "I received a call before we left to come looking for Alex. The man on the phone said he'd kill Alex if we didn't bring him the witness." Her fingers dug into his arm. "Please, help me bring my baby back." Her eyes shimmered with tears. Her eyes were older, but Alex's looked so much like hers, it hurt Ed to stare down into them.

"I'll bring her back, Mrs. Boyette," he swore.

"Alive," she whispered.

He nodded, praying he could. He glanced

around at the Boyettes. "Go home and call the sheriff. Then get on the phone with every one of your neighbors and ask if they saw anything. Cars, strangers, anything out of the ordinary. Tell them to watch for strange cars, any cars and write down the license plates and the direction they're heading."

Dolley stepped forward. "We've been watching the road and the canal for signs of your return."

Madison finished, "Not a single car has passed in twenty minutes."

"Good, that means he might have taken her on foot." Ed glanced around. "Anyone know of a tracking dog in this area?"

Sport's eyes widened and he stepped forward. "Yes."

Calliope put a hand on his arm, her eyes rounding, filling with moisture. "No."

He stepped up to the man who'd lived with Alex. "If you know of a tracking dog, get it out here. The sooner the better so that he can pick up the trail."

Sport nodded, patted Calliope's hand and said softly. "I have to do this."

Calliope threw her arms around his neck and sobbed into his shirt. "I love you, Sport. Don't do this."

Ed turned to Mrs. Boyette, every instinct telling him they were running out of time. "Go, make those calls."

The Boyette family turned as one and ran back to their house.

He turned to Joe. "Top off the fuel in the airboat. We're going to need it."

Joe nodded and jogged back to the marina.

He gripped Calliope's arm and dragged her free of Sport's embrace. "We don't have much time. Show me where you found the phone."

She swiped an arm across her damp face and ran toward Alex's little cottage, bursting through the open front door.

He followed, stepping into Alex's empty house, his heart squeezing tightly in his chest. He had to bring her back. This sunny little cottage wasn't the same without Alex's determined, vibrant personality filling it.

"There." Calliope pointed to the floor in the hallway where pieces of hard plastic had been scattered.

Ed searched every room, working his way toward the back of the house where the back door stood open, the screen door not firmly latched. "They went out this way." He ran out in the backyard and found a ski mask lying on the grass. He lifted it, sniffed it, and wished he had the abilities of a tracking dog himself. By the time they got one there, Alex's kidnapper could have taken her away from Bayou Miste.

"Ed." Sport emerged from the house, Calliope clinging to his arm. He clutched a small pouch in his hand. "I know of a dog, but I will need help from Madame LeBieu."

Ed's head jerked up, his gaze narrowing on the man standing before him. "The Voodoo queen?" Why?"

"She can help. Trust me. She might be our only hope." Tears streamed from Calliope's eyes. "Take Sport. It's what he wants. With Madame LeBieu's help, he can find Alex."

Desperate and running out of time, he nodded toward the other man. "Then you come with me."

"I'm going, too." Calliope clasped Sport's hand, her face set in sad, but determined lines.

"No, it's not safe," Ed put out his hand to stop her.

She glared at him and growled. "You'll take me or I'll follow you anyway."

"You don't understand. We've been shot at and almost killed out on the bayou today."

"I'll take my chances. I'm going with Sport." She slipped her arm through Sport's and refused to let go.

"Then hurry. We have to get back to town before the kidnapper does something stupid." He didn't even want to think of what might happen to Alex. The men Leon Primeaux hired to do his dirty work weren't known for the mercy they showed their victims. The only bargaining chip he held was Primeaux's ex-girlfriend. The one person whose testimony would put Primeaux away for life, thus saving countless other lives from his ruthless machinations.

The three of them ran back to the marina and climbed into the waiting airboat. Joe cranked the engine and spun the craft around, heading across the water. Clouds had gathered over the bayou, sinking low and heavy, threatening a deluge that would wash away all traces of Alex's scent from the ground. Ed shouted, "Faster!"

"Goin' as fast as this crate will move," Joe shouted back.

They held on as the boat skimmed over man-made mounds delineating different areas of the swamp, through stands of marsh grass, and skidded around an alligator lazing in the middle of a tributary. He and Sport hung off the sides, peering around the giant fan to the rear, searching the bayou for any signs they were being followed.

When he thought the swamp might go on forever, Joe entered the sinister gloom of a cypress forest, where the Spanish moss hung low enough they had to duck to avoid being slapped in the face.

A small dilapidated house appeared, nestled in the watery forest, its eaves sagging, bright green moss growing on its porch rails. Madame LeBieu's home. It never changed.

In the shadows at the side of the house, movement caught Ed's attention. He strained to see what or who lurked in obscurity as they sped closer.

About the time he could make out Marcus's form, the man stepped into the open, carrying an automatic rifle at the ready. Oscar Mills emerged from the opposite end of the house, sporting a rifle and a handgun.

Joe slowed as they neared the rickety dock, and then shut down the engine. They skimmed in, to bump against the wood planking. Ed jumped onto the pier, Sport close behind him, Calliope bringing up the rear.

Ben Boyette pushed through the front door, frowning. "What's happened?"

He stopped and stared up at his friend. "They have Alex."

The man's face paled, his lips tightening. "Damn." He shoved a hand through his hair. "They want to trade for the witness, don't they?"

"I have a name, dumbass." Phyllis Ragsdale shoved Ben aside and stepped out onto the porch. "You told them hell no, didn't you?"

"It's not safe for you to stand in the open," Ben said. "Go back inside."

"I'm tired of being bossed around. I want out of this stinkin' swamp and back to the city where I belong." She stood with her hand on her hip. "And I'm not gonna stand by and let you swap me for some swamp bimbo. I got my rights."

Ed clenched his fists about to launch himself at the bitch, when a large, mocha-skinned woman dressed in a bright red, pink, and orange muumuu with a scarf tied around her head emerged behind Ben and Phyllis and raised her hand. "Silence!"

All eyes turned to the commanding presence of the legendary Voodoo queen he had only heard tales of about from Ben. She was every bit as intimidating as Ben had promised and then some.

"I'm not taking any more orders from some fat lady in a Hawaiian tent," Phyllis stated.

Madame LeBieu held up a hand and clamped her fingers together.

Phyllis was in mid-rant, "Get me out—" her lips moved, but no sound came out. Her eyes widened and she clapped a hand to her throat, her mouth continuing to flap, but blessed silence reigned.

Had he seen right? Ed stared at the witness who'd been non-stop talk since they'd picked her up four days ago. This was the first time the woman was quiet. What had Madame LeBieu done to get her to stop? Magic?

He shook his head. He didn't believe in magic. But he sure wished he could conjure a crystal ball to help him find Alex.

"Dog, come to me." The Voodoo queen waved her hand toward Sport.

He frowned. Why had she called Sport *dog*?

Sport climbed the steps and handed her the pouch he'd been carrying since they'd left Alex's house.

She took the pouch in one hand and reached out with the other to brush her hand across his forehead, pushing the shaggy hair out of his eyes. "What brings you to Madame LeBieu?"

Ed shifted impatiently, ready for this visit to be over so he could head back to town and begin his search for Alex. "Sport said he knew of a dog who could track Alex."

"I say silence!" Madame LeBieu held up her hand. "Let de dog speak."

"What dog?" he asked. "We came to get one."

The old Voodoo queen glared at him until he closed his mouth and waited.

She gave her attention to Sport again, her expression softening. "You want for me to break de spell?"

Sport glanced toward Calliope, his brown eyes sad. When he turned back to the mistress of Voodoo, he nodded. "Sport find Alex, but not like this." He held his arms out.

Calliope flew up the porch and grabbed Sport's hand. "I love you."

Sport squeezed her hand. "We always knew this could not last."

The old woman shook her head. "De dog be right. De *cunja* not meant to be forever."

"Will he remember?" Calliope whispered, pressing her face to Sport's palm.

"No." Madame LeBieu shook her head and reached out for Calliope's hand. "But you will. Do you want to forget?"

Calliope stared up into Sport's eyes. "No." She leaned up on her toes and kissed Sport.

Ed shook his head, the conversation going on in front of him getting more bizarre by the minute.

"Come." Madame LeBieu beckoned Sport to enter her house, holding the door open for him.

Calliope hesitated, but the old woman nodded, allowing her to pass as well.

When Ed started forward, the Voodoo queen blocked him. "De rest o' you wait here."

"But—"

Ben gripped his arm. "Do as she said, and trust her. She's Lucie's grandmother and one of the most respected Voodoo artists in all of Louisiana. Her magic is very strong."

"Magic?" He couldn't believe it. "Alex is missing and we're playing in the swamp with a Voodoo queen instead of searching for her."

The door closed behind Madame LeBieu, shutting him out and Sport and Calliope inside.

His patience at an end, Ed spun and marched back to the dock. "Joe, take me back to Bayou Miste. We don't have time for this nonsense."

Joe stood still, shaking his head. "We go when Madame LeBieu says we go."

"Are you kidding me?"

The marina owner crossed his arms and stood solid.

He searched for the jon boat Ben and Oscar had used to transport the Ragsdale woman to Madame LeBieu's. He spotted it concealed in the brush near the shore, twenty yards away from the house. As he dropped over the side of the dock onto the marshy island, he could swear he heard the beat of drums.

His footsteps faltered and he glanced back at the house.

All gazes focused on the front door as a low melodious sound resonated through the wood siding, growing in strength as it continued, combining with the drumbeat.

Shivers slid across his body, raising gooseflesh on his arms. A buzzing whine filled his head as the sound increased from inside the building. Ed pressed his hands to his ears, his vision blurring and his thoughts growing hazy.

A brilliant flash of light and sound erupted from the house and the front door blew open, the screen door slamming against the exterior.

From the dark interior, a golden retriever leaped out into the open and barked.

Calliope emerged, followed by Madame LeBieu.

"Go," Madame LeBieu said. "Save my Alex from de evil mans."

The dog bounded toward the airboat and jump aboard.

Ben hooked Phyllis's arm. "Come on, we're all heading back and we might need you for collateral."

The woman dug in her heels and shook her head, her mouth working but no sound escaping.

Marcus stalked up the steps, flung Phyllis over his shoulder, and carried her to the airboat, dumping her onto a seat. Ben and Oscar climbed aboard.

Ed heaved himself up on the dock and ran to get into the airboat as Joe started the engine. The huge fan blade spun, the sound echoing off the canopy.

"What about Sport? Isn't he coming?" he called

out as Joe spun the craft around and headed toward Bayou Miste.

Calliope bent over, crying, and no one else spoke as the airboat zigzagged through the cypress forest maze and out into the open fields and canals.

Ed, Marcus, Ben and Oscar each held tight to the boat with one hand while pointing weapons outward, ready to take on any assault.

All the way back to Bayou Miste, he prayed they weren't too late.

Chapter Sixteen

Alex awoke to the smell of oil and gasoline, her cheek lying against greasy concrete. Pain ripped through her head and her mouth felt like the Sahara Desert. Her wrists were bound behind her back by what felt like a zip-tie and her ankles were bound the same way. She listened for voices or movement, her sight adjusting to the dim light coming from dirty windows. Where was she? Better question—where was the man who'd abducted her?

She lifted her head, wincing at the sharp stabbing pain, and looked around at what appeared to be the interior of an auto shop. Long derelict, the building had old tires piled against the walls, what was left of a hydraulic lift anchored to the floor, and gnawed-on pegboard attached to the wall with hooks. Across every surface was a nasty layer of grime. And she'd worn her favorite baby blue tank top. A car that looked like the one that had hit Sport stood in one bay with a dent in the front fender.

Laughter bubbled up inside her and would have escaped but for the wadded sock stuck in her mouth. Her gaze returned to the metal plate that had at one time anchored the hydraulic lift. One corner of the plate had been pried upward, leaving a jagged edge. Just what she needed to break through the plastic handcuffs.

Rocking back and forth, she built up her momentum and rolled, scooted, and inched across the disgusting, slimy floor to the metal plate. For a moment, she lay still, breathing and listening for the return of her captor. When nothing stirred, she rolled on top of the plate, the jagged edge scraping her arm several times before she wiggled her body into position where her wrists lay over the metal edge.

With awkward persistence she sawed at the tie, gouging hunks of flesh from her arm in the process. Blood mixed with grease, making it even more difficult to hook the plastic. Her arms and belly aching from holding the uncomfortable position, she finally broke through and rolled to the side, rubbing the feeling back into her hands.

Metal scraped against metal as a door opened in the back of the building.

She swung her feet around, jammed the zip-tie over the sharp edge of metal, ripping her jeans in the process. After three attempts, the tie broke and she lurched to her feet, ducking low behind a counter.

A man entered the car bays. Enough light shone through the dingy windows to silhouette his form. He carried a handgun with a very long barrel on it, like it had a silencer attached to the end. "Ms. Boyette, it's time to go."

When he arrived at the location where he'd dumped her body, he grew still and turned in a three-hundred-sixty-degree circle.

Hidden behind the only counter in the shop, she realized it was only a matter of time before he found her. If she wanted to live, she had to get out, now. She felt around on the floor for something to throw, her fingers curling around what felt like a lug nut. With all her strength, she threw the nut to the opposite end of the shop from the door her abductor had entered. It landed near the pile of tires.

The man spun and ran toward the sound. "You can't get away from me."

Oh yes, I can. She balled up her muscles and launched her body from behind the counter and ran, zigzagging toward the back door.

As she reached the exit, something pinged on the metal wall beside her. She ducked and swung the door wide, rushing through and to the right. The back of the shop opened out on the canal. Alex's mad rush gave her so much momentum she plunged over the bank and slid into the water.

Knowing the man with the gun would have an easy target if she came up for air, she stayed below the surface, swimming as fast and as far away as she could. When she thought her lungs might burst, she ran into a bed of lily pads. She tipped her head up, pressing her lips to the bottom of a pad and lifted it ever so slightly, breathing in enough air to go under again.

A bullet pierced the water beside her, so near she could almost feel the current it produced. She pushed away from the lily pads, afraid their movement on the surface would give her position away. As she swam through the dark canal water, she prayed she didn't get hit by a bullet or a boat, or that she'd be eaten by an alligator. When she came to an opening off the canal that led out into the bayou she swam toward it, hoping her attacker would stay on dry ground and give up his chase. As she slipped deeper into the bayou, she heard the sound of a boat engine start. Oh, hell, the man had found a boat. If she didn't find a place to hide, soon, she didn't stand a chance.

As she surfaced for another breath, she prayed, *Please, Ed, find me!*

The sheriff had an airboat sitting at the marina when Joe pulled in and practically ran over the pier. "Sorry!" he shouted as he shut off the engine.

Ed didn't wait to explain anything to the local law. As soon as they stopped, he hopped out of the boat onto the dock. The dog leaped out beside him and ran.

"Follow him!" Calliope yelled.

Ben ordered Marcus, "Stay with the witness."

Ed chased the dog across the street, dodging sheriff's vehicles and bystanders. Mrs. Boyette was standing on the porch at Alex's house talking to a deputy holding a notepad.

The dog raced between their legs and into the house.

Ed squeezed Mrs. Boyette's shoulder and said, "We'll find her," then set her to the side, rushing into the building after the dog.

"Hey!" the deputy yelled. "You can't go in there. This is a crime scene."

With Alex's life hanging in the balance, he didn't have time to waste talking to the man. When the dog ran out the back door, he followed, running on blind faith that the animal knew what he was doing.

In the backyard, the dog put his nose to the ground, sniffing. He followed a scent to the edge of the property and beyond, crossing streets and ducking through yards moving farther and farther away from Alex's home.

He kept the animal in sight. He looked back once to see Ben racing to catch up. They spread out, running parallel to each other behind the dog.

At the edge of town, the dog stopped and sniffed the road and a curb. He whined and looked up at him as if he wanted Ed to look there as well.

Ben staggered to a stop, breathing hard. "What is it? What did he find?"

Ed bent to study the dark stain on the curb. "Blood. And by the way the dog is whining, I bet it's Alex's." His gut clenched.

The dog spun in a circle, picked up a scent, and headed for an abandoned building that might once have been an auto mechanic's shop. The metal sides of the building had rusted, what paint was left had long since faded.

The dog scratched at a door. Ed reached for the knob, but the door was locked.

"What is it Sport?" Ben asked. "Is she in there?"

Ben went one direction and Ed the other. When they reached a back door, it was wide open.

"Alex!" He ran inside, picking his way past old tires and discarded, broken equipment to a fairly new car standing at the other end with a big dent on the front panel. As if it had hit something.

Sport circled the car, growling, then he sniffed at the floor, whining. He picked something up with his teeth and trotted over to Ed.

He bent to take what the dog had in his mouth and walked to where Ben and Marcus stood near the door and held it up to the sunlight. A zip-tie like ones they used in the department. And it had blood on it.

Sport slipped through their legs, pressed his nose to the ground outside, and took off running, barking as he went. He threaded through tall grass that ran along the bank of a canal, pulling ahead of Ed and Ben. The tall grass hid him from view. If not for the incessant barking, Ed would have had to guess where he was.

Ahead in the canal, a boat pulled away from the shore, a man with shocking white hair at its helm.

There was something familiar about the man. The shock of white hair, his height, and the way he carried himself. He turned back at the sound of the dog barking.

"Holy shit, that's Gordon Dean," Ed said.

Ben ran up beside Ed. "Are you sure?"

"I saw his face. It's Dean."

"That bastard's the leak in the department," Ben said, breathing hard to keep up with the dog.

"I'll kill him if he hurts Alex," Ed ground out, sprinting to catch up, knowing that if Dean got too far ahead, he could disappear into the bayou. If he had Alex in the boat, he could dump her anywhere and they'd never find her.

A fork in the canal loomed ahead of the man in the boat. If he made it there, they'd never catch him.

The dog burst through the brush and, with a magnificent leap off the bank, landed on Dean's back. The boat swerved, bouncing against the bank. Dean struggled to straighten the boat as the dog sank his teeth into the man's hand.

"Goddamn dog!" Dean raised the hand holding the gun.

"Don't you hurt my dog!" Alex Boyette climbed up a hassock of dirt and swamp grass, screaming like a raging Valkyrie, her hand loaded with a clump of something dark and dripping, looking suspiciously like a wad of swamp grass, roots and all.

As Dean leveled the gun on the dog, Alex swung her grass and launched it into the air, clipping the man in the shoulder. The gun went off with a soft pop.

The dog screeched and fell into the water.

Ed and Ben ran along the bank of the canal until they were parallel with the drifting boat.

Dean aimed the gun at Alex. "Stop or I'll shoot her."

Ed knelt on the grass, whipped his rifle to his shoulder and aimed at Dean's shoulder. "Put down your gun."

"You really want me to kill her, don't you?"

"You shot my dog!" Alex either didn't hear Dean or didn't care. She dived at the boat.

Ed squeezed the trigger.

Dean's hand jerked, the gun flying into the water as Alex hit him with the full force of her body. She knocked him out of the boat and tumbled into the canal with him.

Ed and the others slid down the bank and into the water.

Gordon Dean grabbed Alex by her ponytail and yanked her neck into the crook of his arm. "Come any closer and I'll kill her."

"Shoot him, Ed!" Alex said. "He killed Sport."

He aimed his gun at Gordon's head, afraid to pull the trigger for fear of hitting Alex.

"Throw your weapons in the water or the girl dies," Dean yelled.

"Don't do it," Alex pleaded.

"I have to. I can't let him kill you," he said.

"Let her go, Gordon," Ben said. "The game is over. You won't get away. You kill her and the court won't settle for anything less than the chair."

Alex wiggled in the man's clutches, her face turning red then purple.

About to toss his weapon to the bank, Ed hesitated, spying movement in the water behind Dean and Alex. "Alex, be ready to swim. There's an alligator behind you two."

Gordon Dean's eyes rounded and he swung his head around, trying to look over his shoulder without releasing his captive. Then his body jerked and he screamed, his hold loosening.

Alex pushed away from him and swam to the other side of the canal.

Gordon splashed and thrashed, his head going under, then coming up spitting water. "Help! Please, help me!"

Behind him, instead of a deadly alligator, Sport snapped at him again, sinking his teeth into the man's shoulder.

Ed ran to where Alex slipped and slid on the bank, trying to climb the side of the canal. He reached out and grabbed her hand, pulling her up into his arms.

"No." She struggled to be free, "I have to help Sport."

Ben chuckled. "Relax, Alex, he seems to be helping himself."

The dog snarled and took another bite out of the crooked cop then abandoned the man and paddled toward the bank where Alex had come ashore.

Ed set Alex away from him and dragged the tired, injured dog up the muddy bank.

Alex dropped to her haunches and hugged the dog. "Oh, Sport, why did you do it?"

"He saved your life." Ed squatted beside her. "That dog is a hero."

"Oh, Sport, you sacrificed so much." She buried her face in is wet fur and wept.

Not wanting to part her from her dog, Ed Sport he needed medical attention. "Alex, honey, he's bleeding. Let's get him to a vet." He helped Alex to her feet and lifted the dog.

Ben dragged Gordon Dean out of the canal and up the bank where he collapsed on the ground, muttering, "Damned dog. I should have killed him."

Ben ran ahead to get a vehicle to transport Sport to the vet and Gordon to jail in Baton Rouge.

After Ed settled the dog into the back of Ben's SUV, he slid into the back seat beside Alex.

She leaned into him, her hand resting on his leg.

"There's something I've been waiting all day to tell you." A soft chuckle shook her frame. "I even wore my favorite blue shirt for the occasion."

Covered in mud, grease streaked across her face, and the blue shirt more brown than any other color, she'd never been more beautiful. "Before you say anything..." He kissed her, holding her close, soggy clothes and all. "Alex Boyette, I think I'm falling in love with you."

She glanced up, her eyes shining. "That's what I was going to say."

"Yeah, well I beat you to it." He brushed his thumb gently across her bruised cheek.

"You're not afraid of my huge family?"

"I love your huge family."

"I have a business."

"My job is in Baton Rouge, but I don't mind the commute." He rested his cheek against her hair. "We can play it by ear and find a way to make it work."

Alex sighed. "I'm not afraid to leave Bayou Miste. There's a whole world out there I haven't seen."

"Yeah, but it will be a lot more fun to explore it with you."

The veterinarian bandaged Sport's leg and gave him a mild sedative and a shot of antibiotics to ward off

infection. He prescribed rest and a low-stress envi-
ronment for twenty-four hours. He checked Alex's
eyes for concussion, cleaned and applied bandages to
her head and wrists, and told her to see a doctor in
Morgan City as soon as possible.

She left the vet's clinic in Ben's SUV with Sport
draped across her lap and Ed in the seat beside her,
his arm over her shoulder. Every time she stared into
Sport's soft brown eyes, her heart ached for him and
Calliope. Deep down, she'd suspected that the magic
wouldn't last, but Sport had sacrificed his time with
Calliope to save her.

When they arrived at Alex's house, the adults
were waiting. Ben had called ahead to let them know
Alex was okay and they all wanted to see for
themselves.

As soon as Ben got out of the car, Lucie ran to
him, wrapping her arms around his middle, smiling
and crying at the same time. "Oh, *bebe*, I'm so glad
you're okay."

Her mother engulfed her in a hug so tight, she
croaked, "I'm okay, Mom."

She loosened her hold slightly, tears trickling
down her face. "I was so afraid of losing you."

Alex hugged her back. "It's over."

Setting her at arm's length, her mother pushed
the limp hair out of her face. "*Mais*, then get yourself

cleaned up and meet us back at the house. I'm making dinner for everyone." She brushed the tears from her own face and sniffed. "Don't be long this time."

"But I want to know what happened."

"We'll talk about it over dinner," her mother insisted.

She smiled. "I'll be right there."

"We'll stay and make sure she's there on time," Lucie said.

Calliope stood to the side, her bright green eyes dark as the deepest forest and filled to the brim with emotion. "Where's Sport?"

Alex swallowed hard, ready tears springing to her eyes.

Ed lifted the dog's limp body out of the back seat.

Calliope reached out a hand, tears slipping down her face. "Is he..."

"Asleep," Alex reassured her. "He's going to be okay. The vet gave him a sedative. It should wear off soon."

Calliope followed Ed as he carried the dog into the house and laid him on blanket on the couch.

"Ben promised me some clean clothes," Ed grasped her cheeks between his hands and bent to press his lips to hers. "I'll see you at your mother's."

Alex would have preferred he stayed, but she

wanted to talk to Lucie and Calliope alone. "I won't be long." She kissed him back.

After Ben left, she turned to Calliope. "What happened?"

Through choking sobs, Calliope told of Sport's demand to undo the Voodoo that had made him into a man, insisting he could find her.

"Madame LeBieu said the magic was never meant to last." Calliope knelt on the floor beside Sport and ran her hand along his fur. "He's more of a hero than any man I've ever met."

"Oh, *ma chère*, I'm so sorry." Lucie dropped to the floor on one side of Calliope, Alex on the other, and they hugged her until her sobs stopped.

"We'd better get going before my mother comes looking for us." She hurried into the shower, her body achy, her wrists raw, her heart sore for Calliope, but full of hope for her own future. Soon, she'd see Ed. She scrubbed her hair, careful not to disturb the bandage on her forehead, and washed the swamp out of her skin with scented soap. When she felt human again, she stepped out of the shower, dried off, applied antibiotic ointment to her wrists, cuts, and scrapes, and found her prettiest sun dress and sandals.

Sport was awake and actually perky when she emerged from her bedroom.

"Can we bring Sport?" Calliope asked.

"The vet said he needed rest, but he appears to be recovered somewhat." She smiled. "Yes, we can bring him. He's as much a part of my family as my brothers and sisters and you."

Lucie pushed out of the lounge chair and rubbed a hand over her swollen belly. "I see I'll have to get to work on something for Calliope next."

Calliope and Alex both turned to Lucie at once. "No!"

Lucie held up her hands in surrender. "Okay, okay."

"I hope that once you have your baby, you won't have time to dabble in Voodoo," Alex said.

"I can't let it disappear when Gran LeBieu passes on. It's tradition!"

Alex slipped an arm around her friends' shoulders and hugged them. "That kind of tradition we could do without. Come on, the family's waiting."

When she opened her front door, she stared into the dark brown eyes of the man she was falling madly in love with.

He wore Ben's old fishing clothes that were tight across his broad shoulders and a little short on the pant legs. On his feet he wore a pair of bright orange flip-flops.

Lucie and Calliope slipped around her, Sport trotting after them with only a slight limp.

"We'll see you at your mother's," Lucie called out, leaving her and Ed alone on the porch.

"I couldn't wait to see you," he said, gathering her in his arms.

"Are you going to tell me the whole truth now?"

"Since I'm no longer undercover," he held her a little away from him and gazed down into his eyes, a smile playing at the corners of his lips, "ask me anything."

She tipped her chin up and tried to look serious. "What happened to the witness?"

"Marcus and Oscar are escorting her to Baton Rouge where they will keep her in a holding cell until the trial begins tomorrow morning."

"Who was the man who kidnapped me?"

Ed shook his head. "Sad to say, that was our supervisor, Gordon Dean. Crooked as they come and on Leon Primeaux's payroll. Might mean a promotion for me or Ben."

"And you're not a mediator?"

"No. I'm a special agent for the Special Criminal Investigations Unit of the Louisiana State Police."

"All that stuff about growing up in the foster system?"

"True."

"And you've never been fishing before coming to the bayou?"

"True." Ed raised his hand like a Boy Scout. "Scouts honor."

"Were you ever a scout?" she asked.

"No, but I wouldn't lie to you...well, not if I didn't have to."

"Final question." She paused, inhaling a deep breath before continuing. "Were you telling me the truth when you said you were falling in love with me?"

He gathered her closer, his head dipping until his mouth hovered over hers. "You bet your beautiful Boyette buns, sweetheart."

Alex sighed. "One more question."

He brushed her lips across hers. "Really?"

"Do you believe in magic?" she asked.

He laughed. "I have to. It brought me you."

Epilogue

Raccoon Saloon, Bayou Miste, Louisiana
Four months later

Alex stared around the big table, filled with her friends and some of her family, realizing she'd never been happier. Jean Dupree had even allowed Sport to join them at Calliope's insistence. The burly, old bar owner had a soft spot for Calliope and let her have her way more often than not.

Leon Primeaux was sentenced to life in prison. Phyllis Ragsdale had entered into the witness protection program and hopefully moved clear out of Louisiana by now. Ben and Lucie had delivered a beautiful baby girl and life had returned to normal in Bayou Miste.

She had been seeing Ed practically every weekend, since he'd gone back to work in Baton Rouge, and falling more in love with him each day. With a grand flourish, she raised her beer mug. "I'd like to propose a toast to the new parents."

A round of clinking bottles and mugs was cheered along with, "Here! Here!"

Lucie and Ben grinned, both looking tired, but elated at the new addition to their household.

Ben lifted his mug. "I'd like to propose a toast to Dolley and Madison for agreeing to babysit tonight so that we could have our first night out since Lilly was born, and so that Mom could come out with us."

More clinking, more cheers and hugs all around.

"Can we join the party?" Joe Thibodeaux and Miz Mozelle stepped up to the table.

"Please," her mother scooted her chair back.

"We'll need room for four," Joe grinned and waved toward a man and woman entering the saloon.

"My nephew Craig and his wife, Elaine, are in town for a visit. Some of you know them," Joe said. "They're expecting their first baby." Joe's chest puffed out as he draped an arm over his nephew's shoulders. "I'm going to be a great uncle."

Her mom made the introductions all around and they made room at the table for the Thibodeauxs.

Ed stood and cleared his throat. "I have an announcement to make."

All eyes turned toward him. "After careful consideration, much haggling and assistance from Alex, I've purchased a house, in White Castle, halfway between Morgan City and Baton Rouge." He pulled a box out of his jeans pocket and dropped to one knee.

Her pulse pounding so hard against her eardrums, she strained to hear his next words.

"I'm hoping Alex will like the house enough to agree to move in with me...as my wife." He opened the box, displaying a beautiful sapphire and diamond ring that took her breath away. "Alexandra Belle Boyette, after one failed marriage, I never thought I'd want to take the plunge again, but you gave me hope. You showed me how to really love someone and that it was worth risking my heart. Will you marry me?"

"Yes!" She threw herself at Ed, wrapping her arms around his neck as he staggered to his feet, then twirled her around, planting a kiss on her lips.

Everyone gathered around, congratulating, hugging, and shaking hands, as Ed slid the ring on her finger. When they finally resumed their seats,

Alex glanced across at Calliope, her joy fading. For the past three months, her friend had put on a happy face. But Alex knew her heart would not be mended so easily. Losing Sport as a man had taken the spark out of the normally bubbly and vivacious woman.

Lucie leaned close to Alex. "I've been working with Gran LeBieu on a *cunja* to help bring Calliope out of her funk."

"I don't know, Lucie," she said. "I don't know how much more excitement this town can handle. Neither one of us will be around to bail her out if things get crazy. You know how gullible she can be."

"It'll be okay. I promise." Lucie patted her hand. "There are enough Boyettes in Bayou Miste to help her out of a bind. Besides, look what Voodoo has done for you, me, Craig, and Elaine. Do you think we'd have found our true loves without it?"

Her heart swelled every time she glanced at Ed. "I don't think I'd have changed a thing. I can't imagine my life without Ed in it."

"See?" Lucie winked. "Don't worry. Gran LeBieu and I won't let her down. We'll come up with something."

Alex's mother leaned into the conversation. "I've been giving it some thought, too. I believe we need to find Calliope a man."

"Mommmm." She gave her mother a warning look. "Not everyone appreciates your meddling."

"*Matchmaking, ma chère.*" Her mother lifted her hand. "That's a beautiful ring on your finger, Alexandra Belle." She gazed into her daughter's eyes. "I believe between me, Lucie, and Madame LeBieu, we can help our Calliope find the love of her life."

Alex rolled her eyes and raised her beer. Who was she to doubt the power of love and Voodoo. "*Laissez les bon temps rouler!*" Let the good times roll!

Thank you for reading Deja Voodoo. Interested in more Romance Stories? Keep reading for the 1st Chapter of BEAU.

DAMNED IF YOU VOODOO

A Cajun Magic Mystery Book # 4

New York Times & USA Today
Bestselling Author

ELLE JAMES

Damned if you Voodoo
A CAJUN MAGIC MYSTERY
NEW YORK TIMES BESTSELLING AUTHOR
ELLE JAMES

About Book

A doomed Voodoo spell creates chaos in the bayou...

Desperate to bring back love in human form, Calliope Jobert's Voodoo calamity is unleashed on Bayou Miste. When a dead body surfaces in the bayou, the creature born of her botched spell is blamed. Calliope is in a race to prove to the sheriff's deputy her spell-bound being isn't the culprit.

Ex-Navy SEAL Andre LeBlanc, the new deputy in town, has his first major crime to solve.

Murder...

Interviews with witnesses reveal sightings of a local resident, a red-head, clad in a flowing skirt and mud boots, chasing a strange man in the vicinity of where the victim was found. Already distrustful of women since his wife cheated on him while he was deployed, Andre is fully prepared to suspect the red-headed femme fatale, Calliope Jobert, of collusion in the dastardly deed.

Though she proclaims her innocence and that of her elusive male companion of that night, her peculiar behavior and beauty bears further scrutiny. Andre risks falling under her spell as he joins her frenzied search for the true killer.

As Calliope and Andre near the truth, their lives and that of the beast are in danger. Only love and wicked combat skills will see them through to a happily ever after.

Interested in more military romance stories? Subscribe to my newsletter and receive the Military Heroes Box Set

Subscribe Here

BEAU

BAYOU BROTHERHOOD PROTECTORS BOOK FOUR

New York Times & *USA Today*
Bestselling Author

ELLE JAMES

BEAU
Bayou
BROTHERHOOD PROTECTORS
New York Times & USA Today Bestselling Author
ELLE JAMES

Chapter One

Beau Boyette pulled into the parking lot at the Gautreaux Chateau on the bayou west of New Orleans, Louisiana. Dressed in a Robin Hood costume, complete with a green coat, a quiver of arrows, a thick belt and the signature green hat, he felt ridiculous, mostly because of the goddamn green tights. He prayed his Brotherhood Protectors teammates hadn't seen him leaving the boarding house in Bayou Mambaloa. He'd never hear the end of it.

He dug into his jacket pocket for his cell phone. Having put off this call as long as he could, he needed to get it over with and clear his slate for however long his mission might take.

"Beau, *cher*," his mother, Josephine Boyette,

answered on the first ring in her heavy Cajun accent. "*Comment ça se plume?*" Translated: How's it plucking?

Beau grinned at his mother's favorite Cajun saying. "*Bien, Maman.*"

"Why we have non seen you in da past week? You're gonna be here for da Sunday dinner, *oui?* It will be da first time in eight years since all ten of *mes enfants* have been together."

"*Maman*, I can't make the family dinner on Sunday. I got my first assignment and have to work."

"You no can put it off 'til Monday?" she asked.

"No, *Maman*," he said. "I work 24/7."

"You no in *l'armee* anymore. You come to da dinner."

"No, *Maman*. I'm not in the Army anymore, but I work providing protection for people," he explained for the fifth time since hiring on with the Brother-hood Protectors.

"Surely, you get a day off," his mother said. "Do I need to talk to da boss?"

God forbid his mother should talk to his lead over the Bayou Brotherhood Protectors. He'd never hear the end of the ribbing he'd get from Remy Montagne or the rest of the team. Or she could make it worse and take her complaint to Hank Patterson, the man who'd started the original Brotherhood Protectors organization.

Beau sighed. "*Maman*, you don't need to talk to my boss. I signed on to dis job, knowing it could mean working 24/7 to protect our clients. I'm just calling to let you know I won't be at da family dinner. I'll try to make it another time."

"But—" his mother started.

"*Je suis désolé*," Beau said. I'm sorry. "I have to go. My job starts tonight. *Je t'aime. Au revoir*." He ended the call before his mother could get all wound up and talk for another thirty minutes.

Beau didn't have time to talk. He'd been hired by Senator Marcus Anderson to protect his daughter Aurelie.

Miss Anderson had received a number of death threats over the past week since the senator had announced his reelection campaign. At the same time, Aurelie had stepped in to lead her father's philanthropic effort to preserve the bayou.

Since the senator would be campaigning across the state, he wouldn't have time to be with his daughter to guarantee her safety.

That would be Beau's responsibility.

The senator didn't want his daughter to know he'd hired a bodyguard. At least, not yet. He'd warned Beau that his daughter could be headstrong and extremely stubborn, a trait she'd inherited from her father.

Great. Beau wasn't thrilled with the idea of babysitting a spoiled little rich girl with a rebellious streak. He'd have to be on his toes at all times to make certain she didn't ghost him and land herself in trouble with no one around to help.

What she probably needed was a good old-fashioned spanking to get her attention. He'd almost asked the senator if that was a possibility but had thought better of it.

This was his first assignment with the Brotherhood Protectors. He wanted it to be a success and good advertisement for future gigs. Word of mouth was the best kind of marketing in the security business.

He pulled on the green cloth mask he'd acquired with the costume, thinking it appropriate for this undercover bodyguard job.

The event at the Gautreaux Chateau was a masquerade ball to raise money for the senator's reelection campaign. Only the very wealthy had purchased tickets at ten thousand dollars each.

Beau wouldn't be going to the event if the Senator hadn't given him a free ticket. He'd have been standing guard at the door or pacing the perimeter.

Ten-thousand-dollar tickets?

No way.

He had the money, but he had other plans for his savings—a place of his own with a house and five to ten acres of good land where he could raise a garden, a cow or two, and chickens. If it was on the bayou...even better. He'd always wanted a boat dock and access to fishing whenever he had a spare moment.

His mother had offered to give each of her children ten acres out of the one hundred and twenty acres that had been in their family for over two hundred years. So far, only two of her ten children had taken her up on that offer.

As much as Beau loved his mother, he couldn't see living that close. As it was, being in the same parish was almost too close. He was always running into those of his siblings who hadn't left Bayou Mambaloa to find employment in the bigger cities, like New Orleans or Baton Rouge.

No. He wanted to purchase his own property, preferably on the other side of the parish, with a little distance between them to discourage his mother from "dropping in" whenever she felt like it.

Oh, he loved his mother, but he also loved his privacy. As a widow with no husband to occupy her time, Josephine Boyette took her mothering to the extreme, trying to solve every problem for every one of her children instead of letting them figure it out on their own.

He'd limited his time with her since he'd been back, afraid she'd dig into his problems and find out he wasn't as okay as he'd led her to believe.

He'd been working through his issues with the therapist the VA hospital had assigned since he'd returned from his last mission with the Army Rangers.

As the sole survivor of a helicopter crash, he'd been so messed up he hadn't wanted to get out of bed for a month. That and the broken leg hadn't helped.

But that was in the past. He'd been through hundreds of hours of physical and mental therapy and was more than ready to get on with his life.

His teammates who'd perished in the crash couldn't get on with their lives, and they'd never know the wonderful trouble of being psychoanalyzed by their mothers.

How many times had he been told he was the lucky one?

And why didn't he feel lucky?

A weight threatened to settle on his chest, pushing out the air he'd been breathing.

Now was not the time to backslide into the black funk he'd clawed his way out of over six months ago.

Beau pushed open the door of his truck and dropped to the ground. He squared his shoulders and marched toward the entrance, careful not to limp on the leg that would never be the same.

He was determined to do his best to help the senator, make a good impression for the Bayou Brotherhood Protectors and keep Miss Anderson safe.

A man in a black suit stood guard at the door, checking IDs and tickets of each guest as they arrived.

Out of his element at such a formal function, Beau adjusted his Robin Hood hat. When the guard asked for his ID, he presented his military ID, his ten-thousand-dollar ticket and raised his mask briefly.

Beau entered the 18th-century mansion and was immediately struck by the opulent marble flooring and the double sweeping staircases on each side of the foyer, rising to the second level. A man dressed in a livery suit held out his hands. "May I take your... jacket...or quiver of arrows?"

"No, thank you," Beau said. "But perhaps you can tell me where I can find Senator Anderson."

"The senator is in the ballroom receiving line,"

the servant said and waved an arm toward the sound of music coming from a wide-open doorway.

Beau crossed the marble floor and entered a large ballroom crowded with people in a variety of costumes.

A man wearing an Abraham Lincoln outfit stood just inside the doorway, greeting guests as they entered.

Abraham Lincoln held out his hand. "Welcome to the Harlequins and Heartthrobs Masquerade Ball and reelection campaign fundraiser. Thank you for your support."

Beau gripped the man's hand. "I assume you're Senator Anderson," he said.

The man dressed as Abraham Lincoln smiled. "Your assumption is correct. And to whom do I have the pleasure of speaking?"

Beau dipped his head. "I'm Beau Boyette, an agent of the Brotherhood Protectors. I was sent to help you with your situation."

The senator's smile faded, and his grip tightened on Beau's hand. "Thank you for coming so quickly."

Beau's glance swept the ballroom. "Is the object of your concern here tonight?"

The man with the Abraham Lincoln top hat and black jacket gave a brief nod. "She is."

Beau looked around the ballroom again. "Will you introduce me to her to get the ball rolling?"

Abraham shook his head. "My daughter is a strong-minded, independent woman. She won't be happy that I've hired somebody to protect her. For now, I'd rather let you acquaint yourself with her. If that doesn't work, I'll introduce you as a son of a friend of mine."

Beau nodded. "As you wish. At the very least, could you point her out to me?"

The senator glanced around the ballroom. "She's dressed as Amelia Earhart, in trousers, a dusty-brown jacket and goggles instead of a mask." The man shook his head. "I couldn't get her to wear a dress to save my life."

Beau's lips twitched. "She sounds like she has a mind of her own."

The senator chuckled. "That she does." He lifted his chin, indicating direction. "That's her dancing with my executive assistant. At least the ballroom dance lessons that I paid for weren't wasted. They would've looked better if she were wearing the antebellum dress I had commissioned for her."

The woman in the goggles waltzed past Beau in the arms of a man dressed as a swashbuckling pirate.

Now, that was a costume. Beau wished he'd had more time to find a better disguise than the Robin

Hood one, which was the last decent choice at the costume shop in New Orleans.

He hadn't had time to go to a different costume shop, given that he'd only been notified of this mission around noon that day. His only other choice was a hairy Sasquatch costume.

Although, he was now beginning to wish he'd gone with Sasquatch. He felt very exposed wearing green tights, even though the jacket was long enough, just barely covering his ass.

"Good luck keeping up with her," the senator said.

Beau's lips pressed together as he watched the woman laugh out loud at something the pirate said. "I'll take it from here," he said, leaving the senator at his post receiving guests.

Beau wandered into the ballroom, his gaze on Amelia Earhart, a.k.a. Aurelie Anderson. He stopped at a table serving lemonade and what appeared to be mint juleps. He chose a lemonade and stood back, watching Miss Anderson dance around the room with the pirate. As he sipped the lemonade, he thought through the different scenarios where he could introduce himself.

The woman appeared relaxed, dancing and talking with the senator's executive assistant. Her movements appeared effortless, a testimony to the dance lessons her father had paid for her to take. An orchestra provided the music, playing various reimagined modern songs in an 18th-century style.

As the song came to a close, Miss Anderson and her partner slowed to stop. The pirate gave her a sweeping bow and then waved a hand toward the open bar.

Aurelie shook her head and said something Beau couldn't hear. Then, she walked away from the executive assistant. She ducked through a doorway and disappeared.

Beau set his glass down on an empty tray and hurried to follow. He left through the same door that she had and walked quickly down a hallway. He spotted her pushing through another doorway further down the corridor.

Though he hurried to catch up, he came to an abrupt halt in front of the swinging door with a placard indicating that the room inside was the ladies' restroom.

Since he couldn't follow her through that door, he walked further down the hall and stood in front of the men's room, waiting for Miss Anderson to emerge.

A few minutes later, the senator's daughter emerged from the bathroom.

When she looked in his direction, Beau

pretended to be coming out of the men's room. She only gave him a cursory glance before she headed back to the ballroom, her shoulders back, head held high as if she were marching into battle.

Beau followed and found her standing against the wall, her foot tapping to the beat of the music. Beau crossed to the lemonade table, snagged two glasses of lemonade and walked back to where Miss Anderson stood half-hidden by a potted plant. He stopped next to her without looking at her, his gaze on the people dancing across the floor. Eventually, he held up the glass to her. "You look like you need this more than I do."

She took the glass from him and downed most of it in one long swallow. "Thanks, I did need that."

He chuckled. "Do you always dance so rigorously?"

She lifted her chin. "A wise person once told me to put your heart and soul into everything you do, or don't bother doing it at all."

"Have you ever bothered to do the nothing at all?" He quirked his lips upward on the corners in challenge.

"A number of times," the Anderson woman said.

"Now that you've consumed an entire glass of lemonade given to you by a complete stranger, did you stop to think I might have spiked that lemonade with a date rape drug?" he asked.

Her brow wrinkled. "You don't look like the type of man who would spike a girl's drink."

He looked down at his costume. "Is it the costume?"

She laughed. "Partly. And the fact that you wouldn't have given me the lemonade spiked with any drug with my father watching like a hawk." She lifted her chin toward the man dressed as Abraham Lincoln. "He's been watching me all evening. He even enlisted his executive assistant to have a pity-dance with me to keep me busy."

"I'm sure your father's assistant didn't consider dancing with you in any way pitiful." Beau tipped his head toward the couples dancing to the music. "You held your own on the dance floor."

Aurelie met his gaze. "You were watching that long?"

"I was," he admitted.

"That's kind of creepy," she commented. "I might reconsider my earlier opinion about you." She touched a hand to her throat. "Perhaps you did spike my lemonade."

Beau's lips twitched. "I didn't, but I can under-stand President Lincoln's concern for his daughter," he said. "Considering the fact he was assassinated, he has good reason to be a little paranoid."

Her lips curved into a smile, transforming her face and making it softer and more approachable. "You have a point." She held out her hand. "I'm Amelia Earhart. Nice to meet you."

So, she was going to play it that way. "Robin Hood," he said as he took her hand.

Her grip was firm, not limp like many of the women with whom Beau had shaken hands.

"Robin Hood, you say?" Aurelie cocked an eyebrow in challenge. "I had pegged you as Peter Pan."

He released her hand and pressed his over his heart. "You wound me, madame." Beau shook his head. "I would think my quiver of arrows and the bow would have given it away."

She chuckled. "They are quite impressive. How about those tights? Should I assume anything about your sexuality?"

His hand remaining on his chest, Beau shook his head. "Again, you wound me, madame. I assure you I'm more attracted to Maid Marian than Friar Tuck."

Miss Anderson chuckled. "For what it's worth, the tights look good on you."

He dipped his head. "I'll take that as a compliment."

"As you should." She glanced around the room. "Now, if you'll excuse me, I'm working."

"Working?" he lifted both eyebrows.

Still looking around the room, she answered, "This is a fundraiser. My job is to make sure the guests are happy."

Beau nodded. "And happy guests mean more contributions to President Lincoln's reelection campaign, right?"

Her brow wrinkled. "Of course."

"Then, perhaps, you might consider entertaining this guest with a dance?"

Her lips twisted. "Sir, I believe you're quite capable of entertaining yourself." She started to walk away.

"Then perhaps, you might consider taking pity on a man in tights who is sure to be avoided by every available female in the ballroom and dance with me. I would consider it an honor," he performed a deep bow, "and a heroic way to help me salvage my eligible bachelor status."

She shook her head. "More likely salvaging your ego. Although, I doubt you'll lack a partner. Many of the matrons will be vying for you to join them in a dance."

"Only if I first prove I can dance."

Aurelie canted her head to one side, her gaze

raking over him. "True. Not many men can dance. Or, truthfully, *like* to dance."

"I can and do like to dance. My mother made certain all her boys could represent the family properly on the dance floor."

"Forced to take lessons?" She shook her head. "Me, too."

"More like forced to learn." Beau hadn't always appreciated having to learn to dance with his mother and sisters as his partners. Not until he'd grown older and interested in girls had he understood the value. The ladies usually loved to dance, and most of his male friends didn't or wouldn't. "My mother was a very good teacher. She and my father loved to dance at festivals and parties."

She drew in a deep breath and let it out. "In the spirit of showing the other women in attendance that you can and will dance, I suppose I could spare a pity dance with the man in green tights." She held out her hand. "Come on, Peter Pan. Let's show them what you've got."

"Robin Hood," he corrected as he took her hand and led her out into the middle of the ballroom as the orchestra began a new song.

After the first three notes, Beau recognized the song as "Can't Help Falling In Love," made famous by the late crooner Elvis Presley.

"Good grief," Aurelie murmured.

"It's a sign," Beau said as he glided across the floor, super glad his mother had insisted on him learning to waltz.

Aurelie needed little guidance to execute the dance. She usually had to lead when her male partners couldn't. With Peter Pan, she played a little push-me-pull-me until she finally let him take control. "You say your mother taught you to dance?"

He nodded. "She insisted on us learning to be as fluid and graceful as Fred Astaire." Beau grinned. "She loved all his movies, especially those when he partnered with Ginger Rogers."

"Let me guess..." Aurelie said, "she made you watch the movies as well?"

He nodded.

"And your father had no say in the matter?"

"None," Beau said. "When it came to our education, both in school and on the dance floor, he let her take the lead."

"A hands-off father?" She snorted softly. "What's that like?"

"Oh, he wasn't a hands-off father; he just knew which battles to choose. He taught us other things."

"Like?" She prompted.

"How to open doors for women, the elderly, and...well, anyone." He grinned. "He taught all of us about the bayou, to include frog gigging, how to spot alligators, shrimping, crabbing, fishing, cleaning and preparing the food we caught. He also taught us about vehicle maintenance like changing oil, tires and spark plugs."

"Even your sisters?" Aurelie asked.

Beau nodded. "Absolutely. Our mother could do all those things; she just preferred not to. Before all of us kids, she helped him on his fishing boat. Even after we came along, she still loved fishing with my father."

Aurelie frowned. "How many children did your mother and father have?"

"There are ten of us," Beau said and waited for the shock on her pretty face. He wasn't disappointed.

"Ten?" Her feet faltered.

Beau's arms tightened around her, and he effortlessly swung her out and back into his arms. "That's right. They had ten children."

"That's a lot of mouths to feed," Aurelie frowned. "Wow."

He laughed. "My grandparents considered my father an underachiever."

Her frown deepened. "Why?"

"His brother sired nineteen children. My father didn't even come close."

Aurelie's brow furrowed. "You're not serious, are you?"

"As serious as the heart attack that claimed my uncle's life when the youngest set of twins was only five years old," Beau said, his voice growing soft. He'd been in Iraq when his uncle had passed. His father had done his best to help the family out. Fortunately, his brother had been a shrewd investor and had taken out a sizable life insurance policy when he'd been younger. After selling the family boat-building business, his aunt had managed the investments and the houseful of children like the CEO of a major corporation.

"Youngest set of twins?" the woman in his arms asked.

"That's right," he said. "I think there are three or four sets of twins." Beau twirled her away and back into his arms. "Does that bother you that I'm from a family of many children?"

"No, why should it?"

"Do you even like children?" he asked.

She blinked. "Of course I do."

"Do you have any siblings?" he asked, though he already knew the answer.

Aurelie shook her head. "I always wished I had a brother or sister. You're fortunate to have some."

His lips twisted into a wry grin. "Others might not think so. There's never a moment's peace when we're all together."

"I hope to have children someday. Not just one child. I don't wish that on anyone. It can be very lonely."

"And quiet," Beau said with a sigh.

She laughed. "I take it you value silence."

"I do," he said. "But I love my brothers and sisters very much, even though they can drive me crazy at times."

The five-string quartet transitioned into another song, not a waltz, but one that allowed Beau to slow to a rocking motion. His arm circled the small of her back, and he pulled her closer. "Speaking of silence..." He rested his cheek against her temple. "You smell good."

"What does that have to do with silence?" she asked, her body stiff.

"Nothing. But if we don't talk, we can almost imagine Elvis singing this one."

She moved in rhythm with him to the orchestra's version of "Love Me Tender."

Together, they fit perfectly, a fact that gave Beau pause. The more he held her, the more he wanted to.

Dangerous...dangerous thoughts.

Yet, he didn't relinquish his hold.

Slowly, her body melted into his. As the song came to its beautiful end, Beau dipped Aurelie low in his arms and kissed her.

As their lips met, the music ended.

She opened to him, letting him in for a brief and delicious taste. For a moment, their tongues touched and caressed. For a moment, he forgot where he was and that he was on a mission to protect this woman, not make out with her in front of her father and the rich and influential people there to contribute to the senator's campaign.

When he brought her back up, he stared into her goggles, wishing he could see her eyes. He wondered what color they were, what they would tell him and if she'd enjoyed the dance and the kiss as much as he had.

He might not be able to see her eyes, but he could feel the change in her body where his hands still rested against her back.

Aurelie stiffened. "Excuse me."

She stepped backward, spun on her booted heels and darted for the hallway where the bathrooms were located.

Beau started to follow.

"What the hell was that?" a voice said behind him in a tight whisper.

He turned to face an angry Abe Lincoln.

"I introduced myself to your daughter." He couldn't have come up with a dumber response if he'd tried. But once it left his lips, he couldn't take it back.

"And that gives you leave to grope her on the dance floor? What kind of operation is this Brotherhood Protectors?"

Fuck.

He'd blown it with the man who'd hired him. What had he been thinking, kissing the man's daughter?

"My apologies, sir. It must have been the song." Beau glanced toward the hallway where Aurelie had gone. "If you'll excuse me, I need to follow her and make sure she's all right."

"Damn right, you do. And while you're at it, try not to molest her." As he turned away, he muttered, "What's wrong with the young people today?"

Beau didn't try to answer the man. He strode out of the ballroom into the corridor. This time, he didn't see Aurelie walking into the bathroom. She was nowhere to be seen, as if she'd disappeared.

With the kiss still fresh on his lips, he ran to the ladies' room door and knocked on the contoured panel.

An older woman dressed as the Queen of Hearts pulled the door open.

Beau frowned. "Did you see Miss..." he thought

better of asking if the woman had seen Miss Anderson and amended, "Amelia Earhart?"

The woman shook her head. "I was the only person in here." She stepped out of the bathroom, her gaze sweeping him from top to toe. "Let me know if you can't find her. I'm available all night." With a wink, she walked away.

Holy shit.

His first day on the job, and he'd already lost the client.

Ge ~ BEAU ~ Now

About the Author

ELLE JAMES also writing as MYLA JACKSON is a *New York Times* and *USA Today* Bestselling author of books including cowboys, intrigues and para-normal adventures that keep her readers on the edges of their seats. When she's not at her computer, she's traveling, snow skiing, boating, or riding her ATV, dreaming up new stories. Learn more about Elle James at www.ellejames.com

Website | Facebook | Twitter | GoodReads | Newsletter | BookBub | Amazon

Or visit her alter ego Myla Jackson at
mylajackson.com
Website | Facebook | Twitter | Newsletter

Follow Me!
www.ellejames.com
ellejames@ellejames.com

Also by Elle James

A Killer Series

Chilled (#1)

Scorched (#2)

Erased (#3)

Swarmed (#4)

Brotherhood Protectors International

Athens Affair (#1)

Belgian Betrayal (#2)

Croatia Collateral (#3)

Dublin Debacle (#4)

Edinburgh Escape (#5)

Frankfurt Fallout (#6)

Brotherhood Protectors Hawaii

Kalea's Hero (#1)

Leilani's Hero (#2)

Kiana's Hero (#3)

Maliea's Hero (#4)

Emi's Hero (#5)

Sachie's Hero (#6)

Bayou Brotherhood Protectors

Remy (#1)

Gerard (#2)

Lucas (#3)

Beau (#4)

Rafael (#5)

Valentin (#6)

Landry (#7)

Simon (#8)

Maurice (#9)

Jacques (#10)

Brotherhood Protectors Yellowstone

Saving Kyla (#1)

Saving Chelsea (#2)

Saving Amanda (#3)

Saving Liliana (#4)

Saving Breely (#5)

Saving Savvie (#6)

Saving Jenna (#7)

Saving Peyton (#8)

Saving Londyn (#9)

Brotherhood Protectors Colorado

SEAL Salvation (#1)

Rocky Mountain Rescue (#2)

Ranger Redemption (#3)

Tactical Takeover (#4)

Colorado Conspiracy (#5)

Rocky Mountain Madness (#6)

Free Fall (#7)

Colorado Cold Case (#8)

Fool's Folly (#9)

Colorado Free Rein (#10)

Rocky Mountain Venom (#11)

High Country Hero (#12)

Brotherhood Protectors

Montana SEAL (#1)

Bride Protector SEAL (#2)

Montana D-Force (#3)

Cowboy D-Force (#4)

Montana Ranger (#5)

Montana Dog Soldier (#6)

Montana SEAL Daddy (#7)

Montana Ranger's Wedding Vow (#8)

Iron Horse Legacy

Drake (#6)

Grimm (#7)

Murdock (#8)

Utah (#9)

Judge (#10)

Delta Force Strong

Ivy's Delta (Delta Force 3 Crossover)

Breaking Silence (#1)

Breaking Rules (#2)

Breaking Away (#3)

Breaking Free (#4)

Breaking Hearts (#5)

Breaking Ties (#6)

Breaking Point (#7)

Breaking Dawn (#8)

Breaking Promises (#9)

Hearts & Heroes Series

Wyatt's War (#1)

Mack's Witness (#2)

Ronin's Return (#3)

Sam's Surrender (#4)

Hellfire Series

Hellfire, Texas (#1)

Justice Burning (#2)

Smoldering Desire (#3)

Hellfire in High Heels (#4)

Playing With Fire (#5)

Up in Flames (#6)

Total Meltdown (#7)

Take No Prisoners Series

SEAL's Honor (#1)

SEAL'S Desire (#2)

SEAL's Embrace (#3)

SEAL's Obsession (#4)

SEAL's Proposal (#5)

SEAL's Seduction (#6)

SEAL'S Defiance (#7)

SEAL's Deception (#8)

SEAL's Deliverance (#9)

SEAL's Ultimate Challenge (#10)

Texas Billionaire Club

Tarzan & Janine (#1)

Something To Talk About (#2)

Held Hostage at Whiskey Gulch (#3)

Setup at Whiskey Gulch (#4)

Missing Witness at Whiskey Gulch (#5)

Cowboy Justice at Whiskey Gulch (#6)

Boys Behaving Badly Anthologies

Rogues (#1)

Blue Collar (#2)

Pirates (#3)

Stranded (#4)

First Responder (#5)

Cowboys (#6)

Silver Soldiers (#7)

Secret Identities (#8)

Warrior's Conquest

Enslaved by the Viking Short Story

Conquests

Smokin' Hot Firemen

Protecting the Colton Bride

Protecting the Colton Bride & Colton's Cowboy Code

Heir to Murder

Secret Service Rescue

High Octane Heroes

Haunted

Engaged with the Boss

Cowboy Brigade

An Unexpected Clue

Under Suspicion, With Child

Texas-Size Secrets